DREADITATION
andersen prunty

DREADITATION

Also by Andersen Prunty

<u>Novels & Novellas</u>

Neon Dies At Dawn
Irrationalia
Failure As a Way of Life
This Town Needs a Monster
Squirm With Me
Sociopaths In Love
The Warm Glow of Happy Homes
Satanic Summer
Fill the Grand Canyon and Live Forever
Fuckness
The Sorrow King
Morning is Dead
My Fake War
The Beard
Zerostrata
Jack and Mr. Grin

<u>Collections</u>

Bodies Wrapped in Plastic and Other Items of Interest
Deathtripping: Collected Horror Stories
Creep House: Horror Stories
Bury the Children in the Yard: Horror Stories
Pray You Die Alone: Horror Stories
Sunruined: Horror Stories
The Driver's Guide to Hitting Pedestrians
Hi I'm a Social Disease: Horror Stories
Slag Attack
The Overwhelming Urge

For Skully,
The biggest asshole I know.

part one
THE LETTING GO

one

WE DON'T THINK YOU PAID FOR THE FAMILY
PACKAGE.

I'm in the locker room of my office building's gym, a towel
wrapped around my waist, staring down at the phone in my
hand, momentarily confused. At first I think it's a text message until realizing it's a push notification from an app called
Wellnevermindfulness. I thought I'd turned off all the notifications on my phone. I'm trying to minimize distractions. I
don't need to be bothered by YouTube whenever someone
posts a video they think I might enjoy. If there is anyone who
can understand minimizing distractions, I'd think it would be
the people at Wellnevermindfulness, the most downloaded
wellness and meditation app despite its very clumsy name. I
guess it's aimed at Gen Xers or something.

I delete the notification, spray myself down with magne-
sium and rub it in, put my clothes back on, and head up to my
office where I huff my sandalwood-scented diffuser, blast
some New Age tunes at a volume many would find

uncomfortable, and throw myself into my work while frequently staring out the large window overlooking the city, taking deep breaths, and reminding myself today is a beautiful day and I am alive and part of it and out there is the city, filled with good people trying to do good things. In order to experience your existence, you have to stop and take stock of it. I try to do this at least twenty times a day.

By the time I leave work, that notification still really bothers me.

two

I'm not one to rush into things. Not anything that's going to last a long time anyway. I dated Corinne for five years before asking her to marry me. We were married for three years before we even talked about having a baby. We waited another two before actually doing it. I wanted to buy a house in a neighborhood where we could raise the child through its school years. Now little Wendy is five and soon she'll be starting real school and then . . . that's when I have to stop myself. Thinking like that makes me anxious. None of us are going anywhere for a very long time.

Hi. I'm Scott Champion and I am a cautious, prudent person. My actions are conscious and mindful. That's why it took me months before committing to pay for a premium subscription to an app specializing in mindfulness and meditation. It was many months after those awful words had escaped Corinne's mouth: "anger management."

She didn't tell me I had to quit doing anything, probably because she knew that would just make me mad. That's not really how we do things anyway. We don't tell each other what we should and shouldn't do. What she had said, what she had *implied*, was that if I was going to keep doing the things I was doing, maybe I needed to do this one other thing: take an anger management class to "learn how to deal with my emotions."

My day was already so full it was easier for me to quit doing things than it was for me to start doing more things—adding more appointments and obligations. So I stopped drinking alcohol and started going to sleep a little earlier. I stopped drinking coffee and started sleeping a lot better and wasn't quite as agitated through the day. Ditto with the vaping and the nicotine lozenges. I'd stopped smoking years ago. I stopped with the testosterone and no longer viewed every facet of my life as a competitive event needing to be won at all times.

Still . . . there was something inside me that felt . . . misaligned. There were no more spikes of mad agitation, the spice of life. I felt like I existed in a permanently gray, grumpy fog.

That was when I discovered the Wellnevermindfulness app. I'd heard a celebrity talking about it on one of the podcasts I listened to. With all the money I'd saved by cutting out so many things, I didn't feel guilty about paying for the premium subscription. While I'm now a cautious person, when I find something worth pursuing, I'm all in, especially if there's a trial period. Besides, 250,000 five-star reviews couldn't be wrong.

After less than a week of using the app, it was Corinne who first noticed the change.

We sat on the couch after getting Wendy down for the night—me with my turmeric and black pepper-infused alkaline water and Corinne with her chamomile tea, oat milk, and stevia—ready to watch Corinne's favorite prime-time drama, *Redemptive Misogynist*.

She curled up next to me, a gesture of affection she hadn't expressed since her pregnancy, and said, "Are you doing something different?"

I was embarrassed about using the app. It seemed cliched and almost hokey. "Just sticking to the straight and narrow. Why?"

"You seem . . . different."

"Different good or different bad?"

"Different *good*," she almost purred.

"Like how?"

"Your eyes look different. Like they're filled with light or something. And you're moving with a spring in your step again. You haven't hit snooze on your alarm all week." She wrapped her hand around one of my biceps and said, "You don't feel like you're vibrating anymore."

"Vibrating?"

"You know what I mean. You're not stalking around like you want to chew holes through the world."

During *Redemptive Misogynist* we engaged in a form of heavy petting not even attempted since first meeting in college. The television kept playing long after we stopped paying attention. We didn't make it to the bedroom for another three hours. Most of that time was spent exploring each other's bodies like they were new to us before she slid me into her and did what she wanted for as long as she wanted.

The next morning over breakfast, Wendy with her sippy cup of juice and plate of eggs she ate by the handful, Corinne and I exchanged bashful glances over our cups of rooibos tea.

"Okay," I said. "I gotta come clean."

"Viagra?" Corinne said.

"No . . . not fu— Not Viagra."

"*Fuh-fuh-fuh,*" Wendy sang out, the truncated expletive something she'd heard quite a bit of.

I pulled my phone out of my pocket and placed it in front of Corinne, bringing up the Wellnevermindfulness app.

"I've been . . . meditating," I said, half expecting Corinne to shriek out in laughter.

Instead, she beamed, her eyes glazing over almost like she was ready to cry.

"I'm so . . . proud of you," she said, leaning forward to kiss me. "I want to try."

I was momentarily shocked. This wasn't the kind of thing I thought would interest Corinne at all. Yoga, yes, because it could yield real-world, physical results.

"Um . . . yeah." I thought about the previous night. I thought about *that* multiplied by two. "That'd be great. Just download the app and I'll give you my info. No sense in both of us paying for it."

Corinne started that afternoon after putting Wendy down for a nap and for the next two weeks it felt like our lives opened like a sacred lotus. I was still too self-conscious to meditate in the same room as Corinne but the soothing voice of Wisdom Master Blastneesh gently hummed in both sets of our earbuds, guiding us to a serene world of calm mindfulness. Each time I opened my eyes from a meditation, I felt both a little stoned and hyper-present, as though I could fully luxuriate in every second of the day.

After less than a week, I noticed the change in Corinne too. She was more patient with Wendy. The household chores she busied herself with in between meetings for her at-home consulting gig she'd had to take up since losing her job were met with a sense of dutiful purpose instead of as things she simply had to do. And at night, after we'd put Wendy down, we belonged completely to one another, as though there was nothing and nobody else in the world. I began to see life stretch out in front of me as an endless walk through a summery nature preserve rather than as a rock being continually ground down, which had been my outlook since graduating college. I inhaled life and tranquility and exhaled all the toxins and anxiety and anger and fear the world bombards us with.

Then the notification.

three

Parking the BMW in the driveway of our peaceful tree-filled neighborhood, I'm still rattled by the notification. I decide not to mention anything to Corinne. Things have been going so well the past couple weeks I don't want to bring the mood down. Nor do I want to start paying for the family plan. I have the money. It's just principle at this point.

The night passes as blissfully as most of our recent evenings. Sometimes it even feels like we've passed some of our newfound inner peace onto Wendy. Or maybe we're finally giving her the proper amount of attention she's always needed and she no longer has to act out to get it. It's hard to say.

However, after another bout of exhaustive lovemaking, I don't find myself drifting into sleep as easily as I have been, even when I use the app's breathing technique specially formulated to aid in sleeping. I try to focus on my breathing, counting and timing my inhalations and exhalations, but I just keep hearing Blastneesh say in his slow, dramatic, pause-filled voice:

"We don't think you paid for the family package."

"We don't think you paid . . . for the family package."
"We don't think . . . you paid . . . for the family package."
And that, ultimately, is what I end up falling asleep to.

"We don't think you paid . . . for the family package."
"We don't think . . . you paid . . . for the family package."

four

The next week brings another notification. The same one.

WE DON'T THINK YOU PAID FOR THE FAMILY PACKAGE.

Around the third or fourth one, I notice a hyperlink reading "CLICK TO UPGRADE" has been added. Maybe it's always been there and my fury prevented me from seeing it. For an app supposedly focused on wellness, this seems like the absolute wrong way to go about things. It feels like entrapment. Why don't they just block it from being used on Corinne's phone? They have that ability. The anxious part of my brain wonders if they're racking up a bill I'm going to get hit with once it accumulates to an uncomfortable amount, no doubt with penalties and late fees.

C'mon, I tell myself, *this isn't the IRS or something.*

I lock my office door, kick off my shoes, and drop my meditation pillow on the floor in front of the windows. I put in my earbuds, start another session, and cannot lose myself the way I have been. I find myself agitated, Blastneesh's voice rankling me more than soothing me. Still, I sit for the full twenty minutes and swear that once the final chime sounds, signaling me to open my eyes, Blastneesh's voice murmurs, "Why don't you just pay?"

When I back it up to listen to it again, nothing's there.

Christ. I shake my head. Is Blastneesh going to try gaslighting me through the app now?

I end up spending the rest of the day researching Wisdom Master Blastneesh.

After nearly three hours, I'm left with the conclusion Blastneesh has hired one of those PR firms that has the capability to remove nearly everything negative from the internet. Other than the obvious accusers saying Blastneesh is a fraud, there really isn't anything. Visiting the site for the Wellnevermindfulness app almost restores my faith. It is filled with sunny pictures of happy people and states the app is an extension of Blastneesh's spiritual retreat camp located somewhere in Ohio. Everyone wears yellow. There are several photos of Blastneesh himself, long gray beard, wearing a blue sweatsuit and a silver beanie, those hypnotic brown-gold eyes looking into the camera. Like Blastneesh's voice, the image of him is hard to place. It seems to hint at several different cultural identities and religions without explicitly being any one thing. There has been nothing so much as hinting at any religion in anything I've listened to up to this point. His voice sounds vaguely British, possibly with a hint of Indian, or just American affecting a mash-up of those things. The website says he came from the countryside near Mumbai, but I doubt the validity of that. It's all sanitized to the point of escaping nearly any accusations of cultural appropriation.

I feel off all evening. Over dinner I snap at Wendy for not eating all her vegetables, mocking her when she says she's full. In bed with Corinne, I'm unable to maintain an erection and am pretty sure I hear a snort of contempt in her voice when she tells me goodnight and rolls over. When I try to place a hand on her still naked hip, she brushes it off. Insomnia grips me and I find myself wandering through the house, coming to a stop in front of the well-stocked liquor cabinet we keep around for friends.

"Why don't I just pay?" I mutter to myself in the dark.

That settles it. I'll get up in the morning and upgrade to the family plan. I've been cheap and stubborn and ridiculous. It isn't really that much more. After all, can you really put a price on mental and spiritual health? Is holding on to this anger really worth it? Seems simpler to just pay with my bank account rather than my mental health. Blastneesh is providing us an undeniably useful service—with results. With the exception of our povertarian phase, we've always made sure to pay a premium for natural, organic foods without thinking twice about it. How is this any different?

Already, the tightness in my chest and shoulders and neck begins to loosen. Today just hadn't been a very good day. It happens. Drinking to the point of blacking out isn't going to make it any better and will certainly make tomorrow a lot worse.

five

NOT PAYING IS NOT MINDFUL

Why the all caps?

Sitting at my desk and slugging back my morning kombucha, whatever lingering thoughts I've had about upgrading are immediately gone. Maybe I'll just cancel my subscription completely and try to find a free app even though it'll make me feel poor.

This afternoon I do not meditate at all.

At home, Corinne can tell something is up. Like the old days, she will overstep me on nearly everything involving minor chores and caring for Wendy because she knows if I have to do anything it will devolve into a dramatically frustrating struggle. She bathes Wendy, reads her a few stories, and gets her down for the night.

By the time she comes back downstairs, I'm sitting on the couch, staring blankly at a reality TV show about a rich family called *The Soulless*. She comes up behind me and begins rubbing my shoulders. I have to fight the urge to brush away her hands.

"You feel tense," she says.

"Maybe a little."

"Rough day at work?"

I shrug.

"Are you keeping up with your practice?" she asks.

"Huh?"

"Your sitting."

"Still don't know what you're talking about," I say, even though I know what she's talking about but her easy acceptance of the app's vernacular bothers me more than it should. Like I refuse to call it that simply because they want me to and I'm totally aware of how petty and absurd this is.

"Your meditation. Are you still doing it every day?"

"Maybe . . . maybe I skipped it today." I can at least be honest with her about that.

"You know I'm going to nag."

"I know," I say. "I'll try to get back on track tomorrow."

That night I again fail to maintain an erection and end up watching Corinne masturbate herself to climax and part of me, looking into her blissed-out eyes as she moans and takes sharp breaths in between parted lips, wants to be where she is.

I resolve to try again tomorrow.

six

I'm already in a rage when I get to work. This rage swells further when I find the door to my office open, a cleaning woman watering the over twenty plants I keep in there for visual interest as well as to help purify the undoubtedly toxic air of the large building.

"What the hell are you doing?" I demand.

Startled, the cleaning woman jerks and turns to me.

"Mr. Harper told me to, sir."

I approach the woman, rip the watering can out of her hand, and throw it out of the office.

"These plants," I throw a hand toward the nearest one, "are central to my well-being. They're *mine*. Not Mr. Harper's. I bought every one of these. I've had them for years. They keep the air clean but it's not just that. They help keep my thoughts organized. The watering, the trimming . . . I have to do it all. It's . . . very zen."

"Mr. Harper said they were all dried up."

I take a deep breath and move in closer to the cleaning woman.

"When you're in public and you're near a baby who's shit its pants, do you just grab them and change their diaper? Ever breast feed someone else's kid?"

The woman wrinkles her nose. "Ew, no."

I again gesture at the nearest plant. "Same. Fucking. Thing."

The woman slumps her shoulders. "Then . . . I guess I can go now?"

"Please close the door on your way out."

I spend the next few hours researching other meditation and mindfulness apps. I try a couple of them. They aren't the same. That afternoon I again try the Wellnevermindfulness app but Blastneesh's tone now seems goading and threatening, even though what comes out of his mouth is essentially the same thing as the week prior.

I consider stopping at a bar on the way home but talk myself out of it.

When I come through the door to find Corinne clearly upset, I'm glad I didn't stop for a drink.

She keeps everything bottled up until after dinner when Wendy is off in her room playing.

"What's wrong?" I finally ask.

She slams her phone down in front of me and activates the screen. There's a single notification from the Wellnevermindfulness app. It reads: CUNT.

"Screenshot that," I say.

"I already did," Corinne says. "I posted it on all my social media sites but they . . ."

"They what?"

"They all took them down."

"I want you to stop using that app."

"I'm scared."

"Don't be ridiculous. It's just a stupid app. Probably just

some prankster in customer service."

"Not about that," she says. "I'm afraid things'll go back to the way they were before."

This gives me pause.

It doesn't stop me from canceling the subscription. The app informs me, since I've paid for the yearly plan, I will still have access to the premium service for the duration, but the plan will not renew. I delete the app from my phone.

This stops the notifications from coming but I notice a not exactly subtle shift in my online life. Now every pop-up, sidebar, and banner ad seems to be for an oddly dystopian post-meditation life and just seeing them makes me feel bad. Guilty, somehow. There are ads encouraging me to seek help if I'm an alcoholic or drug addict, ads for anger management classes, ads for gyms that make me wonder if I more closely resemble the before or after photo of the model. Eventually these spiral into things I didn't even know there were ads for because I'd never seen them: debt consolidation, bail bonds, learning basic life skills, housing projects, buy here/pay here car lots, free clinics.

Even though I drive a BMW away from my light-filled corner office towering high above the city on the way to my beautiful, educated wife and vibrant, healthy daughter in my nice house in a posh, desirable neighborhood, I still can't help feeling . . . dirty.

seven

I add the salutation—"Warmest regards"—to the email I've composed. It took forever to find an actual email address for the Wellnevermindfulness app. I was just going to leave it but calling Corinne a cunt was the final straw. I could weather a certain amount of trolling through notifications but the message they sent Corinne felt like completely unacceptable misogynistic bullying. I hope, given the content of the email, the customer service department realizes the salutation is sarcastic. I hover over the send button and my phone rings.

It's Corinne.

Just seeing her name alights my pulse and sends it racing. I can't remember the last time she called instead of texting.

"Is everything okay?" I say.

She's crying. "*Nooooo.*" It comes out as something close to a howl.

"Calm down," I say, even though *I* am not calm.

I'm taking a deep breath when Corinne says, "You need to come home."

"Just calm down and talk to me." I've forgotten to exhale

and my voice sounds choked and weird.

"It's Wendy."

"I'll be there as soon as I can."

I stand up and swoon with dizziness. I exhale and slide my phone into my pocket.

A few minutes later I open the door to the house and the alarm system is yelling at me. I quickly deactivate it, thinking Corinne and Wendy are not there. I expect panic and disorder but some level of calm seems to have been restored. Corinne sits on the couch, Wendy asleep against her arm.

"What's with the alarm?" I ask.

I can tell Corinne has been crying when she looks up at me.

"*This* is what's with the alarm." She gestures to Wendy's tiny left hand. There's a bandage on it.

"What happened?"

Now Corinne breaks down again into great heaving sobs. Wendy opens her eyes, groggy, and pats Corinne on the thigh with her good hand.

"What happened, punkin?" I ask Wendy.

She holds up the hand with the bandage and makes a scissor gesture with her right and says, "Snip!"

"Aww," I say. "Did you have an accident?"

"SOMEONE CUT OFF HER FUCKING FINGER!" Corinne shouts.

"Wait . . ." I'm still trying to process this. "What?"

"Beardman went *snip!*" Wendy says, almost joyfully. Then her face grows serious and she says, "Now I won't be able to count to ten, Papa."

I have to sit down because if I don't then I'm going to pass out. I sit on the other side of Wendy and pull her close to me.

"We've done everything," Corinne blubbers.

My heart is still racing, my brain awash in confusion.

After a few minutes, Wendy gets bored and asks if she can

go play *Teddy Bear Overlords* on her tablet. Normally she only gets a half-hour to do this as a reward for eating most of her dinner but I tell her it's okay and she scoots off the couch and snatches her tablet before pulling her beanbag out into the middle of the floor and collapsing onto it, smiling as the glow of the tablet illuminates her face.

I rub Corinne's thigh and ask if she needs anything.

"Maybe some tea?" she says.

"Sure thing." I stand and head into the kitchen. Corinne follows me.

While I'm waiting for the water to boil, she gets most of the story out.

Wendy was at outside recess at school. Miss Linda said she came running to her, crying, holding up her hand, now missing a pinkie finger. When Miss Linda asked her what had happened, Wendy told her a man had cut her finger off with big scissors. Miss Linda asked her what the person looked like and Wendy said it had been a man with a big beard and a funny hat. She said he was dressed in blue but Wendy still didn't know her colors very well so that part might not have been accurate. Miss Linda immediately took Wendy in and called the police while her assistant, Miss Pamela, went to where Miss Linda had last seen Wendy to look for the missing digit. By the time Corinne had been notified and shown up, the EMTs already had Wendy bandaged up. With Corinne there, Miss Linda assisted in the search for the missing finger to no avail. Finally, Corinne relented and took Wendy to the hospital to have it stitched up.

"What was everyone looking for, Mama?" Wendy asked.

"Your finger, honey," Corinne said.

"I told Miss Linda Beardman took it!"

I pour the water over the tea bag, gritting my teeth, my blood turning to acid.

"Did you tell them who you thought it was?" I say.

"What do you mean?" Corinne says.

I set the kettle down and turn to her. "Blastneesh."

She looks surprised and appears to mull it over before saying, "Come on. Are you serious?"

"Who else could it be?"

"That's . . . that's ridiculous."

"Ridiculous? It's the only thing that makes sense."

She chuffs. "Are you high?"

"No," I say. "I am way too sober."

"It just seems . . ."

"Like a payment. That's his way of collecting."

"I know this is very hard for you to comprehend but it is very likely this has nothing to do with you."

"I think someone needs to tell the police."

"Scott, it's going to sound crazy."

"It *has* to be him. You heard Wendy's description. Doesn't it seem kind of . . . I don't know, *targeted* to you?"

"How would he even know what Wendy looked like?"

"Are you kidding? You put everything up on Facebook. The whole world could know whatever they wanted about any of us."

"It's not a public page. No one can see it but friends and family."

"There are other ways."

"Fine," Corinne says. "I still say it's crazy but I won't stop you if you want to call."

I call the local police station and tell them my suspicions. They tell me they'll look into it but I can tell they also think I'm crazy and are just trying to get me off the phone.

That night, we re-live the story again as they recount it on the local evening news.

After Corinne goes to bed, I fetch a half-empty bottle of

Basil Hayden's from the liquor cabinet and polish it off. It's not enough. I try to remember where I put the cannabis tincture I'd brought home from a trip to Colorado a couple of years ago. I go to the medicine cabinet where it rests between a bottle of vitamin E oil and a bottle of Oxycodone from one of Corinne's plastic surgery procedures. I notice she has failed to put the cap on the prescription bottle. Looks like she needed some help sleeping too.

eight

We spend the next week spiraling out of control. Wendy only has a couple weeks of school left so we decide not to send her back. I drink my way through the liquor cabinet and find myself at the craft beer store buying two hundred dollars' worth of beer because if I'm only drinking beer then it means I'm not really drinking. Along with the nightly booze, I've been pounding the cannabis tincture like it's a 5-Hour Energy Drink but with the complete opposite effect. One quiet Thursday, I leave work to drive to a legal state and replenish my supply. Technically it's illegal to bring it back to my state, to use it here, but I feel pretty confident I won't get pulled over and arrested. Well-dressed, well-spoken white guys who drive BMWs and live in the good part of town don't get arrested for marijuana possession, if anyone does at this point.

Corinne resumes her regimen of light opioid abuse I thought she'd kicked after her last rehab session following her termination from her six-figure marketing job. On paper, she got fired for masturbating in her office. In reality, she got fired for taking what she called "a pleasure break," something proposed in the latest self-help book she'd been reading. To her, it was a holistic way of delivering intense pleasure, relieving stress, and restoring proper breathing while engaging in light physical exertion without the aid of medication. To her boss, however, it was leaving the door unlocked so an intern who happened to be the boss' niece could walk into Corinne's office to find her lying on the floor, her skirt hiked up over her hips, inserting a large dildo between her legs. Maybe this would have been fine in the seventies but things had changed and, within an hour, Corinne was packing up her desk and leaving the building sandwiched between two security guards whose combined IQs probably did not equal hers.

Despite reaching out to the local police a number of times, we couldn't get any information from them. Honestly, it didn't sound to me like they were even working on the case. That left Corinne and me to deal with our impotent rage and thirst for justice all by ourselves.

Our three-person family unit had been infiltrated and stained, injured. Corinne and I now had to deal with raising a crippled child. The perfect being we had each worked so hard to bring into the world was now less than. Little Wendy would now be fortunate to get a job as an administrative assistant. Even low-level data entry was going to be a challenge.

And Corinne and I were just supposed to swallow the injustice of it all. Suck it up and continue on like nothing had happened.

I troll and threaten the Wellnevermindfulness company via email and whatever social media I can find them on. The threats all amount to essentially the same thing: I know what you did and you're going to pay.

I reach my breaking point on a Sunday. I wake up and notice Corinne is not in bed. I check the time on my phone. It's almost noon. About four hours later than I sleep most

Sundays. I'm still hung over and the beer from the night before sits like a feverish lump in my bowels. I make my way to the bathroom as fast as I can. Wendy, locked into her room by a child gate, is shouting "Mama! Papa! Mama! Papa!" but this is an emergency.

In the bathroom, Corinne is sprawled on the floor, apparently unable to make it to bed last night. I should check to make sure she's breathing but just the act of bending to check would force a shower of diarrhea out of my ass. I sit myself down and it happens before I can elevate my feet on the Squatty Potty, so fast I feel like I start shitting while sitting down. The bathroom is immediately redolent with the smell of weed from all the tincture I pounded with the beers. The relief is immediate and welcome. I grab my phone to check my emails and bank account before turning on the bidet.

There's a charge on my credit card from the Wellnevermindfulness app.

They've charged me for the family plan.

I slam my phone down on the vanity and crank the bidet so high it stings my anus.

I check to make sure Corinne is still alive. Of course she is. Then I go take care of Wendy.

By the time Corinne joins us for brunch I'm feeling more invigorated and alive than I have in a really long time.

Corinne groggily staggers into the kitchen and takes a quick scan.

"You . . . Doordashed KFC?" Her face wrinkles with disgust.

"Yeah. Grab something. It's . . . really a lot of food."

"This yum!" Wendy shouts as she shoves a chicken finger into her mouth and I wonder if I was being subconsciously cruel when I ordered those.

Corinne sits at the table and grabs a biscuit. "So I guess

Wendy's a carnivore now."

"Omnivore, dear."

"Whatever. Why do you seem so chipper?"

"Because I've decided to take care of it."

"Take care of what?"

"Our little . . . mindfulness problem."

She rolls her eyes and rubs her temples. "Can't we just forget about it?"

"I can*not* just forget about it. They have insulted my wife and injured my daughter. That is not okay. I'm going to fight back."

"Just get a lawyer."

"I'm going to do better than that. I'm going to get a gun."

The biscuit drops from Corinne's hand and I can tell by the look in her eye she thinks I'm still spiraling, that this is the latest in a long string of bad decisions that are going to land me in court-ordered rehab.

"You are *not* getting a gun," she says.

Wendy says, "Bang! Bang! Bang!" and holds the chicken finger like a knife.

"I don't see any other way. We need restitution."

"This is not okay."

"I know what I'm doing."

"I am not going to agree with you."

"Then I will do it alone."

"You could just . . . not do it at all. Sow compassion, not hate."

"We can't continue like this."

"Continue like what?"

And I wonder if Corinne is really that blind or if she's just being obtuse.

"Don't pretend there aren't problems. You're virtually unemployed and addicted to opiates. I've been drinking a six-pack of Belgian beer every night, on top of other things, Wendy has special needs now, and we both slept until noon. *Noon*, Corinne. Does any of that sound good to you? If you won't let me get a gun then I'm going to look into a bounty hunter or a soldier of fortune or something."

But she's stopped paying attention. She's looking out the window.

A car sits in our driveway.

nine

It's a really nice car. A Bentley. Super-bright blue. Has to be a custom paint job. Not cheap.

A tall, muscular man wearing a kind of paramilitaristic version of a chauffeur uniform and dark sunglasses gets out of the car and looks around. He tosses his headful of long, well-coiffed blond hair, the sunlight catching it perfectly. He holds something under his arm.

"What the fu—" I mumble.

"Fuh! Fuh! Fuh!" Wendy shouts.

The tall man crouches down and places what he carried under his arm on the driveway. A roll of some kind. He then begins unrolling it. It's a bright yellow carpet.

I know who's in the car. A surge of many conflicting emotions swells within me.

I stand up.

"Where are you going?" Corinne's voice sounds dull and lifeless.

"I'm going to get my dagger."

"I don't think that's necessary."

I feel like it's absolutely necessary only . . . I don't want to miss the occupant of the car's appearance. I feel pathetic.

Once the carpet is unrolled all the way to the front door, the tall man once again appears in the frame of the window to open the rear door of the car.

Blastneesh emerges. He's smaller than I thought he would be. He looks just like he did in all the online photos—long gray beard, silver beanie, flowing blue outfit, and sandals. He begins walking slowly along the carpet, his fingertips pressing together to form a triangle, his beard gently swaying with the motion. The tall man follows close behind.

One of us could meet him at the door but we continue sitting there in something like a collective daze until the doorbell emits its happy but slightly agitated sounding chime.

I try hard to summon my anger but maybe all the drinking has finally got to me because I feel nearly sick.

"I'll get it." Now Corinne sounds almost chipper.

She nearly bounds to the door, Wendy right on her heels.

She opens the door to reveal Wisdom Master Blastneesh in the flesh.

It's like Corinne melts, falling to a heap at his feet, reaching out to actually *caress* his feet. She looks up and says, "Oh, Wisdom Master, I'm so glad you came."

Now Wendy is reaching toward him. I tense up as much as I can but still feel zapped. Nearly tripping over Corinne, Wendy throws her arms around Blastneesh and cries, "Beard-man!" Then she turns to look at me and beams. "He made me special!"

A faint smell of nag champa wafts to where I sit.

I want to explode, to disappear into my study, dig out the dagger I'd purchased on a college trip to Turkey, and come out slashing. My ears ring and it feels like my head will explode if I don't do something. I can't remember the last time my rage and anxiety collided in such a way as to create this perfect storm.

Wendy giggles as Blastneesh scoops her up. Corinne still lies folded at the man's feet. The bodyguard or chauffeur or whatever stands on the porch just outside the doorway.

Still filled with fury, I move toward the group to snatch Wendy away from that monster and tell Corinne to stand up and show some pride, for fuck's sake.

Something happens as I move closer to them, into Blastneesh's scent, into his *power*.

That's the only way I can describe it.

My hand is already raised, my index finger extended with the full intent of pointing it toward Blastneesh's face—right between his eyes—to flay him with all my accusations.

But, looking into those eyes, something happens.

Within only a couple seconds, I feel like my world as I've known it is turned upside down. All the anger and anxiety inflaming my brain and viscera—to the point of me feeling like a swollen red balloon—dissipates, deflating me. That's all it takes and it feels like the old me falls away like so much dead skin. Whatever beliefs, life plans, interests I might have had are completely obliterated. I'm now open to anything.

I would like to say I feel great shame when I kneel at the foot of the Wisdom Master, but I don't. A wild, cathartic joy swells my heart and I begin sobbing, something I hadn't even done at my father's funeral last year. The new me—the me who being close to Blastneesh renders a very real possibility— will be incapable of shame. Negative emotions will not be able to find a home in the new me.

I feel welcome.

I feel safe.

Secure.

Loved.

A love I haven't felt since my dad and stepmom told me they would pay for my college education. A love I haven't felt since meeting Corinne so many years ago. A love I haven't felt since holding Wendy for the first time.

"You know why I have come?" Blastneesh says.

Corinne looks up, her cheeks slick with tears, and says, "Oh yes, Wisdom Master."

He places a hand on the top of her head and says, "Because I am needed."

Wendy's nine fingers have formed Blastneesh's beard into two tufts and she's milking them like teats.

Corinne and I gradually stand. I will not say we regain our composure because I don't feel anything resembling composure can ever be felt again. All composure is a social construct, a dampening of feelings and emotions. What I want to feel is bliss. And I'm feeling it in abundance. My clothes feel restrictive. The house and neighborhood feel restrictive. The entire life I've made for myself and my family feels restrictive.

A shimmering blue glow encapsulates our living room. I feel light, like I now exist on some planet that has less gravity. My breathing slows and deepens as I drink heavily of the oxygen around me.

Corinne and I stumble over to the couch with goofy grins on our faces. Blastneesh sets Wendy down on the floor and she runs off to her bedroom, almost like she knows her mother and I need to be alone with him. Usually, if we have a visitor, it's like pulling teeth to get her to go off and do something else. The only time we can be alone with company is after she's gone to bed, usually after several attempts.

"I am only asking that you listen to me for a few minutes." Blastneesh speaks slowly, hypnotically. The meaning of the words coming from his mouth doesn't even matter. "Tall Rex will make us some tea. We will have tea and talk. When the cups are empty, we will leave. Then we will be reunited and we will all be part of each other for the rest of our lives."

Corinne and I just nod stupidly as Tall Rex wanders into the kitchen and prepares tea.

32

ten

It's the longest fucking cup of tea in the history of humankind. By the time Blastneesh and Tall Rex leave, I feel hol-
lowed out, dragged across hot coals, exposed. More importantly, I have a sense of purpose. I haven't felt this driven
since attempting to rid the house of all unnatural toxins in
preparation for Wendy's home water birth.

Mostly, tea time with the Wisdom Master consisted of a
confessional-style video Corinne had recorded on her phone
and sent to the Wellnevermindfulness Group. The irony of it
was not lost on me. While I was fighting with the same organization, Corinne was pleading with them. Even after the incident with Wendy. An incident I was still certain Blastneesh
was guilty of. But guilt was such a harsh word. He was at the
center of it. He'd orchestrated and perhaps even perpetrated
the event, but it was not without purpose. It was a catalyst,
that much is now very easy for me to understand. Like that
time I got the results my cholesterol was a couple points
higher than the normal range, sending me on a year and a half
of veganism and virtue porn that ended only because my teeth

were deteriorating and I'd developed a gluten rash from eating too many overly processed, seitan-based meat substitutes. But my cholesterol numbers had been great at my next checkup. Plus, think about all the animals we'd spared and what a positive impact that probably made on the environment.

Corinne's video is another such catalyst. I find myself distracted by it as I read Wendy's stories to her and put her to bed. Obviously, my first inclination is toward anger at having been sacrificed—let's just call it what it is—to the gods of shame. However, the more I unpack my feelings to analyze them, the more I convince myself it wasn't really about me. Or, rather, it was, but it was more about how Corinne perceived me.

I'm just relieved she doesn't see me as a monster.

She started all the way back in college when we'd first met. Her delivery was strained and tear-filled. She presented herself as a woman on the verge of a nervous breakdown and I made a mental note to ask her if she'd been unmedicated when she recorded the video. If so, it would have been the only such day since she'd given birth to Wendy.

She told the camera—and, ultimately, Blastneesh—that she was intrigued by me because she'd never met anyone on a coffee and cigarette diet. I thought I'd been joking when I told her that but, to a casual observer, it would have seemed like reality. I just didn't sleep well and those were the things that got me through my studies without falling unconscious. Not long after hooking up, Corinne joined me on the coffee and cigarette diet, enthusiastic about losing weight every day and having so much energy. We ended that after going on a hike that devolved into me having a massive coughing fit and her having to sit down because she was lightheaded and afraid of passing out. Shortly thereafter, we ended up moving in together. Because we were in our last semester of school and

Corinne was overly concerned about paying off her student loans after graduation and we were both worried about becoming your run-of-the-mill American fatasses, we decided to go povertarian. If it wasn't something not traditionally dropped from a humanitarian plane, we didn't eat it. It was lentils and rice and some canned food. Once a month, as an indulgence, we'd eat fast food using two-for-one coupons we found in our mailbox. We bought all our clothes from the thrift store. Even socks and underwear. We continued this way until after graduation when Corinne began applying for jobs and, despite her B.A., the employment agencies kept trying to send her for manufacturing jobs at factories and she said it was probably because she looked like a scrapper. I didn't have that problem because my uncle got me the job at the company I still work for. I was fortunate to not have to go through the whole job-seeking thing but what Corinne said resonated with me and I started wondering if my looking and smelling poor was keeping me from rising above the ranks of email customer service representative. I told Corinne my uncle could probably get her a job, but she said she didn't want any handouts. Listening to her talk about the job search was getting exhausting and I started to panic when I thought about how many minutes of my life it was eating up.

I proposed to her.

She said yes.

Now she could obsess on the wedding and force me to obsess on it too.

We needed to look good. We would probably never be on display for this many people ever again and we needed to look our best. She made Blastneesh think this was all my idea. We bought better clothes. She put all of hers on a credit card. I had to tap into my trust fund. As an early wedding present, I bought us both gym memberships. She said I sent her links to fashion and make-up tutorials of various looks I wanted her to try out but I have no recollection of ever doing this. We would go to the gym and she would try out new looks every couple of days and the sex we had during that time was amazing. Our bodies were changing. Our *brains* were changing as we began wading into the adult world. By the time the wedding came around, we'd both locked onto the looks and behavior patterns that seemed to garner the most positive attention from our friends, families, and co-workers. She landed her first serious job and we bought our first house in the artsy historical district close to downtown and it was five years of upward mobility, craft beer, medical marijuana, trendy new restaurants, Friday nights with friends—concerts, plays, films—lavish self-care weekends. Then she said—and I do remember this—one night after an ayahuasca retreat when we were lying in bed, I blurted out, "Oh my god, we're just avatars!"

That's when she says I forced us on a path to be more authentic, but I again say this was some maternal nesting instinct governed by frugality on her part. We had grown too far away from our true selves. We needed to live a life more natural and primal. We donned our avatars to go to work but when we came home, it was organic everything. No technology. No frills. It was a holistic philosophy that, at the time, seemed perfectly balanced to me. All the extra money we spent on food was saved because we stripped our clothes off as soon as we came home and we didn't have to buy any leisure wear. We canceled our cable and internet. Turned our phones off the second we came through the door. Artificial lighting can alter mood and disrupt sleep so we got rid of all our lightbulbs, blinds, and curtains. The only electricity we used was for the refrigerator, stove, and water heater because we weren't the Swiss fucking Family Robinson. We went off our antidepressants, although I did keep going to therapy, telling Corinne it was the equivalent of seeing a village shaman. She went off birth control. Talking and fucking were our only forms of entertainment once the sun went down and we couldn't read or hike. The hiking could only be done in our tiny, privacy-fenced backyard, since both of us were naked and barefoot. Really more like walking in circles than hiking. It wasn't long before Corinne got pregnant. I bought light-bulbs because I didn't want her injuring herself while stumbling around in the dark. From the moment I did that, it was like the spell was broken. I began to understand how Lucifer could, by being the bringer of light, also be seen as the anti-christ. The light reveals the cruel machinations of the world.

We sold the old house in the cool part of town. We were now in our early thirties. Prospective parents, not party people anymore. Our child couldn't grow up with bars and night-clubs in her backyard. Not to mention all the crime and home-less people. We bought a McMansion in a desirable but boring town nearby. The school's ratings were so good we wouldn't even need to send the kid to private school. That, combined with the narcotizing effect of being new parents, lasted for maybe the next year and a half.

Again, Corinne made the next phase sound like it was all at my instruction, but the only thing I did was ask "What was the happiest you've ever been?" one night after having a long discussion about how stale and stagnant our life had become. She's the one who answered with "Probably college. In the sorority." And that was how our quiet McMansion became the suburban equivalent of a frat house. Wendy was shipped off to the grandparents on Friday and our house was packed with co-workers and people we met in bars and found on craigslist. We were drinking until blacking out. Every weekend was a bacchanale. Every now and then we'd hook up with other people. We probably should have stopped when Corinne caught a case of herpes and I got chlamydia, but we didn't. The last great faux frat party we had at our house was packed. Word had gotten out. I spent most of the night trying to pick up a small, glasses-wearing, artsy twenty-year-old who reminded me of my first girlfriend. Corinne had gotten way too drunk way too early and had said she wanted to see how many people she could hook up with. I was met with nothing but resistance from my quarry, but every time I spotted Corinne, she was leading yet another person to our bedroom. I didn't want to, but I kept count. She had started leading them back two and three at a time. By the time the night had grown late and the party had thinned out, she was up to nineteen. Mostly dudes, but some girls too. Including the one I'd put so much time into. By the time we went to bed, I think Corinne was looped on something stronger than alcohol because she said, "You should let three guys come on you sometime. It's . . . cataclysmic." And I couldn't help thinking about the slightly damp, odd-smelling bed I was lying in. I told her I was going to sleep in the guest room. It was the first night we'd ever slept apart. I felt humiliated, emasculated. Something had to change.

It was shortly after this Corinne got let go for masturbating in the office. The incident report amidst her dismissal papers specifically mentioned the size of the dildo she'd been using. *Why?* I wondered. It seemed irrelevant. I felt like it was only mentioned to make me feel small, in more ways than one. So I vied for a promotion at work. Told Corinne I was tired of feeling like a cuckold. From here on out, we were going to be on the straight and narrow. She was to be the demure housewife. I was going to be the man of the family. I was going to be *a man.* I grew a fabulous, well-groomed beard, started taking testosterone, got the promotion, went on hunting trips with Ted from accounting where we would bag deer and elk and beam at each other because we were *providing* for our *families*. I didn't want to let Corinne and Wendy down. I wanted them to be proud of me. I needed to be around for them. I needed to be healthy and clear of mind. I needed to live forever, or at least for a really long time. I got in shape. Went running. Lifted weights five times a week. Joined an MMA class. In her dumb, one-sided confessional video, Corinne tried to spin this into me being a vain, narcissistic creep, specifically mentioning the time she'd asked me what the hell I was doing after I'd attacked a squirrel that had been ritualistically making a mockery of Corinne's flowerbeds, ripping it apart with my bare hands. She'd seemed appalled, yelling at me, "Your male optimization is turning you into a real asshole!"

Corinne had a way of making everything seem negative. I started giving myself blueberry and flax meal suppositories because I'd read it was good for the prostate. Prostate cancer had affected nearly every male in my family who lived long enough to develop it and I became very concerned. One night, Corinne invaded the bathroom while I was in the shower, thoroughly engrossed in my nightly routine.

"Dear god, what are you doing?" she asked.

"I'm massaging my prostate!" I yelled over the running water. "Give me some privacy!"

"You're fingerbanging your asshole!" I could tell she wanted to laugh. Knew she would be on Facebook talking to her bitchy friends about what she'd caught me doing, asking them if anyone thought this was "normal." Like all these women with obese, fashion-challenged husbands were going to think being a fully optimized male specimen with the potential for immortality is remotely normal.

In bed that night, she told me I could tell her if I was gay, that she'd always had her suspicions.

And there it was . . . after everything I'd done to be a man, she was still trying to cut me down, still trying to emasculate me. That sent me on my most recent spiral.

When we go to bed that night after meeting with Blastneesh, I feel raw. I try to swallow my anger. There are so many things I want to point out to Corinne. How I'm not the only problem. I want to bring up her depression, her haziness, her attention-seeking hypochondria, her borderline nymphomania, her mean streak, her inattentiveness, how she always wants to make herself seem different than the herd when, deep down, we both know she just wants to be like everyone else, she just wants to shop at more expensive stores.

But I don't bring it up.

Because Blastneesh, through his sheer presence, has changed something inside me.

In just a few days, Corinne and I are going to drop Wendy off at her grandparents' and then we are going to get on a plane to fly to Dayton, Ohio, where Blastneesh will have a car waiting to take us to his retreat in Twin Springs, Ohio, and we are going to spend an undisclosed amount of time re-wiring our brains and setting our souls on fire. After that, we are going to re-enter the world and everything is going to be fresh and new. We are going to be "blasted," occupants of our own glorious bubbles, connected to everyone else on the planet whether they know it or not. We are going to feel "exactly good," which also happens to be the title of Blastneesh's latest book he'd been generous enough to leave behind.

My phone vibrates as I close my eyes. I pick up. There's a notification from the Wellnevermindfulness app.

"Prompt payment is mandatory."

I go to my account to look at two charges. The first is for 30,000 dollars, for the two retreat packages. The second is for 18.99, for the book.

I take a deep breath, tamping down the anger and hearing the voice of the Wisdom Master in my head.

"I will teach you to construct your glorious bubble. By the time you leave my retreat . . . you will be . . . exactly good."

Exactly good sounds great.

I sleep for twelve hours and do not wake up or have a single dream.

I'm ready.

eleven

As laid out in the "Pretreat" program available on the app, Corinne and I have three days to prepare for the retreat. This program, buried behind a pay wall and only accessible to those who've paid for the retreat package, is broken up into three six-hour long audio segments meant to be listened to as one sleeps. The three parts are: The Letting Go, The Clearing of the Mind (The Forgetting), and The Preparation.

As I go about making my turmeric-ginger tea that morning and getting Wendy ready to drop off at her grandmother's while Corinne sleeps in, I feel like the guided audio has done its job. I understand why one should listen to it while dozing off or even fully asleep. It's like an instruction manual, except the instructions are absorbed into the brain, eliminating the need to try and process the words or parse their meaning. Going about my morning tasks, I have this phrase echoing in my head: "Be the savage editor of your life." The meaning is clear. Get rid of all unnecessary and unwanted things. Get rid of all that stands between me and enlightenment. I'm not sure if those phrases were uttered in the audio or if that's simply how my unconscious brain chooses to interpret it.

Once my tea has finished steeping, I screw the lid onto my ceramic travel mug. Wendy sits at the table picking at her banana buckwheat pancakes.

"Eat up. We need to go," I say.

"Not hungry," she says. Even though I'm very much in my own head, well on my way to constructing my glorious bubble, I can tell something's wrong.

"What's wrong?"

She holds up her hands, extending her one remaining pinkie. "Do you think it'll fall off?"

"Your finger?"

"Yeah. I want it to be like the other one."

"Fingers don't just fall off, sweetie."

"Maybe Beardman will take it too. Can you ask him?"

I take my travel mug over to the table, pull back a chair, and sit next to Wendy.

"You just think that way because it's still different to you. Just wait. You'll get used to it. You might even really appreciate the one pinkie you have."

"What's that mean?"

"What's what mean?"

"Preciate."

"*A*ppreciate. It means . . . I guess it's like when you stop to think about how much you like something you've always had."

She takes a small bite of her food and a grim look settles over her eyes as she thinks about what I'd said. Then she puts her fork down on her plate and slides it away from her.

"But . . . if I didn't have it, I wouldn't have to ever think about it."

"That's very wise of you," I say. "And maybe if you still feel that way when you're all grown up, you can do something about it."

She sighs. "I can't wait to be grown up."

"Aw, you should just enjoy being a kid. Trust me."

She takes a sip of her organic strawberry and hemp seed smoothie. "I guess," she says. "Maybe Brie's finger will fall off. She always wants to be just like me."

"Maybe," I say. "You never know." I want to tell her once again that fingers don't just fall off but if she's already forgotten about the viciousness of Blastneesh removing her finger, even managing to see it as a pleasant experience, then I don't want to force her to relive the trauma. Only, maybe, it wasn't really that traumatic? She hadn't been afraid of Blastneesh when she'd seen him. Quite the opposite. "Now finish up so we can get you to Grandma's."

"I don't wanna." I'm not sure if she means finishing her breakfast or going to her grandmother's.

"C'mon. If you're a good girl and finish up, I'll have a surprise for you tonight."

"Really? What is it?"

"Now, if I told you that, it wouldn't be a surprise, would it?"

"Guess not. Is it fun?"

"It can be. I guess it depends on what you decide to do with it."

"I'll make it fun," she says.

"I'm sure you will."

"Where's Mama?"

"She's in bed."

"Can I see her before I go?"

"Sure. But let her rest."

Wendy scoots her chair back and bounds upstairs to our bedroom. I finally take a sip of my tea. It's way too hot. Startlingly hot. I spit it out in a scalding spray and throw the mug into the sink where it shatters as loudly as a gunshot. Corinne doesn't come down to investigate the noise.

I grab my keys and stalk to the foot of the stairs.

"Come on, Wendy!" I yell. "We need to go!"

By the time I get to work I'm in a state of high agitation, although this could be due in large part to the incident at the coffee shop. Because I wasn't able to finish my morning tea, I stopped there after dropping Wendy off. I had to go in, as they didn't have a drive-thru. I ordered a double espresso, which they served with a small glass of water. I knew I was supposed to drink the water first, to cleanse my palate, but I was so thirsty for the caffeine I pounded the double-shot first. It had been a while since I'd had coffee and it attacked my tongue with a thick bitterness I hadn't experienced since performing oral sex on Corinne while she was on an Arapahoe canoe bark supplement. I quickly slammed the glass of water before gagging and vomiting all over the counter. Filled with rage, not even thinking about it, I threw the glass at the nearest barista—a tiny woman with dreadlocks down to her ass. The glass missed her, shattering on the table she was wiping down. While I didn't injure her, I at least got her attention.

She turned, shocked, immediately backing away from me.

I wiped the vomit from my lips and said, "Some people are allergic to carbonation! You need to let people know about that shit!"

I stalked up to the barista. Since throwing up, I felt better, as though I'd already purged my body from the evil that carbonation can do, but now it was a matter of principle.

"Look at your menu board." I pointed to the small chalkboard behind the counter. "You or *someone* goes through the trouble of writing 'gluten free' and 'vegan' and 'contains tree nuts' and 'contains soy' and 'non-GMO.' Nowhere on there does it say 'contains bubbles' or 'carbonated.' Just so you know, *some* of us can't handle it. It's a toxin, a foreign entity, an abomination." Now there was a crescent of baristas to either side of the one I'd thrown the glass at and I was sure every customer's eyes were on me. "So I had to get sick all over the counter and embarrass myself. If I ever come back here, I want to feel more informed. Not like I'm being attacked. That's your job—to *inform* the *consumer*. If that's not changed, you'll be hearing from my lawyer. You should be happy I'm not already on the phone with him."

The baristas only stared at me. I wasn't getting anything out of them. That's why they were baristas. Their brains were not optimized to handle my complaint and I couldn't illuminate them with the limited time I had. So I stormed out amidst their laughter. I distinctly heard one of them say, "Aren't bubbles just air? JFC."

In the car, I pulled up Facebook on my phone and sent out a post that said: "Never going to Drip Van Winkle's again. They Lie and Deceive the Customer."

By the time I got to work, the post already had three comments, all from people I didn't know in real life.

The first one said: "Racist."

The second one said: "Fucking incel."

The third said: "Entitle peace of shit."

I hesitated for only a second before deleting my account, wondering if I'd backed the photos up somewhere. There were all those photos of Corinne and me in Bali. The photo of me standing in front of the Porsche SUV, so proud, our first family car. The photo of me in front of the elk Ted and I bagged in Colorado. Maybe this was what Blastneesh meant by letting go. I didn't stop there. I restored my phone to the factory settings, pulled the SD card, and chucked the phone into the parking lot. It felt good. The savage editing of my life had begun.

It doesn't stop there.

When I reach my office to find the cleaning lady once again watering and pruning my foliage, I don't freak out. I don't throw anything. Regardless, the cleaning woman's defenses are up. She flinches when she notices me.

"Didn't know if you were coming in today or not. Mr. Harper told me to take care of this."

"Get rid of them," I say.

"Sorry?"

"Get rid of them. Take them down to the dumpster."

"There must be a hundred plants."

I was pretty sure there were only around twenty, but it probably looked like more if you were super lazy or couldn't count very well.

"That's right. And I'm telling you to get rid of them."

I can tell she doesn't want to do it. Rather, she *does* want to do it, would love nothing more than to take these beautiful things that keep me healthy and greatly enhance my quality of life and chuck them all into the dumpster, but is simply not used to heavy lifting and doesn't want to put forth the effort this requires.

She sighs. "I guess if that's what you want me to do."

"It is. As soon as possible."

As I suspect, she starts with the smallest one and seems to return in fifteen-minute intervals, probably so she can smoke cigarettes or weed with every trip. I sit at my desk and construct a company-wide email explaining that I will be gone for an indeterminate amount of time.

That evening I leave a completely empty office to find my phone sitting on the hood of my car on top of an anonymous note that says: "Thought this might be yours."

I wonder how they knew until I remember paying a fair

amount of money to have Corinne's and my wedding photo laser etched onto the back of the rose gold case.

twelve

After dinner, Corinne and I sit at the table in a food-narcotized daze while Wendy works on a drawing with her crayons. In an effort to use up everything in the pantry, Corinne spent most of the day cooking and I'd come home to veritable mountains of food piled on the formal dining room table. We usually only eat there if we have guests. We ate until we couldn't eat anymore and spent a considerable amount of time feeding the leftovers to the garbage disposal.

Wendy looks up from her drawing and says, "Can I have my surprise now?"

Corinne's mouth ticks up in the slightest hint of a smile. Her eyes are glazed over and I can't tell if she's blissed out, stoned, or on the verge of tears.

"Do you want to tell her what it is?" Corinne says, looking right at me, through me, as though exploring my insides. "I mean, you've been looking forward to this since she was born, haven't you?"

This is clearly a jab and not necessarily true, but I decide to let her have it, not even telling her her unbridled cynicism is not appreciated. Let her believe what she wants. It's based on the cumulative knowledge of our past, but once we have truly let go of everything, there will be fewer things in our lives to fuel her erroneous statements.

I turn to Wendy and say, "What is it you want more than anything in the world?"

She puts her crayon down on the construction paper, purses her lips, and looks up at the ceiling. This is how people think hard on the TV and in cartoons.

"An iPad," she says.

"You already have one of those."

"*Not the latest version,*" she sings.

"That's just what you think you want."

"All my friends have it. I've wanted it since it came out." Wendy's a smart girl and it's fascinating listening to her build her case. "Think about it," she says. "It would be better for the environment. I could do my drawings on that. No paper. I don't know what crayons are made out of but I wouldn't need those either. Not to mention all the money you'd save. Plus I could donate my old one to a poor kid who would just be happy to have one. They wouldn't even care if it wasn't the latest version."

"Those are all very good points," I say. "But we're going to give you something no one else in your school has. Then all the other kids are going to want what you have just like you want their new iPads."

She rolls her eyes in mock frustration but I can tell by the big grin on her face she's excited to learn about it.

"Just tell me what it *is!*" she squeals.

I take her by the hands and look into her little eyes.

"Your mother and I have decided to give you . . . your freedom."

The excitement on her face fades a little and she says,

"Where is it?"

"It's inside you. It's outside. It's wherever *you* want it to be."

Now she pauses, the excitement turning to confusion. Earlier, when I described Wendy as a smart kid, I meant that in more the left-brained, critical thinking kind of way. When it comes to more abstract, philosophical thinking, she might have a way to go.

"I don't understand," she says.

"You're free," I say. "Free to do whatever you want."

"Like a grown-up?"

"Even freer than a grown-up."

"I can do whatever I want?"

"Whatever. You. Want."

She makes her thinking face again and says, "I want to go to Grandma's."

"Then you can go to Grandma's."

"Really? On a weeknight?"

"That's what being free means. I mean, if she lets you in and says it's okay. You can't just break in. No one's above the law."

Wendy laughs and says, "She'll let me in. Grandma never says no."

I boop her on the nose and say, "I think you're right."

"I'd better pack a bag," she says. "Can I go now?"

"Whenever you want."

She bolts from the table and up to her room.

Corinne sniffles loudly.

"It'll be okay," I say.

"I know." Corinne uses a finger to brush a stray tear from her cheek. I'm not overly concerned because it's allergy season and Corinne has them worse than anybody I know. "I'm just so happy."

I take a sip of my tea—bag tea, the bitterness sends a shiver through me—and clutch one of Corinne's frigid hands.

"We should go see her off," I say.

"You're right," Corinne says.

By the time we make it into the living room, Wendy's already packed and coming back down the stairs. I can tell by the way her bag clanks and rattles she's only packed toys and nothing essential. Oh well, she'll have to learn.

"All ready," she says, beaming.

I bend to give her a hug.

"Have a wonderful time," I say.

"Enjoy your freedom," Corinne says.

"Is Grandma already outside?" Wendy asks.

"Did you call her?" Corinne asks.

"No. I thought you did."

"That's not how freedom works, honey," I say. "You can call her to see if she'll come get you or—there's the door—you could go head on over. It's a nice evening."

"Really?"

"Absolutely. You can stop at a friend's house, pet strange dogs, do anything you want. That's freedom."

In that moment, I'm incredibly proud of Wendy. I think a lot of other kids her age would be scared or at least hesitant. Wendy is neither of those things.

She walks to the front door, opens it, turns, and says, "I'll text you when I get there," and I feel like she's already grown up, headed off to college after spending the holidays at home.

"Be safe," Corinne says.

"I will. Love you guys," she says.

"Love you too," Corinne and I say at the same time.

And then our little girl is gone, all alone out in the big world, reveling in her gift of freedom until she lands in her first abusive, co-dependent relationship, probably with Corinne's mother—if she makes it there.

Corinne turns and leans her back against the door. She wipes away a couple of her stray tears and I ask her if she's taken her allergy medication today.

She opens her bloodshot eyes and says, "Fuck me."

I drag her out to the backyard and do what she asks. She weeps the entire time and it makes me harder than I've been since getting ginseng injected directly into the base of my dick.

thirteen

We don't sleep that night.

After our backyard adventure, I decide I don't want to let go of the contents of the liquor cabinet that I decided to re-stock after previously emptying it.

"We're . . . coming back," Corinne says.

"That may be," I say. "But I feel like, for this retreat to work, we need to approach it as though we are never coming back. Maybe these bodies will be coming back but, inside, we're going to be completely different people."

"I'm on so many medications there are bound to be some interactions."

"That'll just make things more exciting."

And while moving all the quarter- to half-full bottles onto the coffee table in the living room, I discover a small bindle of cocaine. I've never been a big fan of coke and have never bought any that I could remember. It's entirely possible one of our friends left it behind. This would make it a lot easier to get through all the booze.

I empty the contents of the bindle onto the coffee table and divide it into four thin rails. I sit down on the couch, preparing to do the first one.

"Do you have a dollar?" I ask.

"I haven't carried cash in years. No one carries cash anymore."

"I might have something in the car."

"Just use a straw."

"We don't have any. Bad for the planet."

I pause, close my eyes, nearly reeling with the incongruity of her not grasping certain things, and take a deep, calming breath. My vagus nerve is not going to reset itself.

"Do we have everything we need?" I ask.

"Everything we need for what?" she says.

"The retreat!" I don't know why this thought occurs to me and feel like it must have something to do with the pretreat audio. "Did we even listen to the same thing last night?" I ask.

She places her hand on my shoulder in that patronizing way she has when she assumes my thoughts are too jumbled to express myself clearly.

"Scott, baby, slow down. I don't know what you're talking about."

So *I* have to do the patronizing thing where I speak really slowly so she knows I think she's stupid and I'm trying to dumb down my speech.

"The audio file we listened to last night . . . Blastneesh said there were three stages we needed to complete before going to the retreat: The letting go, the forgetting, and the preparation. We need to have everything we need all packed before we begin the forgetting."

"I thought packing would be part of the preparation step."

"No. He meant mental preparation. I just need to pack stuff for the flight. We're not allowed to bring anything to the retreat."

She shrugs. "Okay. I don't really need to pack anything except my meds anyway."

I stand up. "You're . . . being infuriating."

"Go pack the fucking car then."

She sprawls back on the couch and slides her yoga pants to her knees, moves a hand down to her bare cunt.

"What . . . what are you doing?" I say.

"I'm sorry. You didn't satisfy me earlier."

Now it feels like I have a million different things I'm trying to deal with simultaneously.

"It *sounded* like I was satisfying you."

"Oh, it felt good. I just wasn't satisfied fully and if I'm going to do blow with you, I'll never do anything later. Besides, the therapist said I need to reach full satisfaction so I don't harbor so much resentment. Having a proper orgasm is one of the few things I can control."

"Who said anything about doing something later?"

"You'll want to. You'll have to fuck me one more time before you can let go."

"We'll see," I say. "We'll see."

But I've lost her. Her eyes are closed, her fingertips making slow circular motions around her clit, my semen from earlier slicking the cleft of her ass.

I run around the house gathering everything I'll need for the flight, making several trips out to the car. On the final trip, I finally remember what had started this and grab a dollar bill from the console. I always keep cash in there for parking, tolls, and the occasional strip club. There's also a homeless woman who loiters around one of my favorite juice bars downtown who gave remarkable head for only a few dollars.

By the time I get back into the house, Corinne's leggings are still down around her knees, but she's finished. She has her fingers in her mouth and a faraway look in her eyes. She likes to taste herself, claiming it's one of the best indicators of something changing within her body.

"How was it?" I ask.

"Something's . . . happening." There's a quality to her voice I've rarely heard. Something light and unburdened.

"Of course it is."

"Something beautiful."

"Something huge," I say. "Who were you thinking about?"

"Devon McConnell."

"The kid down the street?"

"Yeah."

"He's like twelve."

"I was feeling transgressive."

Looking at her, so blissed out, I find myself once again aroused. I approach her, unbutton my cargos, and let them drop to my ankles.

"I'll give you a dollar to suck my cock."

I think she'll brush me off or say something sarcastic. After all, she's just come and usually checks out after that.

To my surprise, she opens her eyes, looks deep into mine, and says, "I sure could use a dollar. I'm so hungry."

I slide my boxers over my erection and move closer to her and say, "I think you have a hungry nose," and she takes me into her mouth and I think about the homeless girl behind the juice bar and how she was, inexplicably, wearing blackface the last time she'd gone down on me.

When I'm close to finishing, Corinne pulls her head back and asks, "Can I swallow it? I need the nutrition."

And just so the illusion isn't ruined, because I always let the homeless girl swallow it, I say, "Sure."

Normally I make Corinne give it back. I thought she liked doing it. It was rare she ever gave me head and I think it's the fantasy for many women, after taking a load in the mouth, to spit that load back into the guy's mouth. It's why women always want to kiss you afterward. I asked for it back because, when you think about and regulate what you put into your body as much as I normally do, you don't just give that shit away. I always let the homeless girl swallow because I imagined my vitamin-rich semen was helping to sustain her. Plus, there was no way I was kissing her. Not with those teeth.

Once we're finished, we each do a line and settle back on the couch, Corrine with a bottle of Cuervo Silver and me with a heavily depleted bottle of Pappy Van Winkle.

"It wasn't as lumpy as last time," she says.

I search my brain for a compliment to return. "Your suction was really on point."

I light a joint, take a swig of bourbon, and settle back on the couch.

"Did Wendy ever text you?" I ask.

"Who?"

"Wendy. Our daughter?"

"Shit," she says. She sits up and digs around in the couch. When she wears yoga pants, she normally keeps the enormous phone tucked into her waistband. She finds it between two of the cushions and brings the screen to life.

"Nothing," she says. "You get anything?"

I pull my phone out of my pocket.

"Mine's not working. I threw it across the parking lot." The screen's all broken. I turn it over and show her the back. "Remember when you had this done for me?"

"What?" she asks.

"The etching of our wedding photo."

She smirks and looks at me like I'm crazy. "You had that done yourself. And it's not our wedding photo. It's your college water polo photo."

I study it harder. "Huh. Guess you're right."

"It's only nine-thirty. I'm sure she'll text soon. We can't afford to worry about it right now."

She turns on the TV and for the next couple hours we drink our expensive booze and watch videos of people popping pimples and multi-limb amputees trying to put on clothes.

Around midnight I say, "Shit. We need to listen to part two of the pretreat."

"You're right." Her eyes are hazy and unfocused. "But it's subliminal."

"That's right."

I bring the Wellnevermindfulness app up on the TV.

"How do you listen to something that's subliminal?"

"By not listening at all."

fourteen

Not long after cueing up the second part of the audio file, I begin going in and out of consciousness. I snort the third line of coke to try and renew my focus, hoping Corinne will forget about the fourth so I can suck that up too.

At one point, Corinne gets really excited.

"What is it?" My mouth feels thick and my words are slurred.

"Wendy finally texted!" Corinne shouted. "She's at the club!"

"Karen, baby, why are you shouting?" Did I just call her Karen?

"My name's not Karen!" she shouts. "Do I look like some middle-management loser whiner!"

"No, babe, you look unemployed." I know I've said the wrong thing right away.

"Oh, I do, do I!" She stands up from the couch and begins ripping off clothes I'd been completely unaware of her even putting on. Pajamas, maybe? After removing each article of clothing, she throws it at me with as much force as she can muster. She's sweaty and vibrating with some form of crazy energy. "I guess I'll go find a job!"

And before I can stop her, she's already gone.

"You say Candy was at the club?" I sit back on the couch, a smile plastering itself across my face. "That's our girl. Little party girl. Trendy Mindy." Wait. I don't think that's her name. Corinne had just said it, but I can't remember. I just had it. "Fuck it. It'll come to me."

There's still a lot of booze on the table but I can feel myself running out of steam. I quickly snort the last line of coke. I turn the volume of the speakers all the way up so Blastneesh's magical, subliminal non-voice can reach through the house. I gather up all the liquor bottles and take them upstairs in a precariously massive armload. I lean over the sink and let them all clink and roll into an even more precarious mountain. I then raise the stopper on the tub and begin emptying the bottles into it and placing the empties in the toilet. It isn't as impressive a bath as I'd hoped it would be.

There has to be some beer in the refrigerator. Everything else momentarily leaves my thoughts. A man on a mission. I quickly go down to the refrigerator and, thankfully, there's nearly a full twelve-pack of Heineken in it. Fortunately, the alcohol mitigates all the nasty carbonation. I can't remember if I'd read that somewhere or if it's just based on experiential knowledge. I'm overcome with gratitude thinking the voice sinking into my subconscious is somehow responsible for this bit of synchronicity.

"Fuck yes!" I pump my fist into the air. Am I crying?

I snatch the beer out of the refrigerator and take it back upstairs to the bathroom. I've forgotten the bottle opener. I'm not going downstairs again. I've seen people open bottles with their teeth and always thought it looked cool and tough but was too chickenshit to ever try it. But I don't feel chickenshit right now. I feel invincible! Like an invincible guy who wants to take a bath in expensive liquor and kind of expensive beer. I bring the cap end of the bottle up and clamp my perfect teeth down on it. I give it a yank. I try it again and again, alternating sides of my mouth. I can taste blood, and when I glance at myself in the mirror, it's slicking my chin. I yank down, the seal cracking and the cap flying off.

"Whoo!" I shout. "Take that, Heineken."

I take it to the bathtub and hold the bottle upside down, pouring hard. The last thing that plops out into the tub is one of my teeth. No worries.

I think about opening the rest of the bottles this way but don't want to lose any more teeth. I catch the next cap on the edge of the vanity and pull down. I continue doing this with the next several bottles. Eventually, a chunk of the counter chips off and hits my cheek like a bullet. I strip off my clothes and climb into the tub. It's a lot colder than I expect but it feels great on my fevered skin. I take handfuls of the stuff and slurp it down. Doesn't taste great and I begin fading hard before I even make a dent in it. I should probably just go to bed but don't feel like drying off or even moving, really, so I just lean my head against the tile and imagine the upcoming retreat. I can't remember the last time I've been this excited about anything.

fifteen

At first, I think I'm dreaming. Rather, I know I'm dreaming but the dream stops making sense. In the dream, I sit across from Blastneesh in some kind of outdoor temple. It looks like we're on a mountaintop, clouds swirling below us, the sunlight bright and warm overhead. Blastneesh has a curious smile on his face and I feel light and good. Then Blastneesh's eyes start to melt and smoke begins pouring from the empty sockets. I try to break out of my lotus position and go to him but, typical dream, I feel paralyzed. It isn't until I open my eyes that I realize something is very wrong.

I can still smell the smoke.

And beer.

And maybe vomit.

I'm still in the bathtub.

I stand up and look around, last night coming back to me like a laser-light show of fun awesomeness. Maybe it isn't morning yet. Maybe the smell of smoke isn't that serious. I imagine Corinne stumbling home from her late-night job search, attempting to make breakfast, and deciding to take a nap midway through without removing the food from the stove. But as I pull on my underwear and leave the bathroom, I can tell this is more than someone burning food. I still can't see any smoke or fire but my eyes start burning as soon as I open the bathroom door.

I stagger down the second-floor hallway shouting "Corinne!" and "Katie!" but neither of them leave their bedrooms so I assume they've already gotten out.

Wait.

Katie isn't even here. She left sometime last night. I think she went to a club and maybe her grandmother's after that. I'm pretty sure her name isn't even Katie and I cannot succumb to the embarrassing neglect I should feel about forgetting my only child's name. There isn't time for that.

I quickly go downstairs to find it thick with smoke. I still don't see the source but know, whatever it is, it's too late to put it out. I charge for the front door, the smoke attacking my eyes and lungs. I pull the door open and stagger outside into the purple pre-dawn, coughing, my eyes watering, barely conscious as I stumble off the porch and collapse onto the dewy lawn, the well-treated, hypoallergenic grass on my bare skin. Christ, I never knew the lawn was this comfortable. I should make it a point to sleep out here some night.

"Stop being so dramatic," someone says.

I turn to look at the source. It's Corinne. She's still naked. I struggle to sit up.

"Isn't it beautiful?" she says.

I blink the remaining smoke from my eyes and look at the house. Flames lick the sky from the back, black smoke billowing.

"It is kind of pretty." I still feel slightly stoned and don't know if it's from the booze and drugs or the subliminal audio.

"We don't need it anyway," she says.

"Guess not. It's just a house."

"Think about it. If we had a home to come back to, then how could we ever give ourselves to Blastneesh entirely?"

It dawns on me Corinne is taking this way more seriously than me. This moment of clarity feels oddly foreign. I've always dabbled in this kind of thing, moving from one fad to the next, usually on the later side of whatever the fad happens to be. If there had been truth to any of them, if any of them changed my life the way they were supposed to, I would have stuck with it . . . maybe. But I get bored with things and move on. At my current age, I have a hard time convincing myself anything will actually stick and have become somewhat quietly aware I've embraced the cliched notion that life is about the journey and not the goal. Which is death. All life ends in death. To ultimately succumb to one philosophy or lifestyle means I will be doing that until I die, thus putting one foot in the grave. I tried the app because it seemed new and interesting in a really boring way and I'd heard a number of celebrities I highly respected say favorable things about it. Then Corinne had taken to it and, if I was being honest with myself, had taken over at that point. I obviously wanted to balk at the cost of the retreat and the disruption to my comfortable lifestyle but I was, ultimately, curious about it. If we paid that much for something, I doubt it's going to be some sort of authentically spiritual, ascetic nightmare. I imagine relaxing, lazy days around some rural ashram, punctuated with softball spiritual exercises and devolving into evenings of partner swapping and group sex. Everyone there will really just be bored rich people like Corinne and me. I'm sure the food will suck, but that will probably be the most uncomfortable part. If it works out, we can make arrangements to attend another one before coming back to our comfortable lives.

The blaze is rapidly consuming the house.

"Why didn't an alarm go off?" I ask.

"I disabled them."

"I could have died."

"But you didn't."

"But I could have."

"But you didn't. If you had, it would have been meant to be."

"Still . . . this is like attempted murder or something."

"It's not attempted murder if I knew you wouldn't die."

"But how did you know that?"

"I saw a green light."

I swallow the smoky, boozy, bloody, sour taste in my mouth and tongue my broken tooth, one of the front ones. "What does that even mean?"

"If you see a green light, it means it's safe to drive through an intersection. You wouldn't call that attempted murder. It's always possible there will be people in the crosswalk but you know it's safe to drive through because the light is green. If you tell yourself you're only going to drive through the intersection when the light is red, hoping you eventually hit another driver or possibly a pedestrian, *that's* attempted murder. If you pay attention to the signals, you can't go wrong."

I find it interesting she's opted for a driving metaphor since she lost her license after her third ticket for reckless op. This got me thinking about tickets and crime and law enforcement.

"We should go," I say.

"Why? Our flight's not till tomorrow."

"We can't just sit here and watch our house burn down."

"Why not? We bought the damn thing. We can do whatever we want."

"It's arson."

"Is it?"

"Pretty sure. I don't know."

"People buy things to burn all the time. They're called

logs. It's called gas."

She has a point. I remind myself to buy a Tesla when we get back.

I say, "Insurance fraud."

"How is it fraud if we never submit a claim?"

"We're just going to throw all that money away?"

"What's the point in having it if we don't need it?"

I clasp my hands around the back of my head and let it hang between my raised knees. My disappointment must be palpable.

Corinne comes over and puts a hand on the back of my head. "Don't worry," she says. "I started it in the kitchen so I'm sure you can file a claim if you want to."

I knock her hand off mine, looking back up at the burning house framed by the now lightening sky.

"We still need to go," I say.

"Shouldn't we be here when someone shows up?"

"You're naked and smell like a teenager's come rag. I reek of booze and look like I've been assaulted. We don't really know where our daughter is—"

"She went home with the band. Some people named Team Klaus. She texted and said they were going to take her to Mom and Dad's later today."

"Okay. Be that as it may, I don't want to be here when the cops and firetrucks show up."

"So we . . . what? Tell them we had a cooking incident, panicked, and decided to go to the airport?"

"We'll just tell them we left a burner on or something. Fuck. I don't know."

"Fine," she huffs. "Not sure we're going to get this chance again but, fine, we'll go if you want to. Spending the day in a LaQuinta Inn watching *Forensic Files* will be so much more entertaining than thoroughly reveling in this once in a lifetime experience."

I stand up, my legs stiff, and walk over to her. I place a hand on her sticky back, warm with the increasing intensity of the fire.

"Look, I just don't want to miss the retreat, okay? We've both been looking forward to this. What if we have to stick around? There *will* be an investigation whether we want it or not."

The extremely rare sound of sirens in the distance couldn't have been timed better.

"You're right," she says. She sniffles and wipes a tear from her eye. The smoke is probably getting to her. "I just . . . we've had so many good times in that house. It feels incomplete to not see this through."

"We can always come back and look at the rubble."

"I guess you're right again."

"My keys are in the house," I say.

"Can't you control it through the app?"

"My phone . . ."

"Oh, right."

I look at her emaciated and naked body and say, "You obviously don't have yours on you."

Then her face lights up and she says, "That's where you're wrong, mister."

She squats down and fishes between her legs, sliding her large iPhone out of her pussy. "Good thing these are waterproof now."

"I'm sure that's exactly what the manufacturers intended."

Corinne doesn't have the BMW app on her phone and we have an intensely anxious few minutes while waiting for it to download, brainstorming until I can remember my log in information, followed by a crash course in how to actually use the app. By the time we're in the car and headed away from the house, I swear I see flashing lights in the rearview.

Once we're out of our quiet suburb and into the surrounding woods, it becomes apparent to me that I'm in no shape to drive. I can't keep the car on the road.

I pull over and say, "I can't do it."

"Can't do what?"

"Can't drive."

"Did you forget how?"

"I just . . . can't." I might be crying a little.

"Maybe I could try."

"Absolutely not."

She doesn't argue. Just sighs and says, "Guess I can order an Uber."

"I think you'll have to."

Downtown, on average, it takes about two minutes for an Uber to get to you. Out here, it says it's going to take twenty minutes.

I rummage around in back until I find the one t-shirt and the one pair of sleeping shorts I've brought. I don't see anything of Corinne's.

"You really didn't pack anything?"

"No. I told you. I should have put on some clothes before setting the house on fire. Guess I forgot."

I continue rummaging until I find a small emergency blanket. I toss it to her and say, "Here, put this on."

"Why?"

"Because . . . you can't get into an Uber naked."

"How do you think I got home?"

"Okay. Well, I'm not getting into an Uber with you naked."

"Fine."

She wraps the blanket around herself and secures a corner

so it stays on. It covers just enough.

"This looks dumb," she says.

"Not packing any clothes is dumb. It makes you look . . . artsy."

"You know, you're going to have to stop treating me like shit. I'm not just your unemployed house bitch anymore. I got a job."

"You got a job at, like, three o'clock in the morning?"

"Yeah, I did, Mr. Breadwinner."

"Where?"

"I'll be dancing and doing other stuff for the Sparkle Lounge."

"Great. So my wife's a stripper now." I try to sound disappointed but I can already feel my cock thickening.

"If we come back, yeah, I guess that's what I'll be doing."

"Our daughter will be so proud."

Corinne laughs derisively and says, "Did you forget her name again?"

My face flushes. "*No.*"

"What is it?"

"What is what?"

"Our. Daughter's. *Name.*"

"Look, it's been a crazy night, okay? I drank too much and the coke . . . weed . . . magic bath. The fire."

"Jesus fucking Christ, Scott. What's your daughter's name?"

"I'm not going to indulge your sadism by telling you. How do I know *you* haven't forgotten her name?"

"It's Wendy, okay? Our daughter's name is Wendy. We named her that because *you* love *Peter Pan.*" Now she casts a withering glare up and down my body. "That should have been a red flag right there."

sixteen

The sun has come up by the time we reach the LaQuinta by the airport. This is ridiculous. Perhaps my biggest failing thus far in life is somehow geographic. I thought we'd chosen the perfect houses in the perfect areas for our various life stages but now, in retrospect, living in an area where a LaQuinta Inn is the best you can do for hotels near the airport feels like we've aimed too low. Like I've unwittingly suffered some bout of aptitudinal shortcoming.

"I'm so sorry." I'm nearly in tears as we stand in front of the doors.

"It's fine," Corinne says. "It's just one night."

I take a deep breath and try my best not to break down completely. Besides, I know this will not be fine for Corinne. It would have probably been better if the Uber had just dropped us off at the airport. Then Corinne could have just complained about how tired and uncomfortable she is. At least, at the airport, she wouldn't be bored. She could wander around and buy stuff, interact with people, thus giving her that many more chances to force some sort of conflict. Not that the conflict would be her fault. We're elevated people. Corinne understands this even more than me. While she's never had to struggle financially, she never had a trust fund. We were born into certain circumstances and work hard to maintain our good life and are therefore entitled to live the way we want and the minimum wage slobs who work in the retail and food establishments of airports aren't able to wrap their heads around it. Oh, sure, some of them can. They're the people who, while probably never able to rise to the level of someone like Corinne or me, would still be able to find themselves with a pretty decent paying job at a pretty decent company. In fact, there have been times when I spot these people—the ones willing to bend the rules to provide me with the optimal shopping or dining experience—and pull out a business card and hand it to them and tell them they should contact my company and see if they have a job in the mailroom. I say something like, "Just don't forget that your rags-to-riches story started with me." The gratitude on their faces is usually all the thanks I need.

We enter the drab, depressing lobby of the hotel or motel or whatever it is, the interesting smells of cigarette smoke, mildew, and Indian food assaulting our senses.

I stop short.

"Do you have your purse with you?" I ask Corinne.

She looks at me like I'm stupid.

"No," she almost laughs. "You booked online, right?"

"No," I say. "I didn't know this was happening. Remember? I thought we'd be going from our house to the airport a little closer to the flight." I smack myself on the forehead. "Stupid. I'm so fucking stupid."

Now the tears I've tried so hard to hold back are flowing freely and I take stock of our situation and realize how easily we can be mistaken for gross poor people. Corinne's barely wearing clothes. I'm dressed in gym clothes. I never go out in public in my gym clothes even though most of the less fortunate living around us dress almost exclusively in athleisure wear. We smell like smoke from the house, old semen, unwashed vagina, vomit, booze, and whatever cheap, pungent air freshener the Uber driver had infused his car with. I've got that broken tooth and a deep gouge on my cheek.

Corinne puts a hand on my shoulder and says, "I'll handle it. Just . . . go sit down."

I drag my suitcase over to what looks like the most uncomfortable chair in the world and sit down. It's as uncomfortable as it looks. Where do people find this shit? I glance up as Corinne approaches the front desk and the anxiety takes a firm hold of me. She leans against the counter, folding her arms over it and leaning in. I can't watch this. I should be the one up there talking to the clerk. Negotiating. Working out a deal. Watching Corinne negotiate will be like watching the slow dismantling of my masculinity. Part of me wants to charge up there and elbow Corinne out of the way. Although once I notice the clerk is male, I begin to feel a little better about letting Corinne handle it. The clerk now stands directly across from her as she speaks. It's low and I can't hear what she's saying. She throws her head back over her shoulder, gesturing to me, and I take that as my cue to leave. I don't want to hold her back. While Corinne has the unique ability to fuck up most things, she also has the unique ability to acquire things, positions, etc. in which to fuck up. I typically do not question how she comes about these things. I always just assume most of it has to do with family connections or some hidden stream of wealth. Maybe I feel like me being there would hold her back or maybe I just don't want to see how it's actually done, as though that will somehow destroy the magic.

My whole body feels like rubber as I step outside, the heat already oppressive.

I haven't smoked a cigarette since college but find myself with a sudden craving for one. I pat the pockets of my gym shorts as though they might contain either cigarettes or a lighter. Of course I don't have either of those things on me. I go over to the ashtray on one side of the door. I read somewhere that tobacco, in and of itself, is not necessarily that bad for you. It's smoking it that gives you cancer, ruins your lungs and teeth, and turns you into a disgusting addict. There have even been studies suggesting it's good for boosting brain power and curbing anxiety. It might even help with Parkinson's and Alzheimer's. Also, the demographic with the highest percentage of smokers is schizophrenics. Not as glamorous as the French or Italian, but more telling. There must be something about nicotine that calms the brain.

I pluck out nearly a full cigarette, rip off the filter and the charred tip, and pull back the paper. I take the fresh tobacco from the paper and place it on my tongue, chewing it a little before swallowing it down. It isn't as disgusting as I think it will be. I go back to the ashtray to grab a few more butts. I find a bench to sit down on and go about dismantling them. I sit, eat some tobacco, and try not to think about what Corinne is doing to get us a room.

I'm not wearing my watch and don't have my phone on me, so I have no idea how much time has passed. I start feeling lightheaded and a little nauseated. The heat is really getting to me. I'm pretty sure I'm going to be sick. I stand up, the world spinning, and head back to the front doors where I'm met with Corinne.

"We're all set," she says.

I turn and vomit into a fake potted plant.

"Perfect," she says.

seventeen

"What did you do to that guy to get the room?" I ask.

Corinne removed her blanket as soon as we were in the room and now stands in front of the window looking out at the parking lot filled with the sad cars of people who've probably come to this squalid hotel to overdose on drugs or have sex with lower quality prostitutes.

"*Do* to him?" She looks at me over her shoulder, eyebrow raised.

"Yeah. You have to suck his cock or what?"

She turns fully around. She looks mad.

"Is that the only way you think women can get anything done? With sex?"

"It just seems like the easiest way. I'd do it if I was a woman."

"If you were a woman, you'd suck some stranger's cock for a night in a shitty motel?"

"I mean . . . it's kind of an emergency."

"If you must know, I told him you were an abusive spouse, that we were on vacation, and I thought this might be my only chance. The cops should be here any minute."

"You what?" Now *I'm* mad. "What about the retreat? Fuck, Corinne!" I immediately start pacing around the room, like I have anywhere to go or any way of getting there.

"Calm down," she says. Now she walks over to me. "I told him the truth. That we lost everything in a fire. He said he understood and that the same thing had happened to his sister last month . . . after I let him fuck me in the ass."

This makes me immediately enraged again. I have to tell myself she's joking because I'm too afraid of her at that moment to ask.

"I'm kidding," she says.

I force out a laugh and say, "I should fuck you in the ass for that. Make sure you're telling the truth."

"What's stopping you?" She surprises me by whipping her hand across my face, the satisfying smack echoing around the room. "I'll tell you what's stopping you." She moves even closer to me and spits in my face. "You're too stupid. You probably can't even figure out how."

"We've done that before."

"Before you lost your goddamn mind. Before you drank it away. Before you started living off weed. Before you gave half your brain and everything we own to some fucking guru charlatan."

I try to stop cowering from her. "That was your idea."

Now she pushes me.

"Was it?" she says. "That was a bad thing I did, huh?" And she pushes me again.

"I didn't say that."

She pushes me again and again, until I'm up against the wall.

"You need the *balls* to get your misbehaving wife under fucking control."

She reaches out and rips my t-shirt off. The yoga has given her superhuman strength.

"That was the only shirt I had."

"What are you gonna do about it?" She shoves me harder against the wall. "You gonna fuck me in my tight little ass so I can actually feel it?" She drops her hand to clutch at my crotch. "Can you even get hard anymore? Are you even turned on by anyone who isn't a teenager or a slimy whore who lives in an alley downtown?"

She yanks the front of my shorts down, my semi-erect penis popping out.

She grabs her phone and starts taking pictures of it, giggling in the most meanspirited way she can manage.

"It's so small," she says.

"Stop it."

"I'm gonna send these to all my friends . . . just so you know why they're laughing the next time we're all together."

I try taking a step toward her but my lowered shorts make it difficult.

I shuck them the rest of the way down, point at her, and say, "Put it down."

"Or what?" She again points the camera at my dick, now rock hard, and very deliberately takes another photo.

"Or I really am going to fuck you in the ass."

She crawls up onto the bed and gets onto her hands and knees, her perfect ass raised in my direction. She looks over her shoulder, phone in hand, and snaps another photo.

"So do it, big angry guy. Take out some of those frustrations on my tight ass."

"Put your face down in the bed."

She does as told. I move in behind her, put my hands around her narrow hips, and yank her back toward me. I spread her cheeks and watch her anus quiver. It is perfect. If you told me everything she did in life was to preserve the integrity of her anus, I would have believed you. I feel almost bad for myself that I haven't given this flawless specimen the appreciation it truly deserves. I lower my head and lick its puckered surface. I move my tongue around it before lowering my head and eating it like an orange. She starts playing with herself while I continue to eat her. A few minutes later, when her asshole tightens with her climax, I pull my tongue out, spit into my hand to lube myself up, and begin working myself into her. I'm surprised she led me in this direction since she hates anal sex. We'd only tried it a couple times at my prompting and both had been aborted shortly after I got past the tip. I'm curious to see how this plays out. She must be feeling particularly masochistic.

Once I've worked the tip in, I spread her cheeks farther apart.

She looks back at me with tears in her eyes and says, "It hurts so fucking bad."

"Keep your face in the bed."

I push myself the rest of the way into her. I've had fully penetrative anal sex on a few other occasions but never with Corinne. That makes the moment feel special. I look at her asshole stretched around my cock and the way she clutches the sheets in her small, bony fists. I'm overcome with gratitude. I push myself as deep inside her as I can, lean forward, cup her breasts, and say, "Sometimes I wish you had a penis so I could jerk you off while fucking you in the ass."

She sucks some snot up into her nose, grits her teeth against the pain, and says, "You like it back there, huh? Like it when I hurt? When I cry?"

"Honestly, I do." I slide myself in and out of her, enjoying the almost painful friction.

She moves a hand to her pussy. "Tell me how you'd jerk

me off if I was a boy.”

I do what she asks and for the next couple hours our sex life moves in a direction it hasn’t really gone before. I shoot my load deep into Corinne’s bowels while she keeps saying ‘fuck’ and begging me to stop. Afterward, she fucks me in the ass with the handle of a hairbrush and I let her because I feel so bad and pretend to enjoy it even though I absolutely do not.

We take showers, sprawl out on the surprisingly comfortable bed, and find *Forensic Files* on the TV.

“So, really, what did you to say to get us this room?” I ask.

She seems shaken and distant, her eyes heavy. “I told him you were my brother who’d just gotten out of jail.” She chuffs out a derisive laugh. “I mean, that tooth . . .”

I tongue my tooth and feel like she still isn’t telling the truth. She probably did something magic with her phone. It’s a LaQuinta Inn, it couldn’t have been that hard.

She’s almost laughing when she says, “Your wallet was in your suitcase, idiot. Turns out places like this don’t need reservations.”

“Really? No waiting list?”

“No waiting list.”

“Huh.”

eighteen

Heads turn as we walk through the airport. I don't give a fuck. We're there two hours early and all I want to do is find a bar, eat a lot of shitty food, and drink as much as I can in the time we have left. Spiritual retreats are like expensive, voluntary rehab for rich people. I know this. It's how people with too much freedom restrict themselves so they have a taste of what it feels like to be oppressed. It's like appropriating an entire third world country's mentality.

I find an Applebee's but the gate's pulled down. I get mad and kick it. Corinne grabs my arm and tries to lead me away from it but I'm already crying.

"Why's it closed?!" I howl. I want this one last thing and it feels like the universe is trying to take it from me.

"It's too early, asshole."

She's been like this ever since waking up from the third part of the Pretreat program—the preparation. She's apparently preparing to be a cunt. I just want to have a few drinks so I can prepare for days of absolute hell. I've just been fooling myself into thinking this is something I want to do. Maybe it won't suck that bad.

As I try to take deep breaths and center myself, I hear a sloppy millennial say to his girlfriend, "Whoa, looks like these two came straight from the internet," and I almost lose it. Corinne must feel me tense up because she again leads me away.

I'm still emotional. "People will never understand," I say.

"Why do you feel the need to explain yourself to people?"

"Because they think I just have a bad sense of fashion or, god forbid, that I'm so poor I have to wear whatever I can find. Or, worse, that I'm some smooth-brained idiot who feels the need to wear a costume."

"And you think the explanations to why we look like this would make it any better?"

"I'm finished talking to you." I turn to walk away from her.

The fact I had the wherewithal to remember my travel gear is truly remarkable but it doesn't make me any less anxious. Corinne's still wearing the safety blanket from the car. It barely covers her nipples, ass, or crotch. If she sits down, her vagina will be fully exposed. I'm hoping they won't even let her on the plane. So gross and unprepared. Embarrassing.

I, on the other hand, am fully prepared. I even have my wallet, ticket, and passport, even though I don't think I'll need it. It was in the suitcase with my other stuff, none of which would be necessary if planes weren't toxic cesspools and one of the most unnatural forms of travel in the history of humankind. Never mind the fear of crashing. If you die quickly in a plane crash, you're one of the lucky ones. A few years back, one of my co-workers flew with an undiscovered blood clot and died in Cabo two days into his honeymoon. To combat this, I have a compression suit. It's like those thin, tight, unattractive socks you see a lot of old people wearing except it's for my whole body, almost like a wetsuit. It would proba-bly look a lot less shocking and vulgar if I wore it under real clothes, but then it makes me too hot. I also have a small ox-ygen tank and mask, but I won't put the mask and goggles on until it's time to board.

So, admittedly, we don't look like everyone else at the air-port but that's just because I'm more prepared and Corinne is . . . the opposite of that. She looks nearly feral.

As I continue stomping away from her, I spot a duty-free shop in the distance. It gleams like god's loving embrace and I nearly run to it. The best I can manage is something like a quick trot. I must have put on some weight since the last time we traveled. The compression suit is very tight. It goes beyond compression to feel slightly injurious.

I go over to the rack of liquor and grab a bottle of Knob Creek. To the left of the whiskey are several shelves of ciga-rettes. I haven't been inside of a gas station in nearly a decade and it seems odd to see a proud display of cigarettes. I grab a carton of organic American Spirits. On my way to the register, I grab a big travel mug to put the whiskey in since I'm not sure if I can drink in the open parts of the airport and I'm not going to ask. The woman running the register seems tired and middle-aged but that doesn't prevent her from staring at me, judging me.

"What you're looking at," I say as she starts ringing me up, "is a fully prepared man who is on a journey. A journey to self-realization. I am about to begin constructing my glorious bubble. I am ready to become *exactly good*."

She just raises her garbage eyebrows and disinterestedly spits the total out at me.

I find Corinne sitting in front of one of the panoramic win-dows overlooking the runway. I sit down, uncork the whiskey, and fill up my travel mug. Corinne looks away from her phone, at me, and starts laughing softly.

"Jesus fucking Christ, what?" I say.

"You . . . have a hole."

"What?"

"You have a rip."

I follow the direction of her gaze. It lands on my crotch. I look down. Part of my shaved scrotum is poking from a tear in my compression suit.

"Great," I say. "Now I need to find some fucking tape. God only knows what'll happen if I'm exposed to all those germs. I'll probably catch Down Syndrome or something."

"You're a fucking idiot."

I take a sip of my whiskey and feel immediately better.

"At least I'll be able to get on the plane."

"What do you mean?"

"I'm not even sure they'll let you on dressed like that. And you don't have your ticket or ID or anything."

"They'll let me on."

I take another sip of whiskey and shrug. "It's no big deal if they don't. This is gonna be real dumb anyway."

She sighs loudly, slowly shakes her head, stands up, and moves about three seats down. The blanket is so stiff it doesn't fall into place when she stands so her entire ass hangs out, a bruise shaped like my hand on her left cheek.

She absently scrolls through her phone as I sip the whiskey out of my travel mug and nibble some tobacco from the cigarettes. I'm fairly hammered by the time they call our flight to board.

I stand up, stretch, battle a totally manageable wave of nausea, and fumble to put my oxygen mask on. Corinne looks over at me and rolls her eyes.

"I'm going on ahead," she says. "I'm embarrassed to be seen with you."

I don't bother responding. She wouldn't be able to understand me through the oxygen mask and the half bottle of whiskey anyway.

She approaches the terminal counter, her ass still hanging out, many sets of eyes on it. A couple people elbow the ones they're with and nod in her direction but most just let their gaze linger. It makes me proud of Corinne and, ultimately, pleased with myself for not only snagging a woman with an ass like that but for having the foresight to select someone who has the ability to maintain it.

By the time I reach the terminal, there are a number of people between us. Our fellow elite. First class. The fact that was part of the package displays a level of professionalism I'm not entirely used to from other people.

My whiskey buzz and the purity of the oxygen I'm breathing leave me feeling light and easy. A few minutes ago, I was ready to turn back. I was sure it would be days of torture. Now, I'm ready for it. I'm still pretty sure it's going to be torture but it'll be necessary torture. It most likely won't be completely uncomfortable, there just won't be any fun. But, I don't know, maybe more adults need to hear their lives aren't supposed to be fun. Fun is supposed to end on your last day of college and, after that, it's down to business. Sure, you're allowed a few outlets, but that's just what they are—outlets. You aren't drinking or taking drugs or going on vacation or fucking weird strangers to have fun, you're doing it to unwind, blow off steam, let loose. It has to be seen as something in preparation to getting back to work. Christ, people are taking psilocybin these days to increase their productivity. Smoking sativa and abusing Adderall to focus. And this is a different kind of preparation. This is preparing to get back to life.

An older woman taps Corinne on the shoulder. Corinne

shrugs and says something I can't pick up through the ringing in my ears. The woman gestures to a young boy whose head comes up to Corinne's exposed ass. Corinne rolls her eyes, reaches back, and tugs her blanket down.

It's Corinne's turn to approach the agent and I watch eagerly, hoping she'll be turned away. I wonder if she thinks I'll turn back too. Then I have a moment of panic.

What if this is all a trick?

What if this is less like softball rehab and more like full-blown rehab? What if Corinne has concocted all of this just to get me on a plane to some horrible wellness center halfway across the country? If it weren't for Blastneesh and the fullness and depth of the Wellnevermindfulness app, I'd almost believe my paranoid thoughts.

I take another sip of my whiskey and watch in astonishment as the woman behind the counter takes both Corinne's hands in hers, nods, and lets Corinne pass through.

Once aboard the plane, I find Corinne in a window seat in first class and sit next to her. She hands her phone over to me. On the screen is a photo of a young girl wearing way too much make-up and smoking a cigarette. I shrug, hand the phone back to her, and take another sip of my whiskey. A few seconds later, I think, "Wait, was that our daughter?" I cannot, for the life of me, remember her name, but don't see how it could have been. I don't think our daughter smokes.

part two
THE FORGETTING

nineteen

By the time we get to the retreat I'm so drunk I'm on the verge of blacking out. Corinne hasn't said a word to me since before the plane left the tarmac. Aside from the driver, Corinne and I share what appears to be a white prison van with two other "seekers" for the ride from the Dayton airport to Twin Springs, the godforsaken, podunk town hosting the retreat. One of the passengers is an older man with a gray beard who's dressed like an accountant or a science teacher from the Midwest and has the kind of wet-eyed look I associate with crippling depression and crying jags. The woman has dark hair, a nervous demeanor, and dresses like she's the type of person who goes to a lot of things like this when she's not at a pottery studio or poetry reading. She's probably in her mid-thirties and, given my current state, completely fuckable, although she strikes me as the type of person who wouldn't stop calling or texting afterward. Most of her relationships probably end with her in the psych ward. I spend most of the ride leering at her even though there isn't much to leer at given the shawl and the sweater and the flowing hippie skirt.

She's wearing sandals, so I mostly stare at her feet. Her toenails are painted a sky blue I haven't really seen a lot and she's forgotten to paint the toe next to the pinkie on her left foot, a clear sign of a disordered mind.

As we get out of the prison van, both of them waste no time in putting distance between themselves and me.

I've unzipped my compression suit to my waist and peeled it off my shoulders because I got hot.

Before I can stagger after the other two as they quickly make their way to admissions or central processing or whatever, Corinne grabs my arm and says, "Promise me you're going to try."

"Try what?" I'm watching the nervous dark-haired woman. She didn't tell us her name. The man had quickly introduced himself as Thomas but the woman immediately recoiled from my eau de Knob Creek like I was sitting in a cloud of defecation.

"Never mind." The disappointment in Corinne's voice almost sounds real. She begins walking after the other two.

I don't want to be the last one standing by the prison van like a clueless fucking douchebag, so I follow her. Also, her blanket skirt is again stuck above her ass and I've already previously extolled the virtues of that particular body part. I wonder if I will be seeing a lot of different asses over the next couple weeks or no asses but my own and that would only be if there was a mirror in my room or yurt or whatever.

"It's just . . ." I bring myself alongside Corinne. "I feel like I'm going to be disappointed."

Corinne stops. "Do it for Wendy, okay?"

I pretend to know who she's talking about and say, "Yeah, sure."

"I mean it," she says. "This is it, Scott."

I completely understand what she means. This *is* it. This is what we'd paid so much money for. This is what we've looked forward to for around a week. This is supposed to be the place that changes us. This whole experience is supposed to make us better people. And, looking around, I just don't see how that's possible. It looks like one of those pumpkin patches that open up around Halloween when everyone collectively decides they're into this ramshackle, rustic bullshit. At least that's what the faded red barn our two fellow passengers enter reminds me of.

"It's not too late to back out," I say.

Corinne makes a face to convey her disappointment. "Why would we back out?"

I stare at the barn, squinting to try and bring it into some kind of focus. "This just . . . doesn't seem like us. Maybe we could find a retreat in California or somewhere a little less depressing."

She shrugs. "This is exactly what I was expecting. Did you . . . even visit the website?"

"Kind of hard when I don't have a phone."

"I mean . . . before you agreed to this."

"I did a fury of research." I don't want to sound like a completely uninformed buyer. Corinne knows how exhaustively I research most of my high-dollar purchases. She's often accused me of liking the research more than the product itself. I visited the website. I read until I got bored.

"Okay then," she says, "if it was pretty extensive, you should know exactly what to expect."

"It was . . . furious. A fury of research." It feels like there are fish swimming in my head.

I know nothing. I've been distracted. I think I researched it but that feels like a year ago. I'm not going to let this fill me with anxiety. I use this simple syllogism to calm my nerves: Corinne knows what to expect. Corinne is excited to be here. Therefore, it can't be that bad.

Corinne is even lazier and less motivated than me. She would not be excited about something that's going to make her miserable. Unless her excitement is about wanting to make *me* miserable. No, she's way too selfish for that. If that's the case, she would have found a way to get me to come to this alone.

"Look," she says, "a hundred thousand testimonials can't be wrong."

I stare at the big, sad barn, think about saying something about how it makes me feel like cattle, and bite it back.

"It just . . . doesn't look like a lot of fun." I shouldn't have said it. I shouldn't have even put it out there because just saying it invites a rush of melancholy and I lift my whiskey mug to my lips and tilt my head back only to realize it's empty. I throw it as hard as I can. It hits the trunk of a big tree and rolls back toward me, stopping at the toe of my shoe designed to resemble a bare foot.

Corinne and I both stare at the mug.

"Life isn't all about having fun," she says.

I want to bawl and raise my arms to the sky and shriek, "Why not?!"

Instead, I just say, "I know," and feel like crying.

"You want to Facetime Wendy before we go in?"

I kick the mug away.

"No. Let's just get this over with."

I start walking ahead of her.

twenty

Once inside the barn, I immediately start feeling not so great. It's just that—a barn. The only real modernizations are the fluorescent lights hanging from the ceiling. They make everything harsh and unattractive. It still smells like whatever animals had been kept in it. I'm going to throw up if I don't shut my eyes soon. After walking away from Corinne, I told myself I'm going to be excited about this. Or at least pretend to be. But it turns out that maybe a late morning/early afternoon bottle of whiskey had not been the way to make that happen. Even with the compression suit half undone, I'm sweating profusely and feel like I could drink a gallon of water.

I find the darkest corner of the cavernous barn and slump down into the dirt and hay. I quickly scan the barn for a table with some food and drinks but don't see anything other than my fellow seekers gathered in the middle. There are maybe twenty of them but I can't be exactly sure through the blurred vision. Corinne comes in and immediately joins them. She doesn't even look around to see why I'm not with them. Fuck her. Fuck all these people. I can already tell this isn't going to be what I want it to. I think about asking for a refund but . . . what would I be going home to? A burned house and a whole lot of insurance and probably police paperwork?

I lift my head and look at the gaggle of people. I can't make out the specific details of anyone so I can't get my hopes up or allow myself to become too disappointed. I know what that's like. You see a thumbnail on social media and think a person is attractive and then you keep clicking on it and by the time you get to the full-size photos on their profile you realize they're hiding a weight problem or some ugliness or abnormality. They're hiding *something*. Everyone on the internet is hiding something. All it would take is one person to keep me here. Some magical unicorn. Either a bangable girl or a cool guy who has a personality I would enjoy emulating. There was a point in my life where I tried not to think this way but realized turning away from these desires is a restriction on my sense of self.

I wonder if I can throw up without anyone noticing.

I don't even see Blastneesh or Big Rex or whatever his name is.

I work to swallow the saliva continually filling my mouth.

There's a screech of feedback like someone has turned on a microphone.

"Welcome, seekers," a voice says. It sounds like Blastneesh but it could be a recording. "I hope you have left your ego at the door."

Great. New Age humor. A wave of laughter ripples through the group and I think I should probably try to join them but also want absolutely nothing to do with them.

"To find comfort," the voice continues, "we must first suffer. So . . ." and here he laughs softly, "tonight will be one of discomfort. But this is how we will get to know one another. Many of us go through life knowing so few people very well.

We build . . . artifices. We . . . armor ourselves. Our glorious bubble must not be constructed . . . from armor. It must be soft and welcoming . . . an open invitation for like-minded individuals to pass through its walls. Think . . . about the most tight-knit communities you can. They are made up of people who are not . . . strangers to suffering. Communities that have been hit by poverty, drug abuse, crime . . . They may be divided at first . . . but once they recognize the problem . . . they draw together to solve it. And because none of them are truly innocent . . . they bond . . . together . . . humbled, gracious, wanting to help. If you are here, I hope you've identified . . . your problem. You have all listened to the Pretreat so you are already on your way. The tools available in the Pretreat will allow you to dive deep over the course of your stay. Confront your problems. Remove the safety suit of the ego so you can see your true self . . . for what it is.

"I now ask that you all form a circle in the middle of the Welcome Center."

Welcome Center is a pretty grandiose name for this place. I stand and stagger, battling a wave of nausea. I should at least make my way over to the group. Don't want to start off on the wrong foot.

"Now I would like you to remove . . . all of your clothing. I trust you each read the entry instructions and have left all your other items at home. Your clothing . . . is the final thing connecting you to the outside world and this is the quickest way of establishing familiarity within the community."

I settle beside Corinne in the circle. I have the beginnings of an erection, feel momentarily embarrassed, and realize that's just who I am. Inappropriate Erection Guy. And maybe that's one of the problems I need to work on.

I spot the dark-haired woman from the van. She looks nervous and hesitant. She turns to the beefy, heavily bearded man beside her and says, "I can't do this."

Corinne, on the other hand, doesn't hesitate. She hooks her finger into where the corner of the blanket is tucked and pops it out, the stiff safety blanket dropping to the floor like a rock. I try fumbling with the lower half of my compression suit but my hands are numb and I really want to watch other people take their clothes off. To me, this is one of the most erotic aspects about sex. Especially the first time. Either the hesitant nerves if you don't feel great about yourself or the long-awaited reveal if you do. That moment where it feels like all your hard work has paid off. And, in the other person, you're seeing something new, something you've never seen before, maybe something you've wanted to see for a very long time.

"Can you help me?" I ask Corinne.

"Are you fucking serious?"

"I can't do it."

She gets down on her knees in front of me, digs her fingers into the top of the compression suit, and struggles to tug it down my powerful thighs. I alternate my slightly blurred gaze between the dark-haired woman, who has removed her shawl and now has her hands clutched around the hem of her sweater, and the beefy man to her left who's sliding down his underwear while staring unabashedly at Corinne. I take in the rest of the half-circle across from us. The only two other women are a small, young looking one with short hair and another older woman who's shaped like a boulder supported by well-muscled legs. I love seeing people like this naked. More as a curiosity than anything else. When it comes to the human body, I don't think there's any limit to how it can warp and mutate. The younger one lifts her worn t-shirt to reveal no bra and small, perfectly shaped breasts. Then she unhooks her gypsy skirt and lets it fall to the ground, an almost predictably large bush between her legs. The older woman stares up at the lights and I wonder if she's having some kind of stroke. I turn my attention back to the dark-haired woman as Corinne gives one more heave, shucking my suit down to my ankles. The dark-haired woman has finally removed her sweater and is now fumbling with the hem of her tank top.

Corinne stands up and says, "Seriously," I'm guessing in reference to my erection.

The dark-haired woman notices me watching her as she lifts up her shirt to reveal a trim, white belly. She lets her shirt drop so she can point at me and shouts, "He's leering! That man over there is a creep and he's leering!"

The burly bearded guy, his flaccid cock very impressive, looks at me and tilts his head, scrunches his shoulders, and raises his arms as though asking, "Bro, what the fuck are you doing?"

So I turn my attention back to the younger, short-haired girl as I step out of my compression suit.

Her gaze is drawn to someone a few people to my right. I lean forward and look. It's a painfully skinny guy with too much body hair, a long beard, a man-bun, and an almost freakishly huge cock. His cock looks thicker than his forearms. I'm glad I'm semi-erect so I look a little bigger. I'm definitely a grower. Then I notice her gaze flick over to Corinne and linger there. Good. Maybe I'd be able to use her as bait.

The feedback again fills the barn and I imagine Blastneesh someplace far away. Someplace I want to be. Some stone mountaintop ashram in California overlooking the sea.

"I would like to now welcome you all to the Wellnever-mindfulness Institute's summer retreat. We will be spending many hours together over the next several days. You will become closer to these people than you are many family members. You will . . . come to know them inside and out. So I would like you to take the next several minutes to get to know

. . . your fellow seekers. You are to do this without saying anything. You are to make eye contact with every other person in this room. As you gaze into this person's eyes—with absence of voice, absence of extraneous conversational gestures—I would like you to pose questions about them . . . and then find the answers to those questions by looking deeply within them. This is also how we can come to know . . . the self. For that is what we are doing. Looking inward. Something . . . has brought all of you here but, obviously, it is not the same thing. This is the purpose of the retreat. We are building . . . a community. We *have been* building . . . this community. You have all tried to work on yourself with the app but have still found your spirit longing for more. No one has ever fixed themselves alone, although you will be offered many chances at solitude. You will look deeply inward to find the tarnished and broken parts. Perhaps you will find the person across from you has the tools to fix . . . those parts. When we break a bone, we do not sit around and wait for it to heal itself. Nor do we fool ourselves into thinking we have the tools to mend it. We go . . . to the doctor. We become the recipient of thousands of years of research and technology. Technology is enhanced and upgraded all the time. It's happening every second. But when was the last time you thought about . . . enhancing the spirit? Or, perhaps you thought about it and didn't know how to even begin. Maybe that was when you downloaded the app. That was a good first step. That . . . is the toolbox. Your box of pencils and erasers and scissors your parents bought you before the first day of school. And here it is: the first day of school. Soon we will enter the grounds, we will visit the school itself. But first . . . you must become acquainted with your classmates. Some of them you will find attractive. Some you will find repulsive. In others, you will be met with a feeling of indifference. Some you will find curious.

Ask yourself why it is you feel this way about your fellow seekers. After all . . . you most likely don't know anything about them. Therefore, it's more likely your feelings about your fellow seekers say more about you than it does them. Explore your judgments. Change the way your brain works. Together, we can do anything. Go forth. Observe. Do not speak. Do not touch one another. You will see. Now, we are strangers with only one common bond. Moments from now, you will all be friends. Friends are closer than family. You will know more about the people surrounding you than most of their friends and family. Let that knowledge . . . fill you up. Let their naked . . . vulnerability . . . give you power . . ."

We all stand in a daze, either waiting for Blastneesh to elaborate on his quite frankly too-long instruction sermon or whatever it is or just slightly hypnotized by his slow cadence.

All I know is I don't want to look into Corinne's eyes first. Which is good because there's already a man standing only a few inches in front of her. He's a decent-looking guy, I guess. A few years younger than me and well-chiseled, although my muscles are larger and more clearly defined.

I begin making a beeline to the small, young woman with the big bush but the skinny hippie guy's already there and, Jesus Christ, it looks like they're already in love with each other. So I move toward the dark-haired woman, who quickly steps in front of the big, bearded guy, affording me a glimpse of her perfectly taut yoga ass. I knew it would be great. I would just take the lady next to her, but she has a very tall, skinny boy or man with her, clinging to her arm. He isn't naked like everyone else, his genitals covered by a primitive loincloth. I'm drawn to his deformed hands that make me think of lobster claws. For a moment, I'm not even sure it's human. Like maybe it's just some kind of companion animal I've never seen before.

The only person who hasn't already partnered with someone is the boulder-like woman who's been staring at the lights. As I approach her, I spot one obstacle to eye contact right away. Her labia are distracting. More specifically, one half of her labia is distracting. It hangs down nearly to her knee and I wonder what could possibly cause something like that—an injury or a birth defect? Once she realizes I'm standing directly in front of her, she brings her gaze down from the lights and stares into my eyes, whereupon I discover the second distracting obstacle: I'm too drunk to focus on anything. I stare into her dark brown eyes, the entire room spinning around her. I have to keep looking down at the floor to try and steady my vision and every time I do this I accidentally catch a glimpse of that super long labial flap and when I raise my head to once again look into her eyes I can't help but think she knows I'm thinking about that abnormality.

So I look deeper into her eyes, trying to find the answers.

I cannot find any answers. What I do find is a seemingly endless well of emptiness. Behind her eyes, I imagine her brain making a sound like a vacuum cleaner or a box fan—no internal monologue, no wants, no desire, no interior landscape. Then maybe I do find an answer. Like, not about any great spiritual or philosophical question, but about myself. The more I stare into her vacant eyes, fighting the urge to glance down at her bizarre vagina, I begin thinking about chewing on that distended flap like it's some kind of dog toy. For whatever reason, I like this idea and fight the urge to smile. I don't want her to ask what it is I'm smiling about, even though I know we aren't supposed to be talking.

Something shifts in my guts and they produce a deep, guttural growl that sounds like it echoes through the whole barn. My erection now juts out from my body and I feel more embarrassed about it, afraid people will think I'm aroused by this boulder-shaped woman with an abnormal vagina. My face flushes with shame. Hot.

Christ, I'm burning up. I keep waiting for them to say "Snowball" or whatever the spiritual retreat equivalent is that will allow me to move away from those empty eyes. I wonder what she's taking away from me, if anything. I wonder if we'll talk about that later.

My stomach shifts again. Sweat runs down my face and from my armpits.

To my shock and horror, the woman reaches out, grabs my tumescent cock, and says, "Honk."

I lose it. There's a rush of bile into my mouth followed by a propulsive stream of projectile vomit all over the poor woman's enormous breasts.

She immediately recoils and starts screaming like she's covered in cobras.

I hear a commotion come from the entrance to the Welcome Center and see Tall Rex—I'm pretty sure that's his name—enter, still dressed like a chauffeur.

All other eyes turn toward him.

Breaking the rule of silence, the dark-haired woman begins pointing at me. "He's drunk!" she yells. "He was drinking the whole way here!"

A small part of my brain thinks, "Corinne will defend me. She'll get my back." And I almost laugh at having that thought.

Tall Rex takes one look at me before angrily approaching a watering hose coiled on one wall. The groups of people withdraw to either side to allow him easier passage as he marches toward me with the hose in his hand. Knowing what's coming, I consider running away, but part of me thinks it might be revitalizing and refreshing.

He depresses the handle and the powerful stream of water

hits me in the face. Not feeling entirely stable to begin with, I go down. He continues spraying, the jet of water so strong and cold it stings my skin. I feel like I could throw up again but the shivering distracts me from it. I'd thought he was going to use the hose to clean up the puke but he keeps spraying me. Now I'm feeling embarrassed because I'm a huge distraction and everyone is staring at me. The second I try to open my mouth to say something, Tall Rex aims the hose at my face and sprays, forcing me to spit water out of my mouth instead of words. This lasts way too long.

Finally, he says, "Stand up."

I stand, wobbly on my feet.

"Are you drunk?" he asks.

"Absolutely not," I respond. A woman guffaws and I don't know if it's Corinne or the dark-haired woman.

Tall Rex pulls something out of his pocket and, for a horrifying second, I think he's either going to stab or shoot me.

It's a breathalyzer.

He holds it to my mouth and says, "Blow."

Why would he be carrying a breathalyzer? Are they going to breathalyze us and drug test us every day we're here? What kind of fascist shit is that? Will I even be here many more days or is this it?

I blow into the breathalyzer. He pulls it away and I do a quick scan for Corinne, finding her standing between the dark-haired woman and the burly, bearded guy. She's consciously not looking at me.

Tall Rex pulls the breathalyzer from my mouth and turns it so I can read the digital display. I have no real idea what the number means or maybe I do know what it means and just choose not to accept it, but the boulder-shaped woman, still covered in puke, says, "Jesus."

Tall Rex grabs me around the upper arm and hurriedly

leads me to the entrance of the Welcome Center. He shoves me out the open door and says, "You can come back when you're sober."

"Fuck this place!" I shout. "I don't even want to come back!"

But he's already closed the door.

I feel like shit. Not in a guilty or moralistic sense. I physically feel like shit. I've clearly taken my bender one step too far. Mistimed it. While I've never said this phrase out loud, it now echoes around in my head: "I'm too old for this shit."

I'm not really sure of what "shit" I'm talking about though. I don't know if I mean the drinking or trying to take part in yet another different form of socializing. Shouldn't we reach an age where we are no longer obsessed with "finding ourselves" or making new friends? Growing up, I didn't know any adults who were obsessed with this kind of thing. Everyone seemed to be alternately content and depressed out of their skulls.

I'm still staring at the closed door.

I just want to find a comfortable spot and lie down.

It's full dark and there are no outdoor lights in the immediate area. I wonder where we'll be staying while here. I don't see any structures besides the barn. On our arrival, I noted the compound or commune or retreat or whatever it is looked like it had been dropped into the middle of a lush forest. All the trees, combined with the dark, are disorienting.

I take a deep breath. The night air smells great. I try to let the sounds of the crickets and katydids and other night insects calm the rage welling inside me.

Well, I can't just stand here looking like a jackass.

I walk around the barn until I come to a tall fence. If I were in better shape, it might be scalable, but I'm not in any condition to do that. Instead of trying to climb it, I decide to punch it. Again and again. Until my hand is a dripping, bloody mess. Take that, you stupid fucking fence.

Among many other claims, one phrase found on the Well-nevermindfulness website was: "Find Yourself Here."

I can't help thinking about that. Is this finding myself? Is this who I am? A naked guy who imagines chewing on labium, vomits on strangers, punches things, shouts at the dark, star-filled heavens? Because that is exactly what I'm doing, holding my bloody hand up so the nearly full moon can illuminate it and shouting every profanity I can think of. And, while I'm furious, I'm also loving it. Where else would I be able to do this?

Given my current state—nude, highly intoxicated—I don't think it would be a great idea to wander too far off the grounds of the retreat. I'd be okay as long as I stay somewhere between the Welcome Center and the road. There are plenty of trees to hide behind.

The woods call to me. Maybe I'm just trying to hide my embarrassment. I still haven't stopped swearing and know I probably won't until I go hoarse. No longer do I want to find a place to curl up and go to sleep. I feel more energetic and alive than I have in a very long time, possibly ever. I'm alone. I'm in a strange place with nothing to distract me. If I were at home, I'd recognize the anger boiling within me and either pop a Xanax or smoke some weed to level out. But there isn't any of that here and that isn't my fault. Therefore, I don't even feel like I need to take any responsibility for my actions.

I put both my arms out in front of me like I'm going to tackle someone and go charging into the thickest area of woods I can find.

"Fucking fuckwad! Goddamn cocksucking cunt! Shit wrapped in shit getting fucked in the ass by shit until it shits!"

I hit the woods, summer thick, at full speed, promptly step

on a stick followed by what feels like a sharp rock and go down into the dirt and dead leaves. My brain races. I can't latch on to a single thought. My throat and stomach are on fire. I roll over onto my side and vomit. It hurts. I get up on my hands and knees, wanting to get all the poison out of me. I can't stop raging.

"Fuck wellness! Fuck Ohio! Fuck Blastneesh! Fuck Corinne!"

I vomit again. It smells awful.

"Yeah, stupid fucking ground. Drink my puke."

I heave again.

"You're just a fucking whore. The only thing you're good for is trash. We'll destroy you and we'll win." I think I'm still talking to the earth.

I vomit again, still screaming incoherently.

Then something fills my head. A voice. Blastneesh's voice, naturally. It says, "Be quiet. Be quiet, seeker."

And I open my mouth to yell again, probably at the voice in my head, but nothing comes out.

I try to force another heave but no vomit comes out either.

I flip over onto my back next to my stinking puddle of puke.

And I listen and I breathe. The insects comingle with the sound of my breathing and very distant traffic and the wind in the trees and I feel an odd sense of calm wash over me. I don't know how long I lie there like that. I never lose consciousness completely, so I know I haven't blacked out. I want to say time slows down but that isn't exactly true. It's more like time ceases to exist. I know it's dark. That's it. And I'm more than okay with that. Everyone else is in the Welcome Center being controlled, being directed, being a slave to time, being a consumer to the well-being they're paying so much money for.

Not me.

I'm free.

Ironically free. Now that I can do anything I want, there isn't anything around to do. I briefly contemplate masturbating but my formerly turgid cock now lies atop my pubic mound like a dead slug. So I just lie there and breathe deeply. I could easily drift off if I was remotely tired, but I feel wide awake. The moon is high above me and, before I know it, it slides from the sky. One measurement of time, sure, but a very liquid, nebulous, natural way to gauge time. Nothing as rigid and machined as a clock or a watch or a fucking phone. Time is a device of control. Why are humans obsessed with controlling themselves? I let my mind extrapolate these deep thoughts, some of them bordering on true genius. I try to catalogue them, hold onto them even though my brain feels like a sieve. They'd make for some fairly impressive talking points if I ever find myself in conversation with the young girl with the big bush. Then I think about her fucking that big, burly guy and my thoughts again turn dark.

Blastneesh's voice is in my head again. "Violent meditation. Let yourself explore this. There is no creativity without destruction."

I imagine myself with my hunting rifle, stalking Big and Burly as he runs terrified through the woods. I wallow in my jealousy and let it become something else.

"Taking a life is the most power a human can have."

I agree with that voice. I've never really understood how one human can kill another until now. It's the intoxication of power. If life is a competition, then the survivor is the winner. Everything is a competition. We could all spend the next couple weeks wandering around, acting wise and spiritual, trying to find enlightenment. It's all bullshit.

"This is not bullshit. Change is real. You will discover

this."

Thick clouds now drift rapidly across the murky charcoal sky.

I hear a voice. Not just in my head this time. I hear a voice, a child's voice. It says, "Daddy?"

I'm pretty sure Corinne and I have a child but I can't remember it any more than I can remember what I do for a living or what state I live in. There are just large chunks of my past that are . . . gone. I can't help but acknowledge this and think it could somehow prove to be wildly beneficial. A decluttering of my brain.

"Daddy?"

Part of me wants to shout "Fuck off!" but it doesn't even feel like my jaws are cooperating at this point.

I pull myself up to my elbows and turn my head toward the voice. A flash of white disappears farther into the woods. I struggle to stand up, expecting to feel pain, and am instead greeted with a very welcome feeling of numbness.

I follow the child through the woods. Again, there is no sense of time or distance. We could be going in circles. Gradually, the jumbled confusion in my brain dissipates, replaced with the singular goal of finding this child. I decide, if I find it, I'll gather it up and run back to the Welcome Center and pluck Corinne out and we'll go home, wherever that is, and start a new life. A different life, although I barely know what I have to compare it to.

I walk and walk and walk, quickly, until my heartbeat throbs steadily in my ears. I'm wearing down. I imagine a video game power meter slowly diminishing.

Then I hit a fence. This isn't like the tall chain-link fence back at the retreat. This is like a fence for livestock or something. I'm in a grassy clearing at the top of a hill. Birds are waking up around me. I must be facing east because I can see the sky lightening and, as I stand there waiting for the sun to make its appearance, I feel *myself* lightening. Maybe I'll get what I want out of this. I look around for the child but don't see any sign of it. Maybe it had all been in my head. Maybe it had only been there to bring me to this exact spot at this exact moment.

I watch as the sun crests the horizon and the sky lightens into blues and oranges and pinks and purples and my eyes get heavy and I lie down in the soft, damp grass and finally shut my eyes.

I wake up to a cow pissing on my face from the other side of the fence.

twenty-one

I stand in a circle where someone has painted the word "EX-AMPLE" onto the dirt. I'm still naked. Everyone else wears their yellow t-shirts and ridiculous baggy yellow pants. I should be embarrassed about it but I'm more embarrassed about being in the Example Circle than being naked in front of everyone else. Presumably, they'd all already seen me naked last night and have spent far more time in the company of one another. It doesn't matter. I feel pretty good about the way I look. I still feel like a wild man, returning from a long night's journey, the only one here who can say that. I clearly exude some wisdom I've obtained in the woods.

I'm not sure if the intent of this particular exercise is to instill shame in me or if it's because, since I missed last night's bonding exercise, this is how I have to make up for it. The rest of the seekers voted to leave their clothes on after the dark-haired woman had chimed in and said I'd "gotten an eyeful" last night, which isn't really true at all. I'd gotten an eyeful of her and big bush girl and stretchy pussy, but a few of the other more boring people I don't even recognize as they come to stand just outside the circle to stare into my red, crusty eyes. I still haven't eaten or drank anything and have a hard time focusing on my fellow seekers as they approach. Other than Thomas and Corinne, I don't know anyone's name, which exacerbates my disconnection from them.

The first one to approach is the dark-haired woman, presumably so she can get it over with. I unabashedly ogle her on her approach, figuring it doesn't much matter since she already hates me, not that there's much to ogle in the baggy, not-at-all-form-fitting clothes that were probably retreat-issued. I wonder when I'll get mine or if I am to remain naked as a symbol of my pariah-hood. The expected hatred is dominant in the woman's eyes, but now there's something else there. Something like superiority. In the contest of enlightenment, last night had been something like a victory to her, especially if she thinks of me as something akin to the rival team. She stands there less than a minute, just long enough to say she's actually done it.

She's followed by Thomas, who's followed by an older woman with short, gray hair, who's followed by a young, chubby woman with a head of massive dreadlocks and a remarkable amount of tattoos and, quite frankly, I thought there would be more people like this here. None of them really stick around longer than they need to. I don't feel any sort of connection with them. Don't get any answers, not that I really have any questions. I want to step out of the circle and wave my hands and say, "Wait, this isn't necessary," because I don't feel like it is. Nobody here wants to give or take away anything from anybody else. Everyone is here for themselves. I don't feel love or acceptance coming from anyone. They're here so they can go home and tell their friends about it or write about it on their chosen social networking platforms so they can either fight with people or listen to people tell them how much they've always wanted to do something like this. It's an exercise in futility.

Then the young, short-haired woman approaches. She'd been standing in line, deep in conversation with the skinny hippie guy with the amazing penis. It looks like he'll be next. But, unlike the others, the short-haired woman doesn't spend the minimal amount of time. She's significantly shorter than me and stands in my shadow. The expression on her face is completely blank but her eyes—brown bordering on golden— are alive. Maybe it's just the spirit of youth, but she doesn't seem completely dead inside like the previous people. Actually, that's not true. I don't think they seemed dead inside, I just think they seemed, I don't know, dug in. Like *real change* is probably not happening with them. They've lived their most likely very comfortable lives up to this point and will undoubtedly return to those comfortable lives once they're finished with the retreat. Looking at this woman—she's either in her early twenties or aging really, really well—I get the impression she's up for anything. There's a thirst, a hunger there. It's something I can respect. Immediately, I regret not having any sort of wanderlust at that age. I briefly imagine myself at the base of the Himalayas instead of some prestigious, staid private college. Roadtripping with my buddies across the United States instead of roadtripping to the nearest state school that had the best frat parties and keggers. Or, for that matter, traveling anywhere that wasn't a part of some class trip. Sitting in a quiet dorm room reading Herman Hesse instead of spending two minutes scanning the latest *Vice* article just so I could introduce some bombastic talking point if I was ever around someone who had half a brain. A corner of the girl's mouth ticks up and, after a few seconds, she starts laughing. She tries to stop herself but only laughs harder. I don't know how to feel about this. While I love to make people laugh, I absolutely hate to be laughed at. She doesn't seem to be meanspirited though. I imagine the endorphins rushing through her, that giant bush trembling somewhere in the depths of those voluminous pants.

She turns to walk away and I notice the bruises around her neck, almost like someone has tried to strangle her.

I want to call out to her, tell her to come back, but the skinny hippie guy is already approaching, reaching his hand out to her, clasping it in a brief but overly intimate way, the girth of his cock noticeable even in the baggy pants.

He has very kind, slightly hooded eyes. As much as I want to hate him, I find it very difficult. He doesn't stick around long before he leaves to join the growing gaggle of seekers who've already stared at me.

Next is the big hairy guy. At first, I'm a little nervous about him because he seemed angry at me last night. But I see none of that in his eyes. There's a bit of the life I'd seen in the short-haired girl's eyes but even more in line with my own zest for life. This guy clearly just wants to party and have fun. He's here for the exact same reasons I am and I can appreciate that. If we were at a bar, I could see us boisterously rooting for our team on the screen, fist bumping each other if something good happened. I think he would even be okay at the end of the evening when he had to hook up with the ugly girl. In short, he seems like a "pussy is pussy" kind of guy. So, fun, but not competitive. My favorite type of male companion.

He's followed by a woman, probably in her thirties, dark hair bobbed to her chin and tipped with faded blue like she's trying to grow out the color. She's short, broad-shouldered, and has a build that could be described as athletic if she chose to work out at all. Her eyes are tired and wary and she spends the shortest amount of time in front of me, leaving me with the sensation I'd just met a barely remembered ghost.

She's followed by the people I dread most. Two people who I guess are counted as one. The washed-out, haggard-looking older woman and the tall, skinny boy or man, I can't tell. There's something almost alien about him. He isn't decked out in the same yellow uniform as everyone else. He still wears what looks like a cloth diaper or a loincloth. I don't know which one of them I should look at. They both look like they need a lot of wellness. I try looking at the boy first but, well, that just isn't happening. His tiny eyes are rolled back in his head, where they mostly stay. Drool escapes from a mouth housing too many crazy small teeth that lean in every direction. If I have to keep looking at him, I feel like I'm going to be sick. So I flash my eyes back to the woman and that's almost as difficult. There is absolutely no filter over her eyes. It's like I stare directly into her soul and there's nothing there but pain and agony. The boy has a death grip on her arm and it crystallizes what I find inside her. Excruciating pain, sure, but a pain she's come to accept and deal with. A pain she's come to endure. It makes me feel both slightly guilty and highly appreciative of my own life. I have a kid too but am so disconnected from them I can't even remember if they're a boy or a girl.

"Mom?" the kid or whatever says. "Mom, I'm bored." I glance at him. His eyes flick down from the inside of his head to land on mine and I swear he mumbles, "Mount Boring."

Then his mom is leading him away and I want to call out, "I'm not Mount Boring!" but decide to let him have it anyway. While it isn't a great insult, it's one that can't really be come back against because it's so lame it's practically genius.

Next is the chiseled, good-looking guy who I'd noticed staring Corinne up last night. Right away, I'm not a fan. And I feel like that is completely reciprocated in his eyes. We could have a meaningful exchange but we both throw up that guard only two men who have similar interests and want the same things can throw up. Neither one of us could ever learn a thing from the other one because we already know the plot. It's like two opposing teams with the same exact playbook. We wouldn't banter, we would only agree with one another, punctuated with an occasional quip meant to one-up the other guy's last quip for good measure, an endless loop of one-upmanship. He doesn't stay long and the way he drops his shoulders and turns quickly from me, he might as well discard me like a piece of trash. If we ever speak, I feel like either one of our opening lines will be, "Do you have some kind of problem with me?"

Corinne is the final seeker to approach. Last night must have been enough for Big Labia. She seems to have been given a reprieve.

Corinne—still beautiful after all these years. How many times have I looked into those eyes? Rather, when had I stopped looking into those eyes? And now she's here, standing in front of me, and I'm reminded why I hardly ever make eye contact with her anymore. It's like looking into the eyes of a prisoner and I can't help but think I'm her jailor. So much history staring into her eyes. We've both been relatively horrible to each other but I get the feeling most of her semi-dangerous, transgressive endeavors have more to do with acting out against me rather than pursuing her own interests. Because we're so familiar with each other, I don't think she'll stand there that long. But she does. I stay there too, making no attempt to move away, even though that would have been it and I'm kind of eager to wrap this up. I continue to stand there, looking deeply into those intelligent eyes. We stand there, our shadows growing longer as a cloud passes in front of the sun. I try to process what I'm feeling but, surprisingly, I don't think I feel a whole hell of a lot. Maybe Corinne feels it at the same time I do. The feeling of hitting the end of the road with something. She still seems so mysterious to me, which should be a good thing, but it's an impenetrable, unknowable kind of mystery. Tears well in the corners of her eyes and, once they escape, she makes no attempt to wipe them away. I might be crying too. By the time she walks away, I know only one thing—when we leave this place, it won't be as a couple.

This feels like some sort of weird, emotional gauntlet. I'm all too eager to leave the Example Circle and begin walking toward the group of fellow seekers, who've splintered into three smaller groups. I'm still not wearing any clothes but I don't care. After all, we'd all seen each other naked. Like Blastneesh said, these people already know more about me than most people I've known. Well, most people I'm acquainted with anyway. For those who know me well, they've most likely seen me naked and we've probably had some emotional evenings although, since those were probably spent under the influence of drugs and alcohol, a lot of it wasn't remembered the following day and one could argue those didn't really count.

Tall Rex cuts me off when I get about ten feet away from the Example Circle.

"What the fuck are you doing out of the circle?" he says.

"I'm joining everybody else," I say.

"What does the circle say?"

"Huh?"

He grabs me by the arm and leads me back to the circle.

"What the fuck does that say?" He stabs his finger at the spray-painted word.

"Ex-amp-uhl," I enunciate very slowly.

He pats me on the back. "Example. Very good. Today, that's you, buddy!" So condescending. I hate this fucking guy.

His flowing blond hair. At least he isn't dressed like a chauffeur anymore. He wears the same t-shirt and pants everyone else wears but they're a different color, somewhere between brown and yellow that he would probably describe as gold and I think looks like a dehydrated person's piss.

I step back into the circle thinking, if the next several days are going to be like this, I'm not going to be able to take it.

The color of his uniform reminds me how long it's been since I've drank something that isn't measured in ABV. I can't even remember the last time I pissed.

"Do you think I could get something to drink? Maybe some clothes?"

He tosses his hair in anger, some strands sticking to his cheek. He scoops them militantly behind his ear.

"Got you covered." Then he's walking quickly away from me.

I'm not exactly sure what time I made it back to the retreat. I'm pretty sure it had been around mid-day, the sun high in the sky. The Welcome Center and the gate to the fence behind it had been locked. There was a button I pressed repeatedly. I imagine it must have alerted someone somewhere. No one approached the gate to let me in. I looked around. I couldn't see or hear anyone but noticed a camera mounted on the top of the fence. On the brink of yelling, I gave it my most welcoming grin. A couple seconds later, I heard a light click—one of those nearly inaudible sounds that only means something in the modern world—and pulled the handle to the gate.

I felt like this was a better way to introduce myself to the retreat anyway, not herded like cattle in the cover of night. I knew it wouldn't be as grand and spiritual as I'd hoped, but it still managed to underwhelm me more than I thought possible. The beauty of the day would have been conducive to the fantasies in my head. I wanted to smell the scent of incense carried in the clean breeze. I expected to come upon the retreat and see stylishly designed eco-friendly cottages or the cool linen of yurts flapping in the breeze. I wanted to see Blastneesh up on a stage, leading my fellow seekers in meditation or yoga.

What I came upon instead reminded me of a dilapidated summer camp. Ten ramshackle cabins—five on one side of an expanse of lawn, five on the other—were surrounded by thick woods. A long building sat at the end of the lawn, probably containing the dining hall and rec center.

Perhaps the most alarming thing was the group of seekers in the middle of the campground. They all had shovels and seemed to be digging. That's when I should have turned around and never looked back. I'd seen enough documentaries on cults to know how this worked. They're led by some manipulative capitalist who squeezes as much free labor as possible from his followers. Eventually there's abuse, followed by a power struggle, and then the cult falls apart as quickly as after a failed end-of-the-world prophecy. And yet, I continued. I didn't know if there was some inward thing compelling me or if I just rationalized there wasn't anything to go back to. Probably a combination of both and, either way, I felt like Blastneesh had orchestrated each scenario.

That was when Tall Rex emerged, seemingly out of nowhere, to grab me by the arm and drag me to the Example Circle where I now stand watching him come back carrying a large bucket.

"Here's your fucking water," he says and holds the bucket above my head. The water is freezing cold and some heavy, waterlogged fabric hits me on the head and flops off and plops on the ground. "There's your clothes. You're required to wear them. Enjoy the rest of your day."

He walks toward the other seekers and shouts, "All of you

need to get back to the Power Hole!"

They immediately do as they are told.

I bend to retrieve my clothes. This is not the same uniform everyone else wears. This is a yellow sweat suit that looks like something you would buy in a dollar store. As I begin separating the wet, heavy articles, I realize it isn't just one sweat suit, it's three. I immediately think it's some kind of mistake and I'm only going to put one of them on. Then I realize this is part of the punishment, part of me being an example, and that it's Tall Rex's intent for me to wear all three of them at the same time.

"One example can benefit the many," Blastneesh's voice says in my head.

So I begin putting on the soaked sweatsuits as I watch my fellow seekers pick up shovels and resume digging the Power Hole.

I think, "This sucks," followed by, "This is exactly what I need," followed by, "I need a fucking drink."

That last statement . . . that's terrible advice. I know that now. Maybe that's the reasoning behind things like affirmations and guided meditation, listening to people tell their stories at an AA or NA meeting—to replace that niggling voice in your head with other, healthier voices. Like a sober person who describes themselves as an alcoholic even if they haven't taken a drink in years. That's them saying they know their own voice, their own thinking, is the enemy. Like some rotten part of them they keep waiting to fall away. That's the sickness. That's the disease.

Before putting the last sweatshirt on, I wring some water out of it into my mouth. It tastes like bad water, new fabric, and cheap detergent.

For the rest of the day I stand in the Example Circle watching the other seekers dig the Power Hole. It looks like a lot of work. Maybe an example is the thing to be. I only think that until the moisture in my sweatsuits loses its chill and becomes warm and then nearly hot. It feels like I'm wearing a tropical jungle. It's so damp and uncomfortable I stop thinking about how hungry I am and begin thinking about how hot and miserable I am. It's like being in a sauna and staying in that sauna long after it stops being pleasant. By the time the sun begins to set, it's all I can do just to remain conscious.

Eventually, I can't even do that. Sweat plasters my hair to my head and runs down my face. The sweatsuits feel like they weigh three hundred pounds. I try to focus on the seekers digging the Power Hole. I can barely discern one from the next. I have to concentrate harder than it's worth to focus on them. Nausea or hunger or both twists my guts and I can't stand up any longer. I collapse in the wet slop of the Example Circle, weakly say, "Help. Please somebody help me," and then begin to slightly lose my grip on reality because I think Tall Rex comes back and says, "Oh, does big boy need help?" before calling over to the digging seekers, "Can I get any volunteers to help the example?" and Corinne and the dark-haired lady and the woman and her retarded boy and the good-looking man all come running up to the Example Circle and point and laugh and pelt me with small pebbles presumably extracted from the Power Hole and, looking up at them from my position in the muck, they all seem jeering and ghoulish and, beyond them, Tall Rex stands and watches with a smarmy, self-satisfied expression on his face and I feel like I'd rather lose consciousness than deal with their mockery and the next thing I know it's dark and I'm now fully lying in the slop of the Example Circle. I hear and smell the sizzling of meat. I manage to pry my eyes open and track where the sounds and smells come from. Tall Rex, standing in front of a large grill to my left, pulls what looks like human limbs from a plastic tub and throws them on the grill I'm certain was not there previously.

"Almost dinnertime," he says before snapping the tongs he used to turn the meat at me.

I study the carnage in the plastic bin, waiting for it to morph into something else. But it doesn't. It is undoubtedly the corpse of a dismantled child.

"None for you," he says. "Not today, anyway."

I try to say something but my mouth and throat are so dry and raspy, forcing anything out would send me into another bout of heaving retches.

He throws the remainder of the corpse onto the grill. Maybe it's just meat from an animal. I don't know. I try to think if there are any animals that closely resemble a small human when dismantled. The only thing I can really think of is a kangaroo. Kind of hard to come by in these parts. Do people even eat kangaroo? I don't know. Probably. People will eat anything. Then I think about the child I followed through the woods last night. Possibly my child.

As if on cue, Tall Rex says, "Found this in the woods this morning. Wasn't going to let good meat go to waste."

I think, "So glad we spent so much money to be treated with value-based spirituality." He throws his blond locks back and flips a slab of the corpse. "Meat," I remind myself. We don't call edible meat corpses. Like, they have a meat counter at the supermarket, not a corpse counter.

"Chop this shit up and put it in a curry and Blastneesh and the other seekers are going to be very happy."

My stomach grumbles and the dryness in my mouth is replaced with profuse, Pavlovian salivation. If I could stand up, I would push Tall Rex out of the way, steal a piece of the meat, and run off into the woods before he could apprehend me.

I try to stand but it isn't happening. I lift my arm, covered in soggy fabric, and try to suck some of the moisture from the sweatsuits. I gag. It's sweat. All the sweatsuits are now drenched in my sweat.

I try to say, "I think I need some electrolytes," but nothing comes out and I decide to sit quietly and conserve my energy, not that I really have any other choice.

Then Tall Rex is stripping the meat from the bones. The sound it makes does nothing to assuage my hunger. He places the cooked meat in a separate stainless-steel bin and tosses the bones out into the woods.

I think, "Evidence."

"Probably didn't think it was going to be like this, huh?" Tall Rex says. "That's how we get you here. You came here thinking you're going to get what you want but we're here to provide you with what you need. Unlike a lot of other wellness institutes, we're here to actually help people, not just make money from them. That's hard for a lot of people to understand. Of course,"—here he snaps the tongs together again— "once you're here, there's no leaving until it's over. I mean, you're allowed to go when you want, but you won't. No one leaves until they find what they're looking for."

I want to ask if anyone has ever been kicked out but instead just watch him toss what looks like a small ribcage and spinal column into the woods and wipe his hands down the front of his shirt before grabbing the stainless-steel bin and heading up to the long house.

My stomach continues to grumble as the scent from the cooling grill wafts over to me. I think about one of the last books I read. I've never been a big reader. I occasionally pick up the latest book it seems like everyone is reading but, as I've gotten older, I've lost any capacity to read fiction. What's the point? Why should I waste my time reading some bullshit story a mentally unstable egomaniac has spewed out? That feels like a waste of time. Like giving someone money to make their life better while ingesting their words to make me sicker. Because, let me tell you, mental illness is as contagious as the plague. Why do you think there's been such a spike in depression and suicide since the widespread use of the internet? So now the only books I read are books on diet and mental wellness. Actually, I don't even read them. I listen to them. If anyone asks, I can proudly tell them there isn't a single book in our house. The last book I listened to was a diet book written by a medical doctor, a cardiologist. The premise of the book was on the curative properties of meat. The doctor advised the reader to eat nothing but three-to-five pounds of meat a day and take a bucket of supplements along with it. I simultaneously thought it sounded like both the stupidest and the greatest thing in the world. Now I can't think of anything else but burying my face in that bin of grilled meat and not stopping until I gobble up the last morsel. If that had, in fact, been the child I'd seen in the woods last night, it probably only yielded about ten-to-fifteen pounds of edible meat, if that. Given the fact I haven't eaten any solid food in at least two days, I don't think this is unrealistic at all.

I'm surprised by my current predicament. I certainly didn't think, on the second night of the retreat, that I would be sitting in a muddy circle, wearing multiple dollar-store sweatsuits and longing to eat a human child. I thought the diet here would be vegetarian, a lot of lettuce and lentils and bread. Probably kale. I can't really remember if I'd read anything about diet on their website but suppose I'd really just gone from downloading the app because it seemed like everyone else had to researching Blastneesh when I thought he was harassing me. Who has time for research? People like Corinne. They are the ones who have time for research. The pampered, bored housewives of the rich and successful. I trusted her to do the research and, as of right now, I am strongly disappointed in her.

Then that voice is back in my head: "This isn't about her. This is about you. Dive deep within yourself."

I close my eyes and take a deep breath, try not to think about dragging myself into the woods to retrieve a bone—not only to see what nutrients I can suck from it but to keep it, to hold onto it, and prove what I saw. To hold the retreat accountable for the horrible atrocities I'm sure they're committing. I think about all those people laughing at me. Laughing because they're afraid. The voice is right. This *is* about me. Of anyone here, I'm the most equipped to become the most enlightened. Just look at how I've lived my life so far. It isn't just bourgeoise trend hopping. I am *open*. I am *receptive*. I am a neophyte. When something new comes along, I'm eager to pounce on it, suck everything I can from it, hold it up to the light and examine its value. At the end of my life, I'll be one of the few people able to say I've lived fully engaged with my time. Born a Champion, I'm certain to die a Champion.

If I die at all.

Perhaps this is one of the driving forces of my thirst for life—that I want it to last forever. It's one of the reasons I'm not a religious person. Religion just substitutes laws with morality and gives you a blueprint for death involving mainly imaginary conceits.

I'm not sure how long I sit like that, eyes closed, breathing slowly in and out, focusing on my own immortality. Maybe a life well lived is the answer, rather than a life lived loudly. That's really all I'm trying to do—suck the marrow from the bones of life itself. I was born lucky and fortunate enough to have the resources to do this. I always knew I'd have to slow down at some point.

As I sit here, the world slows down with me. The birdsong becomes more somnolent. A soft evening breeze makes ocean sounds with the trees. The incessant trill of the cicadas begins to slow. I've completely blocked out the smell of the grill.

Somewhere in the distance, Tall Rex shouts, "Dinnertime!" and I finally open my eyes to see him clapping his hands at the digging seekers. Once they all drop their shovels and begin heading toward the long house, Tall Rex begins walking toward me.

"The Wisdom Master wants you to join us for dinner, Example. No eating though. Not for you." Then he's again walking away.

It might be hard to stand but a lot of the discomfort has left my body. There's a brief moment where the ground turns liquid and I have to stop to get my bearings. My sweatsuits are still damp and I feel hot and bloated. I'll be glad when I'm allowed to take the damn things off. I almost roll my eyes at myself. "Allowed to?" How long has it been since I've had to worry about being "allowed" to do anything? I'm the definition of the entitled, affluent, white male. I've been doing whatever I want, with absolutely no real consequences, my entire life.

Nevertheless, the walk to the long house feels like the most freedom I've had since being confined to the Example Circle and I take my time with it. The sky is starting to darken, the few security lights around the retreat ticking to life with a fluorescent hum.

I walk into the long house to find everyone sitting around an appropriately long table. They smell terrible and look exhausted, most of them sitting in front of empty metal plates with their heads down. I expected more joviality, the excited chatter of a dinner party or something.

And it doesn't look like they're all there. Naturally, the

first person I search for is Corinne, just to make sure she looks as miserable as everyone else. She does. She does not make eye contact with me, only reaffirming my earlier opinion—that this retreat is not meant to bring us closer together, but to show us how unnecessary us being together is. I wonder if Corinne is having the same memory problems as me. I don't think she is. Maybe she hadn't really listened to the forgetting part of the pretreat. Or maybe it's a different kind of forgetting.

I nearly stop in my tracks after having that thought. Maybe she's forgetting me. Maybe we really *will* be leaving here having cleaved a clean break. She could go off to whatever life with our kid and I could begin a new life having mostly forgotten about both of them.

As I get closer to the table, I notice it's the girl with dreadlocks who's missing.

Tall Rex wheels out a cart with two large bowls and some pitchers of water on it. He sets the bowls on the table—one of plain white rice and the other filled with the child curry. While I've never tasted human flesh, the smell of it once again sends my stomach into a hungry roil.

The skinny bearded guy looks at the massive dish of curry and wrinkles his nose.

"Is that . . . meat?" he says.

"Yes," Tall Rex says.

"Ugh. Guess it's just rice for me."

"You'll eat what everyone else is eating."

I expect more pushback but he just closes his eyes and looks like he bites back a response. Part of me will be really satisfied to watch him tuck into a bowl of meat. At least this cult of humiliation is democratic in its targets.

Corinne sits between the burly bearded guy and the good-looking guy. I contemplate forcing myself in beside her but feel as though I've been embarrassed enough. It's cafeteria, bench-style seating and everyone is spread out to where I'll have to wedge myself in between somebody if I want to sit down at all. And I feel like I need to sit down. The combined lack of food and water, along with being uncomfortably hot, makes me feel a little disoriented in a very unpleasant way.

The small, short-haired girl sits at the end of the table closest to me. I sit on the sliver of bench to her right and she scoots to her left, setting off a chain reaction of annoyed grunts and exaggeratedly loud shuffling.

"I'm Scott," I say, feeling like everyone else is listening because no one is talking.

"Fee." She holds out a hand for me to shake. I take it and she says, "Never mind the blisters," and rolls her eyes.

"You all worked on that hole all day, huh?"

"I can barely lift my arms. I just want to eat and go to sleep."

"Looked like it kind of sucked."

"It was amazing."

"The . . . digging the hole?"

"Yeah. Everybody did such a great job. Nice to sweat out the old and make room for the new, you know?"

I tug on the three sweatsuits covering my torso and say, "I feel like I invented sweating."

"Why were you over there?"

"In the Example Circle?"

"Yeah. Is it because of what you did last night?"

"I guess. Total accident. She touched me inappropriately. That's why I threw up. Guess no one mentioned that."

"Nah. Everyone just assumed you threw up cause you were drunk. Is that your wife?" She nods to Corinne, who stares down at her empty plate.

"Yeah."

"She didn't exactly come to your defense."

"I didn't imagine she would. She hates me. Pretty sure we're getting divorced after this."

"First one?"

"Divorce?"

"Yeah."

"Uh, yeah. Guess I didn't really think about that."

"Happens to everyone. And it's okay. You'll find somebody else. It's so easy to meet people online nowadays and everybody's pretty much turning into the same person so it doesn't even really matter who it is."

"I can't tell if that's optimistic or completely resigned."

"It's just the truth."

Now others are engaging in softly murmured conversation.

"Is this your first one of these?" Fee asks.

"Yeah."

"What do you think so far?"

I'm not even sure why she's asking me that. I think it sucks, so I'm also not sure why I say, "Oh, yeah, it's pretty great. A little different than I expected but it feels like I'm getting what I came for." I'm pretty sure the only reason I say that is because I had paid for it and don't want to feel like a sucker. Either that or the voice that has gotten into my head is now controlling what comes out of my mouth.

"You're gonna love it, man. It just gets better and better."

"So you've done this before?"

"Oh, yeah." She gives me a blissed-out smile. "It's pretty much what me and Branch do." She nods her head toward the skinny hippie guy. "Usually three or four a year. So it's nice to see this one actually come to our hometown."

"You live here?"

"Yep."

"So you can just go home at night, huh? Sleep in your own

bed?"

"Not allowed to leave. Or, well, it's frowned upon. I wouldn't want to anyway. I want the complete experience."

She leans her shoulder into the skinny guy and says, "Branch. This is Scott."

He leans forward and peers at me around Fee.

"Oh, hey, man. I'd shake your hand but I can barely lift my arms."

I can understand why. His arms are skinnier than most women's.

I reach around Fee and clap him on the damp back, establishing male dominance early by demonstrating I still have full mobility of my arms.

"No worries," I say. "Nice to meet you."

And, like that, I feel like I have friends. I feel like I belong.

I start to say something else but as soon as I open my mouth, Fee turns her attention to the front of the dining hall along with everyone else.

Blastneesh walks out onto the stage followed by the chubby girl with dreadlocks. She looks absolutely radiant, beaming from ear to ear. She walks down the stairs from the stage and goes around to the opposite side of the table, everyone scooting down to make room for her with no annoyed grunts.

She looks at Fee and I'm pretty sure Fee mouths, "Did you?" and the chubby girl nods and her smile turns into a soft giggle. I automatically take this exchange to mean the chubby girl has fucked Blastneesh and, judging by her giddiness, liked it quite a bit.

The feedback from the speakers jolts the table of exhausted people.

Blastneesh sits in an ornate chair, adorned in a white robe. Tall Rex sets the microphone stand down beside him with another squeal of feedback, positions the microphone in front of Blastneesh's mouth, bows, and comes down to join us at the head of the table.

"Tall Rex, you didn't say we had visitors," Blastneesh says, everyone laughing politely at his terrible joke. "Is everyone hungry?"

It isn't loud but everyone says, "Starving," or some variation thereof.

"Starving!" Blastneesh says. "I should think not. Perhaps you are a little hungry in the belly . . . but you are not starving. In fact, your soul is full nearly to the point of bursting." He holds out a hand to the lack of response. "It's okay. You may not realize it just yet.

"Okay," he says. "I will let you eat. We will talk about starvation . . . afterward. Tall Rex has prepared a wonderful dinner. Now listen: Don't eat too much. Do not talk while you are eating. Chew each bite of food for the count of thirty before swallowing. This will help with your mindfulness and keep you from overeating."

Everyone stares at the two huge stainless-steel bowls. No one makes an effort to grab them until Tall Rex slides them in front of his plate and spoons out some rice followed by some curry and pours a glass of water. Then the bowls are gradually slid down the table, presumably because everyone's arms are too tired to lift them, until they make it to me. There's still quite a bit left in them but I don't even have a plate in front of me and, by the way Tall Rex is glaring at me, I don't think it would be worth it to just start spooning it directly into my mouth. He would either take it away, realizing that having just a taste to whet my appetite was worse than having none at all, or he would force me to regurgitate it, which would probably lead to another night in the woods and another day in the Example Circle. I'm not in a hurry to do that. Given the state of the retreat, I'm not idiotic enough to convince myself the beds will be comfortable, but they have to be at least slightly better than the ground and I'm completely exhausted.

I look at everyone around the table. It looks like they've all taken at least one bite. No one seems to have a problem that it's a meat-based dish, which is surprising. The lady with the retarded boy seems to have extracted just the meat to feed him, a couple glistening hunks of child sitting on his plate. I look over at Branch, slowly masticating for the required thirty seconds and looking like he's going to throw up. Fee is sweating. Looking around the table, she isn't the only one having a hard time with it.

I hear the boy bellow, "Too hot!" and look at him just in time to see him lean over his plate, the bright red meat and drool dripping out of his mouth.

His mom delivers a vicious smack to the back of his head and says, "Not here."

Then he just sits and quietly cries.

Blastneesh sits in his chair on the stage, looking from seeker to seeker with slitted eyes.

It feels like dinner takes two hours, everyone sniffling and coughing through their modest plates of food.

I wonder what their reactions would be if I tell them they've just eaten a human child.

"I feel like my insides have been scoured," Fee says.

"I think I'm going to be sick," Branch says.

"Better not let anyone see you throw up," I say.

Fee smiles. "You were drunk off your ass."

"I was just trying to get it out of my system before we got here. I guess I took it too far."

I glance up the table at Corinne, chatting with the good-looking guy—Brent, I guess. Seems like an appropriate name.

Fee says, "Your wife's name is Corinne?"

"Yeah," I say.

"She's pretty."

"Thanks."

"You probably didn't have anything to do with it."

"I mean, like, thanks from her. Or, like, thanks for complimenting me on my taste."

"Oof." Branch belches and holds his hand in front of his mouth.

"He hasn't eaten meat since he was ten," Fee says.

"Yeah?" I try to act impressed or surprised or something but I'm pretty sure it just comes out as condescending. I've tried both veganism and vegetarianism but neither one of them stuck so I dismiss both particular ways of eating and most of the people who choose to eat that way. "What kind of meat was it? It looked really good."

"Hm. I don't know," Fee says. "I think I was too hungry to care. Maybe pork?"

"Wow. They really don't give a fuck about dietary restrictions, do they?"

Fee looks at the table, now mostly devoid of food, wrinkles her brow and says, "Well, at least it was gluten free?"

"Mine was also calorie free."

"You poor thing."

"I would have given you mine," Branch says.

"Thanks, but I'm pretty sure they would have just beaten me with sticks or something."

Tall Rex comes around the table gathering everyone's plates, stacking them up and dumping them into the huge stainless-steel bowls before placing everything on the service cart and wheeling it back to the kitchen.

Fee gets up, goes to the other side of the table, and slides in between the girl with dreadlocks and the blue-haired girl.

"Have you guys met Scott?" she asks.

"We did the staring thing," the blue-haired girl says in a lifeless monotone.

"This is Gemini," Fee gestures to the girl with dreadlocks. "And this is Cassie." The girl with blue hair.

"You all know each other?" I ask.

"Just met Gemini yesterday. Cassie roomed with us a couple years back but lives . . . where do you live now?"

"Durham," she says.

"That's right. Me and Branch should come and stay with you sometime."

"Okay."

"Anyway, Cassie's in an electronica band—Team Klaus. Ever heard of them?"

"Sounds familiar," I say. Cassie rolls her eyes. "I probably have them on a playlist somewhere. Are you on Spotify?"

"We are now. We used to be cassette-only." There's more life than I'd previously seen in her eyes.

"Cassette-only. That's an interesting choice."

"You probably wouldn't get it."

"You're right," I say. "I don't know a single person who owns a cassette player but it's probably just because everyone I know is old and incredibly rich."

Cassie cocks a finger at me and says to Fee, "That's why I don't like him. I knew there was a reason."

Fee turns to Gemini and says, "So, how was it?"

Gemini, still looking pretty blissed out, says, "I'm never going to forget it. I think I went somewhere else. It's going to take a few days for things to recover."

"Me and Branch are hoping to do a twofer with him."

I thought they had been talking about sex but now I'm not completely sure. Branch looks miserable and lowers his head to the table and I'm once again pretty sure they've been talking about sex, which is something I'm way too famished, tired, and dirty to think about.

The microphone once again squeals to life and everyone immediately turns their attention toward the stage, toward Blastneesh. Even Branch rolls over onto his cheek.

"I hope everyone . . . enjoyed the feast," Blastneesh says.

A number of affirmations are hurled toward him:

"Perfect!"

"Awesome!"

"Amazing!"

"It was great!"

Blastneesh just smiles and his self-satisfaction is evident even from where I sit. Yet, for some reason, it doesn't really bother me. He's exactly what I expect and possibly even want from a guru or cult leader or whatever the fuck he is. He has to think he's filled with intelligence and wisdom in order to guide everyone else. And if he isn't self-satisfied, how could he ever teach us to be satisfied with ourselves?

"What was I going to talk about? Gemini? Do you remember?"

Gemini smiles and I'm surprised to see her teeth are white and perfectly straight—rich girl teeth. I imagine her opening her mouth to take Blastneesh's large, brown cock. If it's going to take her days to recover, he must be huge. Unless she'd been referring to some kind of spiritual trip.

"Starvation!" she calls out.

"That's right," he says. "Starvation."

He fiddles with his flowing robes, uncrosses his legs and re-crosses his legs and I assume this is because his pubes are itchy with drying come. He takes a deep breath and makes a couple seconds of eye contact with the seekers. I glance up the table at Corinne, who is, of course, completely enthralled.

"The body . . ." Blastneesh lets this trail off almost to the point I think he's forgotten what he's going to say, ". . . is a vessel. Nothing more. It holds only the essential mechanisms to keep it running. Everything else you have to provide for it. It will keep us warm . . . but only so warm. It will keep us awake and alert . . . but only for so long. Occasionally, like a car, it needs filling up so that it will take us to our next destination. We fill our stomachs and our minds. Fill the stomach up with too much or too often and what happens?" Here he puffs out his cheeks and holds his arms out from his body to indicate his new, hypothetical fatness. "You look like our friend Gus here." There are polite chuckles from around the table. Gus—the fat, bearded guy—laughs the hardest. "You can fill it with so much so often you don't even care what you're filling it with. Food loses its taste. Loses its purpose. Becomes . . . an addiction. Like an alcoholic once concerned with buying the brand he likes who eventually just starts reaching for the bottom-shelf stuff because . . . it's the alcohol he needs. Why pay for marketing? Food is too abundant here. Everything is too abundant here. For addicts surrounded by the subject of their addiction, it is impossible to achieve total hunger. To achieve the level of *want* necessary to appreciate what you're putting in your mouth whether it's a piece of chocolate cake or maybe . . . a dead child you found in the woods. To the starving, it will be delicious. Because once you break the habit . . . once your stomach is not just rumbling to remind you it's time to do that eating thing . . . it howls because it needs *nutrition*. This is when we are reminded that *food* is a necessity. One of the very few necessities we really have. Only then will your body respond to food . . . in the appropriate way. There are many on the internet who espouse eating like our ancestors, cave people, hunters and gatherers. Yet they overlook this simple fact: starving has been the way we ate since the beginning of time. If you clean your house every day, do you even notice it's clean? Of course you do. But what is the point of cleaning if it's not dirty? Can you even clean something that's already clean? Is eating when you're not starving even eating? Of course it is. But is it nourishing? Is it nourishing to end up with heart disease, obesity, diabetes, Alzheimer's disease, arthritis? No. Those are . . . debilitating diseases. Therefore, you should only eat . . . when you're starving. Only eat when you think you can no longer function. And then, eat slowly and only until your belly is full. This will ensure your body does . . . what it's supposed to do. It will keep you alive for as long as the universe intends without sending you to a premature grave. We must stop eating just because we are bored. This is hard because no one likes to be bored and almost everyone likes to eat. Especially in this country. This, one of the only countries that seems to have invented food designed specifically for eating and not nourishing. Avoid those things the most. They are as devastating as alcohol and cigarettes. So . . . why have we succumbed to this? Why have we relented to this . . . mindless self-indulgence? Why do we feed the problem and kill ourselves when we should be trying to fix the problem? You are the exceptional ones. Most people would rather eat a bag of potato chips than read a book of philosophy. Why is that? Laziness, perhaps."

He pulls at his robes. A few moths chase each other around his head. He again looks around the table as though giving each of us time to ask ourselves how lazy we are.

"There is this . . . other part of the body that hungers."

He pauses again. This time I think it's just to gauge the level of attention he has.

"That is why you're here. Because your mind is hungry. We have to feed the mind to nourish the soul, the spirit. Fortunately, we can feed this as much as we want to with no repercussions. The spirit cannot get fat. If you keep it nourished, it will always remain . . . exactly good. You are building . . . a universe in your mind. It starts as a small town when you're a child. Everything you put in there is another building, another park, another parking lot, another street, another avenue. And those avenues become highways connecting you to another city you may not have even remembered building. And then . . . and I'm sure some of you have experienced this, it is time to leave this earth. It is time to build your colony on this, your spaceship, to travel through the rest of the universe. And this is . . . infinite! We forget about some of the towns and planets we've created, but they're there, waiting for us to come back. Occasionally, we create one that is so perfect we stick around for a while, but we know there is more work to be done, so we keep doing that. Sometimes, it is good to stop putting things into the brain. But does it get hungry? Does it starve?" He pauses, looks at Corinne, just over the transom from the stage. "Corinne?" Coming from his mouth, her name is a purr. "What do you think?"

For some inexplicable reason, I find myself furiously jealous.

"No?" she says.

He doesn't confirm her answer. He again looks around the table. "What do the rest of you think?"

Everyone says "No." I shout, "Maybe?" and everyone turns to stare at me with withering, sickened expressions. The enlightened equivalent of telling me to shut the fuck up.

Once everyone quiets down, he continues to remain silent until he finally says, "Of course the brain cannot starve. Because . . . it . . . entertains . . . itself. Deprive it of conversation . . . and it will make its own. Deprive it of stories . . . and it will write its own. Deprive it of knowledge . . . and it will *think* its own. And it will be *pure* because it will be yours. Imagine if the stomach . . . made its own food. The closest we have come to that . . . is breast milk and cannibalism and one of those things has a time and place and expiration date while the other is universally reviled. So, like we develop a taste for certain foods, we also develop tastes for what we put into our mind. This is the blueprint for our internal universe . . . our glorious bubble. While the mind cannot starve, it can get dirty, dusty, rusty, and you have to go in there to give it a sweep and a polish . . . knock the cobwebs down. Which is why you are here. I ask you to dig the Power Hole so that you can dig down into your mind . . . remove the dirt. This distraction is necessary. Like the tired saying 'A watched pot never boils,' it could be said that a watched mind . . . can never achieve enlightenment. I make no promises that you will leave here as an enlightened individual . . . but you *will* leave here with the tools. Maybe you will spend the rest of your life in the golden bliss of your glorious bubble. Maybe you will live the rest of your life constructing . . . your glorious bubble. Maybe you will throw your hands up in the air, declare enlightenment as rubbish, and go back to the life that made you so sick in the first place. We're all like recovering addicts, only we're recovering . . . from modern life. While we may not be able to physically quit modern life, we can mentally create our own modern life, our glorious bubble shrouded around us, welcoming the nutritious and filtering out the toxic. True enlightenment is about being exactly good all the time. To realize that all other feelings, *any other way of being,* is fleeting and temporary because those feelings are ignited by things that came from outside our glorious bubble. The e. coli on the romaine leaf. Hostile invaders. Soaring heights that come with crushing lows. Soul-dampening lows that feel like they're never going to end. But . . . if you're *exactly good* . . . what more can you ask for? It is perfection if you're enlightened enough to know

. . . that everything is flawed."

He falls silent. This time he looks down at his lap instead of out at the seekers and I think this is probably it. I almost stand up, eager to go grab Corinne, get back to our cottage, and try to sleep away the hunger and exhaustion.

But Blastneesh looks up from his lap and says, "Everything I said wasn't exactly true. I'd almost forgotten about the other parts of the body we can fill up." He raises his eyebrows and everybody laughs with a perhaps imagined tinge of bawdiness and I get excited because, tired as I am, I think this might be when we all take off our clothes and get to know one another on a physical level and, yes, I tell myself, I am okay with fucking Big Labia to get to Fee or the woman with the retarded son to get to the dark-haired lady, but instead he says, "But that's for another night," and raises his arms to all of us and stands up slowly and exits stage right.

As soon as he's gone, it feels like someone throws a heavy lead blanket over me, a kind of deep mental and physical fatigue I haven't felt since taking care of a newborn. Everyone is already standing and I imagine their muscles ache even more than mine. I stand too, suppressing a groan, and walk straight to Corinne, still engaged in conversation with Brent, who laughs softly and places his hand on her upper arm. I perform the same gesture on him to gently move him away from Corinne. He gives me an are-you-serious? look that goes completely ignored.

"I'm wiped out," I say. "I think I'm going to bed. Do you know which cabin we're in?"

"She doesn't want to talk to you, dude," Brent says.

"Look, if you don't mind butting the fuck out, I asked my *wife* a question."

"And she doesn't want to talk to you."

I try to give Corinne a stare-down but she just looks at the floor.

"Fine," I say. "I'll find it myself."

I turn to walk away. It looks like a lot of the seekers have the same idea as me. Half of them have already taken off. The big, burly guy taps me on the arm as I walk past. I turn on him, eyes blazing. He throws up his arms to indicate he isn't a threat.

"I was just gonna tell you that all the room assignments are posted beside the cabin doors," he says.

I let the anger empty from my eyes, remembering that not everyone was as mean and awful as Corinne.

"Gus, right?" I say.

He looks surprised. "Yeah, man."

"Thanks," I say. "I'm Scott."

"Cool. Nice to meet you."

"You too. I'm beat."

"Get some rest, man. You'll feel better tomorrow."

I walk away already feeling a little better.

It's now full dark outside, the air warm and steamy, alive with insect sounds. I decide to start with the row of cabins to my left, looking for my name. I'm going to look for Corinne's name too, although I'm pretty sure she's rooming with that Brent creep. He probably already fucked her senseless last night. The thought makes me kind of hard.

The first cabin is for Fee and Hildy. I don't know who Hildy is. Has to be Big Labia, the short-haired older woman, or the dark-haired lady. I feel lucky when I get to the next cabin and see my name, along with someone named Carol. Again, I don't know who that is and feel like it must be one of the same three suspects. As tempting as it is to just go in and finally lie on a bed and get some sleep, I need to know which cabin Corinne is in. It ends up being the next-to-last cabin on the opposite side and, fuck, I knew it, she's rooming with

Brent, and if I weren't so tired, the flare of jealousy could have been a truly monumental thing. Only I'm not so sure if it's jealousy or resentment. I can't really be jealous of Corinne. We've both slept with other people since getting married, probably while we were dating even, and I ultimately find that it makes me more attracted to her. Maybe because it re-affirms her sexual allure and vitality—her desirability. Also, I have come here with express plans to hook up with other people. What I resent is how easy they make it for her. It doesn't seem fair. I would be okay if they'd put me in a room with Fee or Cassie or even Gemini—I don't mind getting weird. But I don't even know who Carol is.

The angry resentment rapidly dissipates.

What if Carol is the dark-haired lady?

Now I feel excited to get back to my cabin. I stop lingering in front of Corinne's cabin like a stalker and make my way back to mine, passing a couple smaller groups of seekers and paying them no real mind. I take the three steps up to the small porch, contemplate knocking, decide not to, and throw the door open to my cabin . . . to see the older woman and her son sitting on the bed farthest from the door.

Whatever excitement I'd been feeling plummets out of my body. Why hadn't there been *two* other names on the paper? Better yet, there are more than enough cabins here, why don't they get one to themselves?

The woman just stares at me, her eyes filled with accu-satory suspicion.

I'm so pissed and tired I don't even want to fool with being polite so I just say, "Hey," and strip off my three sweatsuits and collapse into the bed, pulling the sheet up to my shoulders and closing my eyes.

"I'm Carol," she says. "This is my son, Jorry. He's six."

There's no way that guy is six. I open my eyes and turn my

head to her. She still sits on the edge of the bed, Jorry next to her. He's leaned forward, swiping at his tongue with that weird claw hand.

"Too hot," he mumbles.

"I'm Scott," I say but it goes unacknowledged.

"We're from Florence, Kentucky," she says. "I've lived there my whole life. I live in a small ranch house at the end of Grove Court. There are a lot of bad people who live there. I do not talk to any of them. I can't even leave my house anymore. Every time I do, even if it was to take my trash down to the curb or get my newspaper when I still received one, Mr. Bloss would be out in his yard wanting to have sex with me. He was that same way even when I was a little girl. I tried to send Jorry out to get the paper when we still received one but it wasn't any different. Mr. Bloss would still be out there, wanting to have sex with Jorry. But they stopped sending the paper because they were afraid I was learning too much. The same reason they stopped putting cable television on my TV. They want me to watch what everyone else is watching. They don't want me to form my own opinions about anything because then I'd be too powerful. So I set my alarm to sunrise every morning and I make oatmeal and I take it into the living room where I've got this big bay window that looks out over the street and watch all these bad people doing bad stuff all day long. Kyle Davis, who lives at 12 Grove Court, gets into a 2011 black Kia Soul every day and goes into town to buy drugs from people at the bus hub. Then he comes back and stays in his house all day until night falls and then he goes out looking for people to rape. He rapes one person a day. He doesn't even care. Men, women, children, he'll rape anything with a pulse. Even immigrants, if you can believe it. Animals. But I don't see that. I don't hear their screams. Because I go to bed at sundown. I have to. The darkness opens up the brain and lets the signals from the transformers and towers come in. I should already be asleep, especially being so close to the signal. It comes from a place called The Point in Dayton, Ohio. That's only like half an hour away. It makes people do bad things. But only average people. Not the elite. The elite have special linings around their brains. Average people are just entertainment for the elite. That's why this signal makes people do bad things."

I knew she was insane before she ever opened her mouth. There was a moment where I tried to pay attention to her but I recognize this for what it is: a schizophrenic's spiel. She says this exact same thing, possibly with moderate variations, to anyone who does not completely dismiss her. She has a soft voice with just the slightest hint of an accent so, as far as monotonous drones go, there could have been more unpleasant ones to fall asleep to.

I don't know how long I'm out. I wake up to a loud slurping sound. I prop myself up on my elbows, allowing my eyes to adjust to the murk. I look over. Carol and Jorry lie side by side in the narrow twin bed. Carol's top is off, her pale, pendulous breasts hanging to either side of her torso. Jorry's mouth is attached to her right breast. At first, I think I'm going to be sick and then I remember how hungry I am. I couldn't have been asleep long. It feels like I'm still in half a dream state.

I throw the sheet off, cross the room, and kneel beside Carol's bed.

"Do you mind?" I say.

And she raises her left arm and places her hand on the back of my head and gently guides me to her swollen breast, inviting me to suckle.

twenty-two

After a few moments of careful observation, I plunge my shovel into the dirt of the Power Hole. This is the first time in my life I've ever used a shovel. It feels liberating. Each time the shovel bites into the soil that I heave over my shoulder, it feels like another chunk of the old me is being removed. I don't know if I think that thought or if it was put there by subliminal means. It's still my thought, right? I mean, we all learn things, incorporate the things that don't clash too horribly with who we really and truly are and use those teachings to apply to ourselves.

After only a few minutes, the already high sun is beating down and I've broken my first sweat of the day and I'm grateful to be wearing what all the other seekers are wearing—voluminous pants and flimsy t-shirt, both yellow. I've stationed myself roughly next to Fee for a whole host of reasons, the first being that I notice Branch is in the Example Circle and I'm curious about what he did and also want to take the opportunity for her to grow comfortable around me in the absence of Branch, even though he doesn't really strike me as a jealous guy and they probably have group sex all the time.

Also, my first pick for a digger buddy would have been Corinne, both so I could figure out what she was up to with that Brent guy while trying to make her feel bad or jealous in some way, but she is absent. This gives rise to many negative thoughts but I put all those thoughts into the dirt and throw them behind me and think to myself that I could be a decent guru if it just means coming up with really obvious metaphors. The final reason is that Fee is not wearing a bra and I am going to low-key ogle her all day. The first time she lifts her shirt to wipe the sweat from her brow—about ten minutes into the dig—I know I've made the right choice.

Tall Rex circles the hole with a long metal rod of some kind. I hadn't noticed this accessory before but maybe that's because I wasn't at the hole yesterday. It's entirely possible I am the reason for the rod, being the most physically intimidating and aggressively hostile seeker here. I find that flattering.

"Do we get any breaks?" I ask Fee.

She tosses some dirt over her shoulder and shrugs.

"What's that mean?"

She glances at Tall Rex, who's passing us on the perimeter of the hole about a foot higher than us. The seekers really made excellent progress yesterday. He shoots me a barbed look and slowly taps the rod in the palm of his free hand. Maybe we're not supposed to be talking or maybe Fee has some insider knowledge about the break situation she doesn't want Tall Rex to overhear.

Fee waits until he's farther down the perimeter and says softly, continuing to dig, "They explained to us yesterday . . ." She pauses to toss some more dirt over her shoulder. "The only breaks we're able to take are . . . when our mind and body break . . . several times during the day . . . We're supposed to acknowledge what we're feeling . . . but press on . . . *That,*

Blastneesh explained . . . is how one *breaks through*."

I toss another load of dirt and say, "Sounds retarded."

Fee visibly cringes.

"What?" I say.

"Dude, that's not a cool word to use."

"I wasn't using it to describe something cool."

"You know what I mean."

"I thought only calling someone a retard was bad. I mean, that has become a, uh—what do you call it?—kind of an epithet." I nod to Jorry, who stands with his hands down his cloth while his mother shovels and looks like she's ready to die. I try not to focus on her pendulous breasts and definitely try not to think about the delicious nutrition she harbors inside them. The only nutrition sustaining me. "Like I'd never call that kid a retard but I might describe him as retarded."

I've more or less stopped shoveling to talk. It's too hard to do both at the same time.

"And that's your right," Fee says. "And it's my right to take offense at your choice of words."

"So what would you describe him as?"

"A *human*."

I roll my eyes, toss some dirt. "Well, okay, but he's definitely not like you or me." I think about going on, but Tall Rex is once again within listening distance to us so I put my head down and shovel harder.

When he once again gets out of earshot, Fee says, "That's my point. We're all just humans . . . No two of us are alike . . . so why do we have to have these harsh-sounding words . . . to describe the *similarities* . . . between a certain segment of the population."

She doesn't fall into the trap I'd set for her—I wanted her to say she would describe him as mentally disabled or mentally challenged, maybe even intellectually disabled, so I could make the argument that if those weren't already out-dated words, they soon would be—so I'm left kind of silenced. While I wouldn't describe myself as a former edgelord, I will admit to having dabbled. When it comes to arguing, she's clearly on some next-level shit. She's either gone to graduate school or takes social media way too seriously. I think about pressing her and then remember I'm trying to groom her for sex or woo her or something, so I just say, "I guess you're right. I'll try to do better."

And hopefully me saying that shows I'm adaptable and willing to learn, thus putting me into a "project" category. Women love a project.

We continue digging quietly as Tall Rex makes a couple more rounds. No one else seems to be talking either. Not even covertly. Fee is really sweating now, her thin t-shirt plastered to her shoulders and breasts, her nipples protruding and almost visible through the thin fabric. She's so focused on the digging she doesn't even notice me ogling her.

I wait for Tall Rex to pass again before asking, "So, why's Branch in the Example Circle?"

"He barfed up his dinner last night . . . out in front of the cabin . . . I guess Tall Rex heard him . . . and Branch told him how uncool it was . . . to force someone to eat meat . . . This morning Tall Rex dragged him out there . . . and said no one can find enlightenment if one does not learn to bend their will."

"When in Rome," I say and think I should have shown more sympathy or at least not have used such a tired cliché.

"Yeah . . . I guess he'll learn . . . I just hope he's okay . . . Branch is . . . fragile."

I want to congratulate her on finding someone with such a huge cock but think that isn't proper spiritual retreat talk. I feel like maybe I should just watch Fee and take cues from her. She and Branch both seem like wizened retreat specialists so they probably have it down. I shouldn't have left all the research to Corinne. Should have known how anxious it would make me. I'm rarely an impulsive person because of this. It's not that I lack a sense of self, it's that I feel like I'm unlike most people. I'm able to stand back, explore their weaknesses, and then exploit them for personal gain. Like, if invited to a party, I would often spend hours on Facebook researching the attendees so I could immediately connect with more people there, increasing my chances for both profitable business opportunities and sexual encounters. Whenever the party or the social evening or whatever was over, I'd have to ask myself how I did. Did I win or lose the evening?

Here, it looks like I'm going to have to take the role of novice, which is something I've had to do before and found it to be not completely without its merits. It allows the other person to feel superior and drop their guard. And that's when I can pounce. I am determined to leave this retreat as the most enlightened seeker.

Tall Rex is on the other side of the Power Hole and I'm enjoying my conversation with Fee, so I ask her, "You and Branch ever lived on a commune?"

After heaving a shovelful of dirt over her shoulder and wiping sweat from her forehead with the back of her hand—a gesture that lifts her shirt and reveals a strip of tanned, trim flesh and just the slightest bit of the band of her green underwear—she makes a pained smile and says, "Actually live on one now."

"Whoa. Here?"

"Yeah . . . There aren't many of us . . . It's just a couple campers and some tents . . ."

"Must suck in the winter."

"It can . . . if it gets too bad, a lot of us . . . go back home."

"Makes sense . . . Corinne and I have a pretty big house in . . ." I'm drawing a blank. Why can't I remember what state I live in?

This doesn't seem to bother Fee. "Sounds nice . . . You two have any kids?"

"Yeah." But I don't go into detail because I can't think of the specifics. I'm still pretty convinced that was our child wandering the woods the night before last and that the other seekers helped consume them last night. It suddenly dawns on me that it may have been a blessing not being allowed to eat. I decide to gloss over it and get into the real reason I asked about a commune. "You and Branch would be welcome to stay with us sometime. We love visitors."

A curious expression crosses her face and I'm about ready to ask if she's seen Corinne when a searing pain crosses my shoulders and I look up to see Tall Rex holding his long rod. That's when I realize it's not just a rod, it's a discipline stick.

"Focus," he says.

But I'm blinded with rage. I want to scramble out of the hole and attack him. Then there's that voice in my head.

"He's right. Focus. Dig deep. Violent meditation has its time and place. That is not now."

I can sense Fee and some of the other seekers watching me. While the attention is nice, it also adds an unwelcome sense of gravity to my impending actions. Tall Rex's blow was so hard it caused me to drop my shovel. Still making eye contact with Tall Rex, I try to force some of the hate to melt away, put the palms of my hands together, bow slightly, and say, "Yessir."

And it's like my obedience unlocks something in him because his cold, steely demeanor briefly retreats and he says, "The journey is long, friend, and we must focus our energy on the earth, not the thought-waste spewing from your mouth. The freedom to not think, to not talk, should not be taken lightly." As if to make his point, he brandishes the discipline stick at me and walks away.

I pick up my shovel and resist making a snide comment to Fee. For now.

Again, I hear the voice: "Dig deep. Expand the Power Hole. Bide your time. You are uncovering the power at your core."

Look, I know how important the core is. The more I tune into that voice, the more I know it's not mine. I wonder if anyone else is hearing it. I wonder if this type of focus is what happens when the fog of alcohol has lifted. I glance at the other seekers around me. They're like machines. Focused digging machines. And I realize I'm behind. I'm behind and at a disadvantage. I haven't eaten real food in I don't know how long. My stomach grumbles and I can't help but focus on Carol's breasts, surprisingly large for such a frail woman. I glance up from her breasts to notice her mouth constantly moving and I wonder if she's talking to Jorry or just muttering more nonsense. I once again plunge my shovel into the dirt, knowing I will get to eat with the rest of the seekers this evening, think about possibly returning to Carol for another nightcap when we retreat to our cabins. I can't recall the last time I'd slept as soundly as I did last night.

So I spend the next I-don't-know-how-long mimicking my fellow seekers, hoping whatever it is they appear to be accomplishing will happen to me. I toss shovelful after shovelful of dirt over my aching shoulder. I don't like how all the dirt is just tossed into a few random piles. I think we should have our own piles of dirt so Tall Rex and Blastneesh know who did the most. Surely the size of my dirt pile would be a direct reflection of my focus and dedication to becoming enlightened.

This makes me anxious. This drives me to work harder, dig faster. I try to put Corinne out of my mind. I try not to think about Fee taking credit for the size of our—eye roll—*communal* dirt pile. I feel like it's a race and everybody else has had a head start. Big Labia stomps her shovel into the dirt, sweating and driven, and I imagine her reaching a point where she can toss aside her shovel and proudly shout, "I've reached enlightenment!"

Imagine the embarrassment of losing to someone like her.

"The power at your core."

That's all I can think about. I go back to the period of time when I was really into exercise, when I actually went to the gym and punished myself on a near-daily basis, before I started using "the gym" as an excuse to hang out at the bar with people who were younger and cooler than me or to get reduced-cost blowjobs from the girl living in the alley. You reach the point where you feel like you can't go on anymore and then you just keep going. That was how I gained mass. That was how I transformed the doughy, skinny-fat guy I saw in the mirror into the Greek statue I wanted to become. That's what I dig for. The spiritual equivalent of a Greek statue. I want to be able to seem as self-satisfied, as accepting of the world, as some other people I've encountered. I want wisdom and knowledge. I want to know how not to feel swollen with rage or like breaking into tears when a barista makes a mistake. I want to get back to feeling like I have a handle on the world. I want to feel the power I felt in my twenties with the humility that not everyone is spiritually adept enough to achieve that.

When Fee says, "Whoa, slow down there, tiger," I can barely hear her over the blood roaring in my ears. I feel driven and inexhaustible and like I don't want to be doing anything else but uncovering the power at the core of my being. Then I start to feel like I might be having a heart attack.

I keep going.

twenty-three

"Everyone!" Tall Rex announces. "Put down your shovels and meet me at the Example Circle."

I get excited and try to shout, "Do we get to pelt rocks at him!" but my mouth and throat are so dry, my heart is racing so fast, I don't think any sound comes out.

Dirty and sweaty, we climb out of the Power Hole, everyone exhausted by all their hard work but excited to have the closest thing resembling a break we're going to get. I haven't glanced around at my fellow seekers in a while and am not entirely surprised to notice Corinne is still nowhere among them.

I snort and swallow enough to coax a modicum of moisture into my mouth and ask Fee, "Have you seen my wife?"

She runs a hand through her sweaty hair and says, "Maybe she had special counsel with Blastneesh?"

"Special counsel?"

Fee shrugs.

I assume special counsel means she's getting fucked by Blastneesh. Meaning she's going to feel superior and more special than me. She'll be absolutely insufferable the next time I talk to her. I remember the glow on Gemini's face last night and the thought of that glow bestowed upon Corinne sickens me. I was the one who had the initiative to download the app. I was the one who prepared. I was the one who got us here. And Corinne is going to be the one to reap all the enlightenment. *She* is the one invited to sit at the foot of the master, so to speak. Christ, sometimes I wish I had a pussy.

As we collectively approach the Example Circle, I can't help but feel an overwhelming sense of schadenfreude at the sight of Branch. He's wearing the multi-layered sweatsuits and I wonder if they're the same ones I wore yesterday. Were they even washed or were they still crusty with my sweat when he put them on? The sweatpants are so thick I don't even notice his monster cock, so my schadenfreude isn't even tempered by this resentment. It's unbridled. And something about that makes me feel great. Reveling in the misfortune of others is simply a part of modern life. Put in another light, it's called appreciation. Appreciating that you have it better than others. Sure, you can lend a hand, try to pull them out of their doldrums or misfortune or whatever, but why do you want them to be on your level? Or, maybe that's the point. If you're the one who helped pull them out of it, then you are always ahead, thus cementing a feeling of superiority, augmented by the notion of "having done the right thing." This is the only way I can see that behavior as making any sense whatsoever.

I made sure to grab a handful of pebbles. I don't want to be the first one to throw them but will happily join in if someone else starts.

Branch stands, looking at us in a beseeching way.

Tall Rex stands in front of Branch, towering over him, a slop bucket in hand.

"On your knees," Tall Rex says.

Branch immediately drops to his knees and I wonder if Tall Rex is going to degrade him by making him blow him. Honestly, though, Day Three seems a little early for that.

Tall Rex places the bucket on the ground in front of Branch. It looks like it's filled with the leftovers from last night.

"Eat," Tall Rex says.

Branch again looks up and around at the seekers. I wonder if he feels forsaken. I had him pegged as the retreat golden boy, but now if he's going to ascend to that hallowed level, he must overcome this trauma-inducing obstacle.

The voice in my head says, "No one is going to save him," and I wonder if that's the true purpose of these shamings. Is it a way for Blastneesh and Tall Rex to establish dominance or is it an exercise in humanitarianism? Like, are they waiting for one of the other seekers to step forward and tell them to stop, tell them what they're doing is wrong, volunteer to take Branch's place? That all just seems so status quo. The type of thing that would only happen in a terrible, aspirational movie or something. I contemplate being the one to step forward, really just to be seen as a nice and caring guy, but I'm not going to take that chance on someone like Branch.

Branch looks at the slop bucket and slowly shakes his head. "I don't know if I can do it."

"You have no choice."

Branch looks up from the bucket. This time I know he's looking directly at Fee, who is looking very pointedly at the ground.

To make him feel worse, to make him feel like his long-term partner has also forsaken him, I move closer to Fee and wrap an arm around her shoulders in the most comforting and least lecherous way I possibly can. I'm pretty sure I see a shadow of hurt darken Branch's eyes.

The tension over the next several seconds is nearly unbearable. As exhausted as I am, as gross as Fee feels beneath my undoubtedly gross arm, I feel anticipation welling inside of me. If he gets up and walks away—if that's even an option—my chances with Fee will be greatly enhanced. If he chooses to plunge his hands into the bucket of meat slop, possibly a human child, and begin eating, the satisfaction I'll feel at his debasement will be something I think about with regularity at least over the course of the retreat.

Big Labia breaks the tension by shouting, "Eat it! We gotta get back to work!"

"Yeah!" Brent shouts. "The Power Hole isn't going to dig itself!" I can hear the sexual frustration in his voice. The jealousy at having to give Corinne up to Blastneesh for the day, both of them in Blastneesh's deluxe cabin, each of them trying to blow one another's minds, probably with their genitals.

Branch again looks imploringly at Fee and I can feel her head slowly nod beneath my arm. He reaches out a frail hand and dips it into the bucket, puts a piece of meat in his mouth, and begins chewing.

Tall Rex hoists his discipline stick into the air and says, "A round of applause for Example Branch!"

We all begin banging our tired and sore hands together. Tall Rex begins circling the perimeter of the Example Circle.

"Faster," he says.

Big Labia is the first to take it up and turn it into a chant.

Then we're all—Fee included—chanting "Faster! Faster!" and Branch, looking absolutely miserable, is taking handfuls of the slop and shoving them into his mouth. He's barely even chewing the stuff, just shoving it in, his massive Adam's apple bobbing as he works it down his esophagus. The bucket is probably the size of, like, six human stomachs so I'm wondering if it's even possible for him to eat the entire thing without vomiting at least a couple of times. It gives me something to look forward to. Kind of like an intermission.

Everyone is still shouting. He pauses. Both of his hands are covered in the red sauce. It hangs from his chin and plasters his shirt to his noticeably distended stomach.

I pause in my chanting to lean into Fee and say, "He looks really uncomfortable." Then, quickly, because I'm afraid I sound almost happy about that, I say, "I feel really bad for the guy."

I'm not even sure she hears me. She keeps chanting along with the others, even more frenzied now. It must be somewhat satisfying to take part in this completely socially sanctioned bit of torture. Even though she and Branch seem pretty hippie-dippy and blissed out, they must have their disagreements. Who smoked the last of the weed? Why didn't you get the organic beans? Whose turn is it to burn the shit hole?

Getting back into it, I take up the chanting again. Branch looks like he's ready to throw up.

Tall Rex yields his discipline stick, shaking it, saying, "If you throw up . . ."

Branch again leans over the bucket and commences shoveling. It gets kind of boring but, as he pushes on to the point where I think the next mouthful could either lead to a ruptured stomach or the aforementioned vomiting followed by the promised beating, I'm once again rapt. I even find myself looking forward to what's going to happen to the next example.

We've all moved in closer to the Example Circle so we can see the disappearing contents of the bucket. He doesn't have much left.

I again move close to Fee and put an arm around her, hopping up and down excitedly. "I think he's going to do it!"

He pauses, swallows deeply, closes his eyes, and plunges

both hands into the bucket, scooping up the remainder and two-fisting it into his mouth. The chants of "Faster! Faster!" are immediately replaced with elated cheers and applause. While I would have much rather seen him require medical attention or, at the very least, throw up and get beaten, I can feel a sense of joy in his accomplishment. Like a severely underdog team winning a game they really shouldn't have won. You feel kind of bad your team lost, but you still feel kind of happy for the other team.

After fully swallowing the last bite, Branch collapses back into the circle, his hands over his stomach. Now I imagine him out here in the hot sun, wearing all those sweatsuits, so stuffed and uncomfortable. Feels pretty good.

"Let's get back to it," Fee says and I'm not sure if she can't bear to watch Branch any longer or if she just really likes digging.

I follow her back to the Power Hole, wishing the provided uniform for this retreat was yoga pants instead of these flowing harem pants. I was so drunk the first night I can barely remember what Fee looked like naked. I'd be willing to make the sacrifice and wear yoga pants too, for the sake of equality. I'm pretty proud of my ass, although that pride has waned somewhat on my approach to middle age and since putting on these few extra pounds.

As we begin digging again, I think about my few extra pounds. I'm pretty sure, no matter how miserable the other seekers are while they're here, they will be happy and consider it a tremendous success if they manage to shed some extra weight before they leave.

The brief time away from the Power Hole was just enough time for my muscles to stiffen up somewhat and it makes going back to the digging that much more difficult.

Even though I'm sure I could find a way to make it

interesting, I'll spare you the details about my digging. I don't know how long it goes on for. Probably just a couple of hours that feel like three days. I'm trying to do anything but think about how much pain I'm in or how exhausted I am. I ogle Fee as much as I possibly can. As she becomes more saturated with sweat, her pants begin sliding down her hips, affording me a glimpse at the top of her ass crack. Her shirt becomes glued to her and she lifts it farther and farther to wipe the sweat from her face. I fantasize about fucking her in the dirt while the other seekers look on.

I also find myself watching Brent and thinking, kind of, about Corinne. I think about charging across the Power Hole and bashing Brent with my shovel. Clearly, there is no way he's going to become the most enlightened, but I have to admit he's probably the best-looking male here. I also have to admit that maybe it's a point of pride he'd chosen Corinne as his object of fancy. If Corinne and I end up splitting, I hope I'll be able to find someone as beautiful as her. Preferably younger. Preferably less mentally ill. I'm pretty sure I can do it. Then I'm thinking about fucking Fee while Corinne and Branch watch. Then I imagine Branch fucking Corinne while Fee gives me a blowjob. Then I'm embarrassed to glance at Fee and see her staring at the turgid erection tenting my pants. But, I don't know, maybe she's into it. I haven't come since fucking Corinne in the La Quinta. It feels like a lifetime ago. If the group orgy doesn't happen tonight, I'll have to sneak off somewhere, not that I think Carol will really mind if I just pound off in my bed. She seems kind of unaware of things happening outside her head.

And there's the voice. It now feels like it's constantly murmuring, rising in volume so I can hear every word clearly before fading to a background static running corollary to my own thoughts. The voice strengthens and guides me. It's the most intimate advice I've ever received. This voice clearly knows me, knows what I want out of life and, at this point, it might be the only advice I listen to. It emboldens me. Makes me feel powerful and less alone.

My revery is disturbed by a blood-curdling scream.

It's coming from the Example Circle.

Branch.

I don't know how Fee has the strength or energy, but she drops her shovel, scrabbles out of the Power Hole, and sprints across the grounds.

"Emergency meeting!" Tall Rex calls. "Everyone to the Example Circle."

I drop my shovel, suddenly conscious of blisters on my palms, and head to the Example Circle.

Branch lies on his back, clawing at the ground. Fee is on her knees beside him, holding his shoulders. They are both focused on the area below his distended stomach, where his sweatpants are extended to maximum capacity.

"Oh god, it hurts so bad!" he screams.

Fee scrambles along beside him, grabs the waistbands of his sweatpants and yanks them down. This act causes Branch to again cry out. Fee's eyes widen at the sight of his cock, swollen to monstrous proportions. Branch's curry-stained hands shoot to his penis, clutching it.

"Fuck," he mutters through clenched teeth before shouting "Fuck!" open-mouthed.

At a loss, Fee strokes his forehead and looks plaintively at everyone gathered around.

"Can't one of you help us?" she pleads.

"I could probably drag him somewhere," Gus says.

"I'm a doctor," Thomas says. He seems spacey and out of it. "But I don't know how to help. I've never seen anything like this. I am not a doctor of penises."

I want to tell her maybe he's just backed up and she should try jerking him off to relieve some pressure and tension but I don't really want to help and I certainly don't want to watch Fee give Branch a handjob. Actually, maybe I do. It'd probably be kind of hot and the closest thing to group sex I'll get in this place. Instead, I keep my eyes glued on Branch's dick, which seems to be growing before my very eyes. I wonder if any of the women are thinking about jumping on that thing and make the mistake of glancing over at Carol, who's staring fixedly at Branch's penis and greedily rubbing her gnarled hands together while murmuring sub-audibly and licking her lips with a dry tongue.

Jorry looks concerned. "What's happening, Ma? Why's his pee-pee so big?" He's clutching his own crotch through the weird diaper/loincloth thing and shifting his weight from foot to foot, visualizing the discomfort undoubtedly felt by all the dudes here.

Now Fee shoots daggers at Tall Rex and says, "What did you do? What did you put in the food?"

Her challenge to authority is commendable and a mistake. Tall Rex lashes out with the discipline stick, catching her on the upper arm.

Branch again unleashes a howl. It's a sound I've never really heard an adult make.

Then his penis explodes.

Fee gets most of it, her yellow uniform turning almost completely red. The rest of us get spackled with it here and there.

Fee moves up to Branch's head, lifting it and cradling it in her lap.

"We need to get him to a hospital," she says to no one in particular.

"He's dying," Thomas says. "It wouldn't help."

And we all stand around as the last bit of life leaves

Branch's body. Aside from the sense of exhaustion surrounding my fellow seekers, I can also sense a feeling of relief. With one fewer seeker, our chance of becoming the most enlightened increases exponentially.

"Back to the Power Hole!" Tall Rex shouts. He points the discipline stick at Fee and says, "You too."

To my surprise, she lets Branch's head drop into the dirt of the Example Circle and accompanies the group of seekers back to the Power Hole.

twenty-four

Having completed a full day at the Power Hole, I have new-found respect for my fellow seekers. I can't imagine waking up tomorrow to do the same thing. Not only will it be *more* physically exhausting with sore and achy muscles, it will be a hundred times more boring without the dramatic upheavals of today.

Fee was understandably quiet throughout the rest of the day. I was too tired, too focused on listening to my guiding voice and digging to try and cheer her up or make her feel better. If I'm going to make any moves, I need to act quickly, establish myself as a voice of comfort and concern.

In the dining hall, everyone sits about where they sat yesterday. Thomas approaches Fee in that creepy, spacey way he has and says, "I'm very sorry for your loss." I'm immediately somewhat jealous. He makes it seem so easy. Nevertheless, it unlocks something within me.

"I'm here for you . . . you know, if you need anything," I say.

"I'll be okay," she says.

"I'm sure you will," I say. "Just . . . you know."

Her uniform is still caked in blood. She's sweated most of it from her face. She smells horrendous.

"Wonder what we're having for dinner," I say. I'm starving. I figure we'll probably be eating Branch and I'm unperturbed by this. At least it will be substantial, solid food, and since Branch was vegan or vegetarian or whatever, he should be fairly tasty.

Carol approaches Fee, nervous, wringing her hands, Jorry twitching along uncomfortably behind her.

"Men'll always get in trouble with those things," she says. "My pops choked to death on his. It was really embarrassing for everyone, messy, and I was nearly driven from my home."

"I'm sorry to hear that," Fee says.

"Just be glad you're young." Carol takes Jorry's lobster-claw hand and walks him up toward the head of the table.

Corinne emerges from the back area, looking radiant, and doesn't cast so much as a glance in my direction. Then Blastneesh emerges onto the stage, the seekers bringing their tired hands together for as much applause as they can muster. I would have thought maybe he would look somber or heavy-hearted, but he seems just as lofty and ebullient as he did yesterday.

"Gaining power," the voice in my head says.

I try not to think of how much of Blastneesh's semen is inside Corinne. A full day of "special counsel," whatever that entailed, had to be better than a day at the Power Hole, not to mention what an advantage it must bestow on someone's path to enlightenment.

"You all act like someone died," Blastneesh says, laughing along with all the seekers. I hesitate until I see Fee laughing too.

For a moment, I feel like I've missed something. Like what

I witnessed with Branch was some kind of spiritual re-enactment and he would come strolling out to the table at any minute.

"We will not talk about death. For the living, it doesn't exist . . . but more on that later. Who's hungry?"

A wall of chatter rises from the famished table.

"There were too many distractions for today to be bountiful," Blastneesh says. "So we eat accordingly."

Tall Rex wheels out a cart of what looks like sandwiches.

"You may come up to the front and grab your . . . wet lettuce sandwiches!" Blastneesh says and, instead of grumbles and moans, there are appreciative *mmm*s and *can't wait*s.

What the fuck is a wet lettuce sandwich? I don't even care. I'm so hungry, if they were serving my dead child from the night before, I'd gleefully eat it.

I'm again toward the back of the table so I'm the last one in line. Because I'm so hungry, it's not exactly dread I feel as I watch everyone get served before me, but my hunger doesn't exactly mount at the prospect of a wet lettuce sandwich.

Tall Rex stands behind the serving tray, a small stack of sandwiches consisting of a substantial amount of lettuce on basic, plain white bread. Next to the sandwiches is a large bucket of water. Before handing the sandwich to the seeker, he plunges it into the water.

As Gus steps up to the serving tray, he says, "Can I get mine dry, man?"

"Only wet," Tall Rex says.

"Wetter's better, I guess, huh?" Gus laughs and takes his soggy sandwich slapped down on a paper plate.

Gemini's in front of me. I say, "The budget must really be shoestring here."

She turns and smiles, possibly still radiant from yesterday, possibly just brain damaged enough to be happy all the time.

"I think it's kind of like a metaphor. Like, you now, if you're so hungry, it doesn't really matter what you're eating? You know, like, what he was talking about last night? I'm just thankful there's food."

I have virtually no recollection of what he talked about last night and am not looking forward to tonight's egotistical diatribe either.

I get my wet lettuce sandwich and head back to the table. I think everyone has the same idea I do—to eat it as quickly as possible—and the sound of eleven people scarfing down wet lettuce sandwiches is perhaps even more disgusting than the sandwiches themselves. As soon as I'm finished with it, I try to forget about it. It's one of the most revolting things I've ever eaten.

There isn't the same chatter around the table there was last night. Maybe it's as much of a pall as can be felt amongst so many positive people seeking enlightenment, although I suspect everyone is just very tired.

Gemini sits and stares, smiling at Blastneesh on the stage. Fee looks down at her empty plate and picks at a blister on her hand. Corinne, near the head of the table, glowing, also stares blissfully up at the stage.

Tall Rex, having wheeled the sandwich cart away, comes back to the stage and arranges the microphone in front of Blastneesh, who sits with his creepy half-smile, not saying anything, for an inordinately long amount of time. Part of me wishes he wouldn't launch into his self-important lecture or speech or meditation or whatever he calls it. I do not get my wish.

"Sometimes . . ." he practically purrs, "bad things happen."

There's a wave of sad agreement and I'm too far away to see if Blastneesh's expression is remotely conciliatory.

"But what a way to go, huh? BAM! Wow!"

The sad mutterings are immediately replaced with laughter. Even Fee is smiling. Corinne is blissfully nodding her head. I wonder if she even knows what he's talking about. Someone had to have at least told Blastneesh. Maybe she overheard while his cock was in her ass or halfway down her throat.

"There must be carnage for the living to live. Afterward, I encourage you to all go look at poor Branch, still in the Example Circle, still . . . the example. But an example of what? An example of someone who is . . . too weak to keep down a modest bowl of food? It occurs to me our first two examples have been . . . *men* who were unable to keep things in their body. The first, our Champion back there, because he didn't know when to stop putting things in his body. The second— poor, deceased Branch—because he never wanted it in his body in the first place, so he rejected it. His *mind* rejected it . . . not his body. As we spoke about yesterday, the body does not reject nourishment, it welcomes it. His *mind*, his rigid ideology did not want to accept it and . . . *blaargh*! It all came back up. And then what happened today . . . so tragic. Maybe his body was too accepting. Maybe he'd been so malnourished for so long, his body took in all of that nutrition at once— greedy for it—and, well, his penis exploded so clearly his body did not know how to handle it."

He pauses and scans the seekers, letting his gaze linger on a couple of us.

"When we go to look upon Branch's corpse, let us not feel mournful. After all, he was here. He was ready. He was ready to leave his body. He was as full as he could possibly be. He had the most . . . rigid erection he'd probably had since being a teenager. He was loved by those around him. What more could a person ask for? And now his energy, his life force, is completely without restraint.

"It is said there's a demon that inhabits these woods—silent, invisible, always looking for its next host. This demon finds happiness in carnage, compelling its host to perform the most violent acts, pitting human against human."

Dear god. Could that be the voice I'm hearing? All its talk of violent meditation. Could a demon be inhabiting my brain? I need to remember this so I can bring it up to Blastneesh if I'm ever able to force a special counsel, which I intend to do either tonight or tomorrow.

"But . . . if they are so weak to succumb to this metaphysical being, shouldn't they be deserving of their fate? To be released from their physical bodies to do battle with this demon on its plane of existence. So the weak host is either removed or removes another person, thus making the earth that much cleaner. And because it is able to consume the soul and not just the body, it is cleaning whatever waits in the spirit realm, as well. Gatekeeping against the imperfection. It's why we have a fence around the perimeter. To keep out the curious . . . the suspect. It's why, unfortunately, as some of you have asked, we must find a way to dispose of Branch amongst ourselves.

"I am not going to go on . . . too long tonight. It was not my intention to be so morbid. So we'll have a short night tonight, and tomorrow, if there are fewer hijinks, if there is more focus and celebration, we'll feast . . ."

I keep waiting for him to say more, but Tall Rex emerges to remove the mic and stand from in front of Blastneesh, who stands and begins walking off the stage.

Thomas, near the front of the table, half-stands, bent over at the waist to call, "Wisdom Master, I have a question."

His request goes unnoticed as Blastneesh exits the stage, seeming to float in his robes.

Tall Rex bends way down to speak into the microphone.

"Everyone to the Example Circle."

On our way to the circle, I sidle up next to Fee and say, "You don't have to look if you don't want to."

"I want to. Like Master said, it's not really Branch anyway." She chuffs out a slightly sarcastic laugh and says, "If you want to know the truth, his cock was the most beautiful thing about him."

I'm a bit stumped. If Fee's a size queen, I'm going to disappoint her. It's not an appropriate time, but by mentioning Branch's appendage, I see an opening to talk about sex. I'm not going to pass it up.

"I guess that probably made you pretty happy, huh?"

"Well, sure, but we were never really exclusive so I was . . . kind of proud of it, you know?"

"Felt lucky?"

"Something like that."

"I guess I'm sorry to see it go too."

We reach the Example Circle on the outskirts of the campground (let's call it what it is). There are a few security lights scattered around the cabins but, back here, it's poorly illuminated and I'm a bit disappointed I'm not going to be able to see the aftermath properly. Thankfully, Tall Rex has a powerful flashlight he shines on the corpse.

"Everyone gather round," Tall Rex says. "Take a good long look. Meditate on it."

"What are we supposed to learn from this?" Thomas sounds disgusted.

"How about you learn not to be a fucking asshole," Tall Rex says.

Thomas doesn't say anything. He just takes it. Of course he does. Fucking pussy.

"Do you . . . need me to hold you?" I ask Fee, thinking it's a generous proposition since she's still covered in penis blood and smells horrible.

"I think . . . if I could just get some space?"

I can respect that. She wants to lose herself to the memory of that cock. I don't want to seem too needy so I give her her space. I don't know if she really meant physical space but I move closer to Corinne anyway. It'll make it easier to ambush her when our meditation session is over.

She's standing next to Brent. When she notices I'm standing on the other side of her, she moves to the other side of Brent, putting him between us.

He shoots me what I'm sure is his best attempt at a withering gaze and says, "She *doesn't* want to talk to you."

"Quiet!" Tall Rex barks.

I lean into Brent and whisper into his ear, "She's *my* wife."

He doesn't say anything. Just rolls his eyes, which I find somehow more infuriating because it's one of Corinne's signature mannerisms.

I decide to put my back to them, moving closer to the Example Circle, focusing on Branch's brightly lit corpse, paying special attention to his crotch.

It's a ghastly sight, virtually unrecognizable as a human penis. It looks like what would happen if you squeezed a banana too hard. Oddly, I derive more satisfaction from looking at the twisted, pained, horrified expression on his face. Branch did not die pretty. I hope when my time comes, I'm able to compose myself and look peaceful or, at the very least, handsome. Branch looks like someone in the throes of dementia or being tortured to death or something.

A loud sniffle comes from Big Labia behind me. I recall how she grabbed my dick the first night here and feel like she probably senses the loss much in the same way Fee does. Mourning the loss of one fewer beautiful cock in the world.

She was probably only biding her time so she could molest him in the same way she molested me.

I don't know how long we're supposed to stand here watching him. It's more boring than watching him eat. Much less dramatic. I feel like we're waiting for something to happen, but we're not. Nothing is going to happen. His spirit is not going to rise from his body. He's not going to get back up and start moving around. I guess we're supposed to feel something, but I don't. The only thing I feel is that I don't want to go out like that. And maybe that's the point. He did die as an example, after all. It could have been me. That makes me feel a little better and I wonder if that isn't the true meaning of mourning or "paying one's respects." We're gathered here today to be thankful we're not the one lying in the casket or, in this case, on the ground with our giant penis exploding through our multiple layers of sweatpants and now resembling a gory, exploded sausage. This is the point of our meditation, the voice in my head reassures me. Immediately after this realization, the true boredom sets in and becomes almost unendurable. This is compounded by the wave of boredom I feel from the other seekers. There's less sniffling, more shuffling.

"I wet myself, Ma," Jorry says loudly.

Carol shushes him.

I don't know how long we continue to stand there. It feels like at least an hour. When I don't think I can take it anymore, Tall Rex says, "You may return to your cabins."

I'm exhausted but I have to talk to Corinne. She and Brent are already a fair distance away. I move as quickly as I can on my sore legs.

"Corinne." She's trying to ignore me.

"Corinne!" She and Brent both turn to face me.

"I need to talk to you."

She doesn't look annoyed and perturbed like I expect. She still has that blissed-out look on her face she usually only has when she's taken just a bit more than the recommended dosage of the right pills and everything else is pretty much going the way she wants it to.

"What is it, Scott?" she says.

Brent says, "How many times do I have to tell you she doesn't want to talk to you?"

I don't look at Brent in acknowledgement, just say to Corinne, "Why's he so aggressive? I don't even know him."

"Because he knows about you. He *listens* to me. I spent all last night talking to him."

"Yeah, well, he's not acting very enlightened."

"Did you . . . want to talk to me about Brent?"

"*No.* I want *Brent* to go away."

To my surprise, she turns to him and says, "Do you mind leaving us alone for a few minutes?"

"You sure?"

"It's fine. Trust me."

I slit my eyes as I watch Brent walk away. "I do not like that guy."

Corinne rolls her eyes and says, "Well, I'm sure the feeling's mutual."

"How was *special counsel*?"

"Oh, fuck, is that what you wanted to talk to me about?"

"Well, yeah, I think if my wife is going to spend all day fucking another dude, even if he *is* a guru, I have the right to know about it."

"So . . . you think . . .? You know what . . . it was great. It's probably going to hurt to piss for a week."

"We tell each other about this stuff. You know that."

"I didn't know you were such a cuck when I married you."

"Well, we've both changed."

"That's for sure. Are we done here?"

I feel like there was more of a reason for wanting to talk to her but I think I really just wanted her to tell Brent to go away—a victory on my part—and to confirm she'd fucked Blastneesh. Since both of those things happened, I'm having a very hard time thinking of anything else.

"I don't know. I'm having trouble . . ."

"I thought maybe you were going to ask about Wendy."

I stop myself from saying "Who?" and realize she's talking about our child. I try to commit that to memory. One child. A daughter. Wendy. It's going to be too much.

"Oh my god," she says. "You've already forgotten about her. Well, I just wanted to tell you—"

My eyes fall on the dark-haired woman, who's now talking to Brent.

"You know what?" Corinne says. "Fuck it. I'm done here."

And she's walking away to join the most-attractive group of post-mourning seekers.

"No, wait . . ." But I can't think of anything. The day has finally caught up with me.

I look at the few groups of people—Brent and Corinne and the dark-haired woman (I really need to find out her name), Thomas and the short-haired older woman and Big Labia, Fee and Gemini and Cassie and Gus (the cool kids), and the thought of talking to any of them is too exhausting. I don't see Carol and Jorry so they must already be back at the cabin. Like losers. Like the indoor kids who stay in the cafeteria instead of going out for recess. The group that doesn't even try. The saddest group of all. My people. It doesn't make me feel great, but I head back to the cabin, telling myself I'm just tapping out early because it was my first day at the Power Hole.

Back at the cabin, Carol sits on the edge of her bed staring into the middle distance with an expression that could be ter-rified or might just be her normal expression.

"Where's Jorry?" I ask.

She hooks her thumb toward a door I hadn't noticed and says, "Bathroom."

"There's a bathroom in here?" I say, already looking forward to taking a shower.

She doesn't need to answer me, doesn't even make eye contact, just continues to stare at that indefinable space between us.

I want to sit on the bed and wait for Jorry to exit the bathroom, but I'm afraid I would immediately fall asleep.

"Does he normally take a lot of time in there?" I'm already pacing the floor of the cabin, knowing I'm done the second I stop.

"I've lived in Florence, Kentucky, my whole life," Carol says in response to absolutely nothing. "I couldn't imagine living anywhere else. But I feel like I've lived all over the place. I'm a part of so many other people. When I was very young, too young to even remember, my parents had all the bones and organs removed from my body so they could sell them to be used by other people. They replaced them with in-ferior lab-grown versions. That's why Jorry's the way he is. Somewhere out there, there's people with my bones and in-sides who've had healthy, beautiful children."

Jorry emerges from the bathroom adjusting his loincloth.

I don't think Carol is really talking to anyone so I slide into the bathroom. I don't have to piss or shit, probably because I'm on the verge of dehydration and the only thing I've had to eat for two days is a wet lettuce sandwich and some breast milk. I strip off my uniform and hop in the small stand-up shower. The water pressure is non-existent, the water smells like a pond, and there's no soap, shampoo, or washcloths, but it feels amazing anyway.

When I step out of the shower, I don't want to put my sweaty uniform back on so I enter the main cabin naked. I can get why we all had to strip down on the first day. It completely eliminates that taboo. Half the reason we're not naked all the time is discomfort and embarrassment. I'm willing to bet the dude who invented underwear was either inadequate (he had a small penis) or jealous (he didn't want anyone looking at his wife's pussy).

Jorry is latched onto Carol's left breast, his head able to rest comfortably on her lap.

She's still talking. "When we get back home, people are going to see us differently. They're going to stop attacking us with their psychic powers."

I approach Carol and ask, "Do you mind? I'm starving."

She doesn't stop talking, just nods her acquiescence.

I sit on the other side of her, lift the flagon of her breast and enclose my lips around the nipple. She's still talking but the only sound I can focus on is Jorry's slurping. It's a bit nauseating so I do my best to tune it out. There's something that seems incredibly nourishing about Carol's breast milk. The grumbling in my belly is immediately quieted. I feel a sense of well-being, almost euphoric, settle over me. By the time I think her breast is tapped out, I feel slightly stoned.

Carol is still talking. Jorry lies on his back beside her, milk drooling from each corner of his mouth.

"I've led an attack on the tower several times. All the wires from the tower are underground so they're too hard to get at, but there's a signal at the top of the tower. Must be 20G, at this point. It's changing all of our brains faster than ever. Faster than newspapers back in the day. It's why it doesn't take things any time to catch on anymore. The tower creates ambassadors for the signal. Converts. Makes them rich and famous so they end up selling technology for the rest of their lives. That's how they become part of the machine. I think that's why the tower's on the hill behind my house. Because it was built using my original brain. My first brain."

I stand, thinking maybe I'll go for a walk. I'm pretty sure I won't need to put on my clothes. Besides, while I am not a hundred percent happy with the size of my penis, I am not ashamed or embarrassed by it.

Before I can walk away, Carol breaks from her crazy talk and says, "You know, men produce milk too."

I am pretty sure she has just offered to give me a blowjob. This, in and of itself, does not make me hard. Then I have to think about the last time I came and I'm thinking about fucking Corinne in the ass in the sleazy La Quinta Inn and my cock is stiffening. Carol places a hand on the underside.

"I've tried getting milk from Jorry but the way his penis is . . . it's like an endoscopy. And the milk is always so sour."

Jorry, laughing, stands up and doffs his loincloth.

I don't even know what he has between his legs. It's like a very long, thin worm hanging down to his calves. Still laughing, he takes it in his hand and begins spinning it around.

I'm still so hard Carol thinks I'm into this, but as she leans to take me into her mouth, I'm totally freaked out by what is happening. For a brief moment it feels like I'm in a horror show, all the well-being dissolved, the comforting voice in my head nowhere in existence.

I back away. "I have to go for a walk."

The second I'm outside the cabin, the voice decides to return.

It says, "You owe her."

I stop moving away from the cabin. Of course the voice is right. To find enlightenment, I must, at times, be selfless.

twenty-five

By the time Tall Rex bellows for us to come to the Example
Circle, I'm so full of fury and rage it has nowhere to go.

When I went to the Power Hole first thing in the morning,
I searched for Fee to take my place next to her only to find
she was today's example. I didn't have to rack my brain too
hard to figure out why. It may have just been her association
with Branch, but my guess was that it was because she crossed
over into the Example Circle in her effort to comfort the dying
Branch. Then when I scanned the other seekers around the
Power Hole to locate Corinne, I noticed she, too, was missing.
As was Brent. My first thought was that it was Brent's day
for special counsel and Corinne was able to glom on because of
her exceptional performance yesterday, but the dark-haired
lady was also missing and I more reasonably assumed it was
probably her day for special counsel and Brent and Corinne
had somehow escaped together. Or were getting a quick one
in before a busy day at the Power Hole.

I couldn't take the humiliation anymore. I charged out of
the Power Hole and to their cabin, where I didn't have to even

bang on the door. It was already open. No one was inside.

An overwhelming pain shot through my lower back and I fell to my knees and heard Tall Rex say, "Get back in the Power Hole. They're not here."

A lot of questions shot through my brain but, first and foremost, I wanted to fight Tall Rex. I'd never actually fought anyone outside of my brief MMA phase and decided now was not a good time to fight someone who also had a weapon.

Besides, that voice was back in my head. "Now is not the time."

So I swallowed my pride and went back to the Power Hole, insinuating myself around the loose group consisting of Gus, Gemini, and Cassie because everyone else was old and gross.

They were already hard at work.

Tall Rex had yet to return to the Power Hole, so I asked, "Do any of you know where my wife went?"

None of them said anything. Cassie gave me the briefest side-eye.

"Nothing?" I said. I went back to shoveling and grumbling under my breath. I don't know what I said but feel like it had something to do with them all being so medicated and brainwashed they had no idea what was happening around them.

It must have gotten under Gus's skin because he said, "Okay, dude, who's your wife?"

Maybe because I'd talked about this with Fee, I assumed they all knew. Maybe the same thing consuming my brain was also consuming theirs.

Getting over my initial shock, I managed to say, "Corinne. The pretty blond."

"Oh, yeah, she's not your wife anymore," he said with, I'm pretty sure, more smugness than was necessary.

"What the fuck are you talking about?" He'd taken the

wind out of my sails.

"Wild night last night," Gemini said.

"I feel like I'm missing something."

"I'll say," Gemini said, never breaking from the digging. The iciness I felt from this group was palpable and I assumed it was because they could sense me getting closer to Fee and didn't want me threatening their dynamic.

"Her and Brent got married," Gus said. "They eloped."

I immediately lost my words. Okay. This is embarrassing to say, but I had a bit of a tantrum. I threw my shovel in the dirt. Threw myself into the dirt. Pounded my fists into the dirt. Raised my head to the sky and shouted, "Why?" and maybe kicked and screamed some.

I was pretty sure I heard someone in the group mutter "DTs," as though any display of emotion was an expression of some chemical imbalance.

Then Gus was above me, strong and comforting. He put his hands under my arms in an attempt to lift me up.

"C'mon, man," he said. "Tall Rex is on his way back."

I didn't want to, but Gus was there, helping me up. That voice was in my head, whispering comforting things. Part of me wanted that voice to go away. Part of me wanted to just lie in the dirt and wallow. But I knew I was going to do what the voice wanted me to. I was going to do exactly what everybody else was doing. I'm pretty sure I was crying.

"I feel weird," I said.

"We need to get back to digging," Gus said. "We gotta be on our best behavior today or tonight's going to be real ugly."

I didn't know what the fuck he was talking about but picked up my shovel and got to digging anyway.

I watched Tall Rex's blond hair emerge above the horizon of the Power Hole. When he got to the far side of the hole, Gus said, "How long you been without a drink?"

"Huh?" I was confused. I didn't know why Gus would be concerned about the status of my hydration.

"Alcohol, dude. How long have you been without alcohol?"

I'd been so exhausted I hadn't even thought about it.

"Oh, a couple of nights, I guess."

"That's why you're feeling weird. Make it through tonight and you'll feel much better tomorrow. Like a new man." Then he quickly bugged his eyes and got back to digging and I knew Tall Rex was close. I got back to digging.

Tall Rex was wheeling the cart around the Power Hole. He tossed down several bottles of water.

"You all need to stay hydrated today. It's very important. Drink your water."

I didn't need to be told twice. I hadn't even realized how thirsty I was. The rest of the morning was spent with him monitoring people's water intake, tossing down another bottle when the previous one was empty. He seemed serious about it. Drinking water seemed to be more important to him than digging the Power Hole, so I spent more time drinking than digging. It should have been a fairly relaxing morning so my mounting fury was undoubtedly caused by Fee and Corinne's absence and my increasing need to pee.

By the time he called us over to the Example Circle, I was contemplating just letting go in my uniform. With all the sweat already drenching it, I didn't think anyone would notice. I managed to hang on.

Now we all—minus Corinne and Brent and the dark-haired woman—stand around the Example Circle. Fee sits in the Example Circle in the lotus position, eyes closed. Previously, I'd put her in the "cute" category of adult women who still cling to some kind of teenagerhood, either by their physique or their outlook. Fee had both. Now I think she looks absolutely beautiful, the relaxed but almost holy pose imbuing her with an exoticism I hadn't really noticed before.

Tall Rex speaks and I feel like it's coming from a script, something written or dictated by Blastneesh. I wonder if Blastneesh lives in the head of Tall Rex. Does he have to talk out loud to him or is he able to put his words directly into his brain? Was the pretreat some way of introducing that virus into the potential seeker? I imagine the viral load increasing as more words are introduced until one's brain is completely taken over by Blastneesh's thoughts and ideas.

"Today's lesson," Tall Rex says, "is about letting go. Our example," he gestures at Fee, "could not let go. She saw a man, clearly beyond help, expiring, and she made the mistake of breaching the sacred Example Circle to cling on to whatever hope she could. What good does this do for the expiring? What good does it do for her fellow seekers? The act of not letting go is an act of imprisonment. Many of you may feel like you are prisoners here. However, you are free to go at any time. Take, for instance, the much more positive example of seekers Corinne and Brent. It's rare that two people find enlightenment and love so quickly and in the same place. We are fortunate to live in a sovereign community under the watchful eye of someone as holy and powerful as our Supreme Leader. A leader who can so expeditiously dissolve the seekers' previous disastrous entanglements and unite them under not just one, but all gods."

I feel like this part is intended just for me. It's hard to think about anything except how much I have to piss but he's just told me that I'm a middle-aged, divorced dad now, and that it's all legal and binding. It stings only about half as much as the pain in my bladder.

"And so, another day, another example. Our first example was a train wreck of an individual. Someone who had never experienced a minute of truly involuntary discomfort in their life. A prime example of everything a seeker doesn't want to be. So we looked upon it. We learned how not to be. We lashed out at it. We looked into it. We mapped the imperfections to eliminate the dead ends from the mazes of our lives.

"The second example was about acceptance. We will learn to accept what we need. A culture that has too much will begin turning away what it needs. It will place value judgments on it. This creates a monoculture. We must accept everything and do the editing in our brains. This is how culture grows. It eliminates hunger. It eliminates creative starvation. For, if we are accepting of everything at all times, there is no reason anyone on the planet doesn't have what they want when they want it. Instead, we live in a culture that has to be convinced they want things because they spend their lives denying so much. We define ourselves by what we do not accept. That's why, outside these gates, there is a sick society getting sicker and more out of balance every day. The little decisions we make multiplied and writ large. It is because of *them* that you are here.

"That brings us to today. Letting go. It's something that was covered pretty thoroughly in the pretreat. It's obvious some of you didn't listen to it. Some of you did not take this as seriously as others. Some of you are serious students and *some* of you are just spiritual tourists, not interested in true change, only interested in a *new experience* or a *quick reset*. That is not what this retreat is about. It *will* make you different. So what do you think of when you think about letting go?"

Jorry lets go of Carol's hand and begins shaking his hands in front of him like they're hot. He makes wild facial expressions.

Gus says, "I don't know, man, the only thing I can think

about is taking a piss."

Tall Rex shuffles back from the Example Circle, bows, and throws his hands toward Fee. "Then, please, be my guest."

"Are you serious?" Gus asks.

"Of course," Tall Rex says.

And I'm pretty sure Gus isn't going to do what Tall Rex clearly wants him to so I'm surprised when Gus approaches the Example Circle, slides his pants down below his sack, and unleashes a torrent onto Fee's chest, further soaking her already sweat-drenched shirt.

Jorry squeals and drops his loincloth and looks at Carol and says, "Can I, Ma?" and she pats him on the ass and says, "Go on," and he's moving closer to the Example Circle, his penis so narrow the urine shooting out of it is a wildly uncontrolled spray.

Now we're all moving closer to the Example Circle, the men in typical urinal mode, even though Thomas clearly looks like a guy who sits down to pee, the women bending over so they can emit poorly aimed arcing streams. I join in but this lewd and disgusting act has also made me kind of hard so I have to lean over a bit and it kind of burns a little. I concentrate mostly on her head and face, hoping she keeps her eyes closed so she doesn't know it's me. It's a good thing the dark-haired woman isn't here pissing on Fee because I'm not sure I could have resisted jerking off. With my cock in my hand, I shift my focus between the increasingly damp Fee and the asses of Gemini and Cassie. Cassie has a narrow, boyish ass and Gemini's is wide and round but perfectly shaped and a desire for them blooms.

There's a sense of elation amongst the seekers as we all let go on Fee and I'm wondering if she feels like this is a cleansing. A great, hot cleansing. No one has refused to do this. We've accepted this and now we're truly letting go of both our moral and sanitary hang-ups, as well as our urine. I imagine us all collectively experiencing that euphoric shiver that accompanies a satisfying urination held onto just a bit too long.

I look away from Gemini and Cassie's asses because I don't want to become any more visibly excited than I already am. Thomas is in a state of absolute bliss. He cradles his average-sized but malformed dick in his fingertips. His head is thrown back and I've never seen a man who usually looks so serious and sad smile so unabashedly and I wonder why this is bringing him so much joy. Maybe it's something he loves to do but hasn't been able to do in a very long time. Maybe it's something he's never done and he relishes the discovery of a ribald new hobby. I'm happy for him. I feel a connection I didn't think was possible. I briefly imagine us hanging out when the retreat is over, hooking up with girls just to piss on them, experiencing this collective joy as much as possible. After all, I don't know what Thomas's marital status is, but I'll be leaving here single.

I then find myself a little sad because this means, if any group sex ends up happening, it'll be that much less forbidden and taboo. I will be fucking someone different than my wife but, if I don't have a wife, then it's not cheating. Plus, I will not be able to watch her getting fucked by someone else, which is a huge part of the thrill. Watching her like she's an actress in a porno. Getting to see her whole body in action. Not having the need to make her feel pleasure. The burning resentment and jealousy. Looking forward to the first time we have sex afterward, both of us performing at our best.

Now it looks like everyone is finishing up. Big Labia slings the last of the urine from her mega-sized skin flap, gives it a little twist and wring, and I wonder if she has to do this every time she uses the restroom. We've turned the Example Circle into mud. Fee still sits calmly in the lotus position, seemingly unfazed.

I'm still going, the last one, and I'm not sure if that means I've won or lost. I'm not sure it really matters to anyone but me. For the remaining few seconds, I enter something like a trance. I'm tired and hungry and I'm in pretty much the most boring place in the world, but I'm pissing on a beautiful girl— the wild abandon, the intimacy of this act, bringing us as close together as we've been this entire time—the sounds of nature are all around us, the sun is beating down, not so harshly to-day, and it feels like the hands of the other seekers are on me, encouraging me, cheering me on, elevating me to new spiritual heights. An example is nothing more than a tool for others to learn from. Fee has served her role as an example to the letter. I can't wait to talk to her about this the next time we get the chance.

Then, with a poorly aimed final squirt, I'm done. I feel like I've won an epic battle. Everyone else seems both slightly dazed and slightly excited. Fee, thoroughly drenched in the urine of several people, slowly licks her lips and smiles myste-riously. I'm pretty sure she's into this.

"Back to the Power Hole!" Tall Rex commands.

We all do what he asks. No more water is given to us.

twenty-six

There's a drum circle because of course there is. It's almost eyeroll inducing but everyone seems to be pretty into it. I guess this is our celebration and we're all so happy to not be digging a useless hole in the harsh sun there seems to be a collective energy driving us.

Toward the end of the day of digging, I smelled smoke coming from up near the dining hall. Someone had constructed a large bonfire. Then came the smell of roasting meat. The smell became more and more pervasive. Looking around at the other seekers, they were aware of it as well. I'm sure, if I were closer to any of them, if I had not isolated myself toward the very far end of the Power Hole, I would have heard their stomachs rumbling as furiously as mine was. It became both harder and easier to dig. Harder because I was so tired. Easier because it felt like it was coming to an end. It's what I imagine a blue-collar guy must feel in the last few minutes of their last shift of the week. You're tired. You want to stop. But your time off is looming and that makes you work harder because it's almost over. I don't know. I usually either called in on

Friday or left at lunch.

Tall Rex appeared at the perimeter of the Power Hole.

"You have one more hour!" he shouted. "If you work hard, you'll get your reward! If you slack off, no dinner! No wisdom from the Wisdom Master! And I'll beat Thomas until he's unconscious!"

I was expecting Thomas to look up with a "What did I do?" expression but he kept his head down, digging harder and faster. I supposed he was singled out because he was the closest one to Tall Rex.

Then Tall Rex was back to circling the perimeter, pausing frequently to observe certain seekers until they started digging even faster. Luckily, I wasn't digging that fast to begin with, so it wasn't that hard to up the pace a little. I conserved my energy when I knew Tall Rex's eyes weren't on me and picked up my pace when he was close by. I wasn't really that worried about getting caught slowing down. I'm sure a dinner that didn't consist of wet lettuce would be great, but if dinner were done away with completely, I had a warm breast of milk waiting for me back at the cabin. That would do. I didn't really care if Thomas got beaten until he was unconscious or not.

Eventually, something I'd never really experienced overcame me. I decided it was easier to just put my head down and work furiously than it was for me to continually monitor Tall Rex and try and game his observations. Again, I had that overwhelming feeling this was something like enlightenment. I lost my sense of self. I was part of the team. I was no different than any of my fellow seekers and we were all working together, all to the best of our individual abilities. How many others were self-aware enough to have this thought? I lost myself in this feeling until we were finally called to dinner.

The set-up was different. Someone had dragged the dining

table out of the hall. A covered stage had been erected immediately in front of the hall. The light from the sizeable bonfire bathed everything in flickering orange light and dancing, ghostly shadows. Near the fire, a couple of spits turned, loaded with glistening hunks of meat. The dark-haired woman emerged from the door of the dining hall. The others had looked radiant and I was wondering if she would also, since I'd never seen her look anything but miserable and depressed.

She was. Beaming. Absolutely stunning. Probably filled with a gallon of Blastneesh's semen.

Blastneesh glided toward his chair and the microphone. Tall Rex scrambled up to the stage to adjust the microphone to Blastneesh's standing height.

Furtive, Blastneesh glanced around at all the seekers. Fee moved next to me and I had to move several steps away. The reek coming from her seemed to have established a kind of gaseous life of its own.

Blastneesh held both his hands out in front of his chest, the tips of his pointer fingers and thumbs touching.

"Nikola," he said, "what is this?"

"A triangle!" she said, clapping her hands in approval of, I guess, herself.

"More on that later. What are these?" He gestured to a pyramid of what I thought looked like bongos.

Nikola, the dark-haired woman, seemed stumped.

"Those are bongos, man!" Gus shouted.

"Very good." Blastneesh then retreated to his chair.

Tall Rex took the microphone and said, "The Master wants to hear some music!"

"Hell yeah!" Gus said, rushing the pyramid of bongos, eagerly handing them out to the other seekers, some looking as confused as me.

And now we're in it. A small circle near the fire, all of us pounding the bongos with our tired arms and sore hands. Sweat sticks our clothes to our skin and, as much as I want to be near Fee, I've chosen to be on the opposite side of the circle as her. I can't even imagine what she must smell like now, with the stink broken open. Gus is really going to town and I imagine he's back in his college—probably community— days. Fee looks as blissed out as she has all day, probably happy to be moving, using her reserves of strength on the drums. Thomas is also really into it and seems to be maybe the only one of us who can manage to make anything resembling a melody. The rest of us are just kind of going through the motions, occasionally throwing glances toward Blastneesh, who sits in his chair with his eyes closed, slightly bobbing his head to the wildly unsyncopated rhythm.

Much like the digging, this goes on for way too long and I lose myself to it. The beating of the drums is shaking something loose in my soul, something primal. That voice in my head is barking, almost chanting. "Harder. Harder. Harder." And I'm trying to do my best. It's like fucking when I'm in peak physical condition. Wanting to break the other person. Pounding them until they can't take it anymore. This has always been the closest thing I've ever felt to love. Two people engaged in the most intimate of contact, trying to bring one another to the point where their bodies lose control and shower the other person in their secretions.

I get to the point where I don't think I can keep going. I open my eyes to look around and realize I'm crying. I see Big Labia through my tear-blurred vision and it's like I'm seeing everything in slow motion, the flickering of the fire giving it an almost strobe-like effect. She's nude. She is holding the long part of her labia in her hand and hammering her drum with it. She's crying out in orgasmic ecstasy. I can't take it anymore. The thing inside of me has to come out. I raise my head to the night sky and scream. I don't stop until I hear Tall Rex, as if from a great distance, say, "Let's feast!"

Ten seekers, including myself, sit around the table. Plus Jorry. I haven't really thought of Jorry as a seeker. I've thought of him as an extension of Carol. But, you know what? He's experiencing most of what everyone else here is experiencing so I'm going to count him too. No reason to exclude him because of his . . . disability or condition or whatever. So, eleven seekers, including myself, sit around the table. Something about it feels post-orgasmic. We're all tired, sure, but there's a deep satisfaction buffering that fatigue.

The voice in my head is silent.

Blastneesh is rattling on about triangles as I feel my body greedily processing the food—probably Branch—I just ate.

"Of course . . . a triangle has three sides. As do . . . many things. Each of you is a triangle . . ."

I'm having a hard time focusing on what Blastneesh is saying. I glance at Hildy, the older short-haired woman, someone I'd nearly all but forgotten about because she's too old to be of sexual interest to me and doesn't have any remarkable attributes like a giant labia or weird son. Her eyes drift closed and her head bobs toward her chest.

"The sperm . . . and the egg from two humans combine to form a third human."

What about twins? I think. Probably more of a square than a triangle. Then I imagine what it would be like to have a triangle-shaped penis. Would that be more pleasurable to the woman, to be gradually stretched? Then I think about some kind of exercise I could do to make the base of my cock really fat so it would have a similar effect. Maybe I could get Botox injected into it.

"Think of the earth as an egg . . ."

I'm so fucking tired.

Blastneesh's pause goes on forever, almost like he's trying to lull us to sleep. Realizing my eyes are closed, I manage to open them. Everyone at the table is asleep. I listen to their rhythmic breathing and the crackle of the fire as I wait for Blastneesh's next words. They do not come. I think Blastneesh is also asleep.

"Fuck this," I mumble. I stand up from the table and begin making my way back to the cabin.

I hear someone behind me and turn to see who it is, expecting it to be Carol and Jorry.

It's Fee.

I enter the cabin and collapse onto my narrow cot, too tired to even take off my clothes.

Fee enters the cabin.

"I think I'm too tired to fuck," I say.

"I don't want that," she says. "I just want to lay on you."

"You smell really bad," I say.

She's already positioning herself on me.

"You'll get used to it," she says.

twenty-seven

I wake up to chaos. I'm unbearably hot. Fee is still lying on me. The heat has caused her stink to further blossom and the stench is almost too much to take. Her head is lifted and there's a string of drool spilling out of her mouth and onto my forehead.

She says, "Will you please be quiet?" and that's when I become aware of Carol's drone.

"The nearest parking lot is less than one mile from this retreat. A parking lot is nothing more than a piece of land covered in asphalt. When I was nine, a group of very evil men attempted to turn me into a parking lot. They flew me somewhere in the Middle East and filled most of my insides with sand, concrete. That's how I know where all the parking lots are."

"Please stop talking," Fee says and now I'm awake. I can feel the tension between them.

I also become aware of Jorry, who's nervously standing toward the back of the room, his loincloth removed, muttering something and swinging his weird penis around with his claw hand.

"We cannot be silenced," Carol says. "People have been trying to censor us for years, but our voices will be heard. The concrete I was filled with has a high metal content. That's what the towers are talking to. All the Point has to do is change the frequency. A lot of people will die automatically. We do not yet know what this mass death event will look like. It could be a bomb. It could be a lot of bombs going off all across the world. These bombs could already be planted. They've probably been planted for years. It could be a virus. A global pandemic. But those of us who are prepared will be turned into something close to gods. We'll finally realize our potential."

"Are you awake?" Fee says and it takes a couple seconds to realize she's talking to me.

"Yeah," I say.

"Want to get out of here?"

"Um . . ." I really just want to go back to sleep. My body feels so tired and achy. I'm not sure I can go anywhere. Plus I'm kind of hungry and wondering if I can get a bit of Carol's breast milk.

Fee is already struggling to extricate herself from me.

Before I can even get my thoughts together, she says, "Or you can just stay here. I don't care."

She's walking toward the door. I'm struggling to pull myself out of the bed. Jorry is howling something that sounds like "Bye-bye" and flicking his penis at Fee like a whip. Carol drones on.

I finally manage to get out of the bed. I haven't felt this bad since getting here. I don't even know why I'm chasing after Fee. I think whatever spell she had over me has been broken by her atrocious stench and her new, judgmental attitude. I flash back to the dark-haired woman, Nikola, dancing around the fire, beautiful and free, seemingly connected to the source of whatever brought me here.

"You're gonna miss these," Carol says. She's unleashed her breasts, and she's right.

For a moment, I'm torn. I could just stay here, fill my belly up with Carol's sweet breast milk and go back to bed, have a good night's sleep.

But Fee undoubtedly feels gross and distressed and who knows what that could lead to.

"Hungry, Ma." Now Jorry is scrambling to the bed, placing his head on Carol's lap and latching on to one of her nipples while his claw hand massages the other breast until he's covered with milk.

"I'll be back," I say.

"You won't be the same," she says. "Not after that bitch gets done with you."

And I'm out of the cabin, wondering if there's been some previous tension between Carol and Fee that I might have missed.

"Hey, hold up!"

Fee has already made it a fair way from the cabin.

I draw closer to her, trying to keep just enough distance so the urine-stink isn't so powerful.

"So what's the plan?" I ask, hoping she'll say something like "Skinny dipping" or, at the very least, "A shower."

"Escape," she says and, before I can say anything else, she says, "But just for tonight."

"Lead the way," I say, wanting to be complicit but also slightly terrified. Of what, I don't know.

We're heading toward the large barn we originally came in through.

Fee notices me looking nervously around and says, "Don't worry. We're free to leave. We're not prisoners here."

"I know. I just don't want to take many detours on my path to enlightenment."

Her lips curl into a smile and I can tell she wants to laugh at me and I become aware of how stupid what I just said sounds.

There's a narrow opening where the fence meets the barn.

"Think you can make it through there?" Fee says.

"Probably," I say.

Fee passes through easily and struggles to pull the fence back as much as possible. Cramming myself into the small space and working my way through, I'm aware of how much weight I've put on over the last . . . who knows? I can barely remember a time I wasn't here.

I make it through and ask Fee if she thinks I'm fat.

This time she does laugh and says, "Does it matter?"

"Yeah," I say. I don't tell her that other people's opinions of me matter more than reality.

"Maybe just a little gone to seed?" she says.

"Wait. That just means you think I'm old too."

"Relax," she says. "It doesn't matter."

Now we're heading down the narrow drive surrounded by massive trees. It's very dark and the woods are alive with an insect hum.

"So where are we going?" I ask.

"Into town," she says.

"What's in town?" I can't imagine anything interesting being in a town like this and, I have no idea what time it is, but can't imagine anything being open.

"I work at this brewery. I thought a drink sounded good."

Now I want to grab her and hug her, despite the stink. A drink sounds great.

"There's a brewery here?" Maybe I don't realize how trendy craft beer has gotten. If breweries have hit the rural

Midwest, their days are probably numbered.

"Of course," she says. "It's a college town."

"Huh," I say.

We reach the end of the drive and I follow Fee onto a narrow blacktop road.

"I guess, technically, it's not really a college town anymore. Shrine College used to be here but now it's called Shrine Institute. The college went under and they were bought by the Point a few years ago. I'm sure you've heard of them. Big global company. Hospitals, pharmaceuticals, biotech. I think they mine cryptocurrency too. All that stuff. Food, of course. Tuition's free but every student has to be a test subject. Works out pretty well though. College students love drugs."

"It seems so quiet."

"It's summer. Most of the students or subjects or whatever aren't here. Even if they were, it kind of depends on what drugs they're testing anyway. There's also the Chappeau factor."

"The Chappeau factor?"

"You've heard of Bill Chappeau, right?"

I have. "Love him." And I'm wondering why I can suddenly remember his television show from the nineties and his more recent stand-up specials but I still can't remember what city I live in or whether or not my kid is a boy or a girl or my ex-wife's name.

"So most of the stores and businesses are closed because Chappeau used the massive amounts of money he got paid to buy them up, assuming the Point, a company of endless wealth, would buy them from him for more than he paid."

"Wait. Bill Chappeau lives here?"

"Yeah. You didn't know that?"

"Why would I?"

"He talks about it all the time. I always thought he moved

here just to be quirky until I learned about the cash-grab thing. Then it started to make a little more sense. I mean, I've lived here my whole life. It's an interesting town but you could find more things to do in a single block in a real city than you could in this entire town."

She turns into a gravel parking lot that doesn't contain a single car. We approach an old white building and I notice the words TWIN SPRINGS BREWERY on the door.

"This must be the place," I say.

"Yeah," she says. "Not really a functional taproom anymore. Mostly just a hangout for Chappeau and his friends when they're in town. But they keep a few of us around to serve them. The tips are pretty great if you can take the abuse."

"Abuse?"

"Famous people are pretty obnoxious even when they think they're not being obnoxious."

"I'm pretty sure I wanted to be famous at one point."

"Everyone has. Instead we end up doing shit that famous people do without achieving the famous part. I mean, you notice how language is changing, right? Eventually we'll have more influencers than celebrities. But that's always what celebrities really were, right? Influencers. They're the ones who inspire us to travel, we want to watch what they're in, we want to read what they're reading, eat what they're eating. But they used to have to be good at something or at least some ad agency had to trick us into thinking they were good at something. An influencer is just a pretty face that's been plied with free products. It's out of balance. Or maybe it's more balanced. I guess we probably have more in common with influencers than celebrities."

"Huh. Guess I never really thought much about it." But I'm already wondering how I can become an influencer. It sounds powerful.

Fee tugs on the door and seems surprised to find it locked.

"Usually the last person to leave is too drunk or high to remember to lock the door. We'll try the back."

I follow her around the perimeter of the long building until we come to a wooden patio or deck or whatever. Fee climbs the few steps and crosses the deck to the back door. It's locked too.

"Hold on," she says. She reaches down the front of her pants, digs around for a second, and brings out a key.

"Was that . . . was that in your vagina?"

"Had to hide it somewhere."

"Wow, you're like the second woman I know who uses her vagina as a pocket."

"They come in handy sometimes."

She unlocks the door and I follow her into the bar or, what did she call it? The taproom.

She pauses and I nearly run into her, stopping short of contact but once again in her bubble of stink. This is not a glorious bubble.

"Something wrong?" I ask.

"Just had to make sure he wasn't here."

"Who?"

"Bill . . . Chappeau. Sometimes he works on his routine here."

"Alone?"

"Sometimes there are people but, yeah, I've heard he performs to empty rooms too. He's a weird guy. Anyway, coast is clear."

We enter the surprisingly modern taproom. The main lights are off but the security lights emit enough of a glow to make things visible. Fee goes behind the bar and pulls a couple beers from the taps. It looks like they have a big selection.

"You didn't even ask what I wanted," I say, feigning hurt.

"It's an IPA. I didn't need to ask. It's the aging hipster special."

"Ouch." Knowing she's watching me, I let my eyes quickly scan her body and say, "I like variety," hoping she picks up on the subtext.

She rolls her eyes.

I take a stool at the bar, my eyes immediately scanning for a television, realizing it's been days since I've had any contact with the outside world. Fee sits on the stool next to me and I fight the urge to move down a couple more stools, putting some more space between us, before telling myself I'll get used to it.

Once she sits down, it's as though we have absolutely nothing to say to each other, like an awkward first date.

My hand shakes as I take the first sip of my beer and I'm not sure if it's from anticipation or the full day of digging and night of savage drumming.

"This is pretty good," I say. While true, I'm sure I would have thought the same about anything with alcohol in it.

"Yeah, well, I didn't make it."

"I know. I . . . was just making a general observation."

She huffs and rolls her eyes again. I have to fight the urge to talk down to her like a child and make the rest of the night uncomfortable.

She must sense my annoyance because she says, "Compliments are fine. When people do a good job or go out of their way to look nice, you should compliment them, when appropriate. General observations are just . . . petty braindead vocal diarrhea, you know?"

These are not the types of conversations I like to have so I decide to placate her with the hope of moving on.

"I get it. It's like talking about the weather."

"Exactly. It's what people talk about when they have absolutely nothing else to talk about. Or have nothing in common."

It's as though she's handed me a gift. It's amazing to me I can still remember the techniques I learned when hooking up with my various extramarital affairs in bars. Unless the girl was one of those rare, combative people with super low self-esteem who wants to get hate fucked by a dude she can't stand—her ideological opposite—then the way to her vagina was traversed by accentuating the things you have in common.

"Well, I guess we've both had Branch in us. We have that in common."

She finishes sipping her beer and looks confused.

"What?" I say, thinking she took what I said the wrong way.

"Who's Branch?" she says.

"He's . . . Are you fucking with me?"

"No. I . . . Things have been foggy since listening to the pretreat."

"Branch was your boyfriend. You acted like you'd been together for a long time. His penis exploded yesterday. I'm pretty sure we ate him for dinner tonight."

She takes another sip of beer, her brow slightly furrowed as though trying to remember.

"Nothing?" I say.

She sets her glass down and says, "Nothing."

"I have it too. The memory loss or erasure or whatever."

"You showed up here with your wife—" She drums her fingers on the bar. "Karen?"

I shrug. "I don't know. We agreed things weren't working out so she left with that model-looking guy."

"Brent." It hurts me that she remembers his name.

"Must have left quite an impression."

"We hooked up the first night."

I almost spit my mouthful of beer out.

"Was my wife there?"

"No. It was just a three-way with him and my boyfriend. Well, I guess Gemini was there too, but she just watched. I think she might have made out with that woman with the real long pussy."

My mind is reeling with both missed opportunities and endless possibilities. I have to ask myself if I could fuck Fee smelling the way she does, then I think about the homeless girl behind the juice bar and I'm sure I could.

"Oh my god," she says. "I can practically tell what you're thinking."

"Oh yeah?" I try to sound playful, take another sip of my beer, make the type of deep, lingering eye contact with her that lets her know how into her I am. "What am I thinking?"

"You're thinking, 'This girl will fuck at the drop of a hat.' Am I wrong?"

I feel somewhat called out, unsure of how to respond. I take another sip of beer to buy a few more seconds.

"I'll admit," I say, "for a minute there, I was feeling really hopeful."

She sips her beer and offers a slanted, coy smile.

"My pussy smells like opium, tastes like brown sugar, and is as tight as a teen virgin. And you will never know if I'm lying or not."

"So, there's no chance?"

"I don't feel like there is, no."

Because the only way to win is to thoroughly assess your competition, and also because part of my coming to this retreat was about destroying my ego, I decide to ask, "So what did *Brent* have that I don't?"

"Oh, it's what my boyfriend—Branch, I guess—wanted. He was bisexual and liked to watch me with other guys sometimes."

I nod. "I get it. I loved watching my wife with other guys. I never did any of the gay stuff though."

"You don't know you hate something unless you've tried it."

"But I don't want to *try* something I don't want to do."

"Also, it's okay to like more than one thing. If you exist in the modern world, you have a right to try and do everything you can. We're all subject to years and generations of cultural conditioning. Sometimes you can't find out who you are unless you've done some things you've been taught not to do."

"Nah. I'm good."

"I just feel like a woman isn't a woman unless she's eaten pussy and a man isn't a man unless he's sucked cock or taken it up the ass."

I polish off my beer, wondering if I've missed an opportunity to score points with Fee.

"So, you're saying I might be attractive to you if I sucked cock?"

"Not you specifically. I just find exploration appealing."

I slide off my stool. The beer hit me harder than I thought it would.

I hold up my empty glass and say, "Got anything stronger?"

"That's the strongest thing here. It's a double IPA."

"Maybe I just need another one then." I slide my glass over to her and she totally doesn't get my joke about the double IPA even though it's cracked up bros and made at least a few girls smile at its attempted cleverness.

She slides my glass back to me and says, "You can help yourself."

It seems like a lot of work to walk behind the bar and pour another glass from a tap I, quite honestly, have never had to use before. Then I remember what she said about exploration being attractive and decide I'll at least attempt it. But then again, I don't know why I'm even trying. She's already taken sex off the table so the rest of the night spent with her will be a boring chore.

Putting my glass under the tap, I look at Fee over my shoulder and say, "Let it be known I've never done this before. I'm ex*plor*ing."

"You're really . . . why are you here?"

I think about her question while the coppery liquid fills my glass. Do I even know why I'm here? I mean, I kind of think I know why I wanted to come, but feel like she's not going to take it well. The beer gets closer to the top of the glass and I release the tap topper. The beer stops flowing. This was remarkably easier than I thought it would be.

I go back to the stool next to her.

I open my mouth to answer her question but she's already talking, practically cutting me off.

"Because a guy like you . . . I'm guessing you got a little bored, things were going kind of stale at home . . . the affairs you have weren't really doing it for you anymore . . . all the recreational and designer drugs couldn't bring back that spark you once had. So . . . you downloaded the app because you heard about it on one of your favorite podcasts and . . . once you started throwing money at it, you were invested in the value-added spirituality racket. And at first you thought the idea of a retreat was lame until your magical thinking turned it into something you could look forward to: a charismatic leader to make choices for you, new people who'd listen to your tired stories with fresh ears, physical labor you'd never do for a paycheck, the possibility of sex with practically anonymous strangers . . . and, if you hate it, you can always go back to your comfortable life."

I sip my beer and slowly digest her words rambling around in my head. I can't figure out if she's trying to seem older and wiser than she is or if she's trying to actively cut me down. Either way, I don't want to give her the satisfaction of being right so I dig deep from some narrative from my half-remembered life that isn't so douchey or self-involved sounding.

"I just . . . needed a change."

"A change from what? Like, I don't think you're getting it. This is what it's like to be poor. This is what it's like to live in squalor. Something you never would have chosen to do if it didn't cost a lot of money."

I can tell she feels self-satisfied right now and I have the realization I don't like Fee very much. I'm pretty sure I had that same thought about buying poverty before signing up. My sights are now firmly on Nikola and I will spend the rest of the time trying to distance myself from Fee.

"It wasn't just about me," I say. "It was about my wife and kid too."

"Your kid whose name you can't even remember?"

I wave her off and say, "That'll come back. My wife—"

"Whose name you also can't remember."

"Okay, whatever. My wife *needed* this. She's a terrible mother. She needed a couple weeks to herself. Some time to get her head straight so she can remember that raising our child should be her top priority. I finally made the decision when I came home shortly after the kid went to bed. They left their iPad downstairs and I turned it on just to see what they'd been doing on it . . ." I take a slow sip of beer, letting the last thing just kind of hang there.

"And?"

"Beheading videos. A whole playlist of them. How could

they sit around and watch this shit with their mother in the room? I had to go review security footage and do you know what I saw?"

"Got me." She doesn't even look interested.

"They were both watching them. My wife and kid, huddled over the iPad, *laughing* at beheading videos."

"That does sound tragic." She's practically mocking me.

I take a quick sip of beer and say, "Well I'm sorry if my troubles don't rank high enough on your misery index. It must be rough being a twentysomething who has enough money and free time to come to something like this."

"I just think your story was a lot of bullshit."

It is. I was the one watching beheading videos during a blackout. I watched myself laughing at them on the security footage the next day, but I'm not going to let her know that. "Okay, so why are *you* here?"

Now she turns in her stool to look directly at me. Something in her gaze finds that part inside of me that's always flailing and presses it up against the wall.

"Same reason as you," she says.

She has beautiful eyes. "And what's that?"

"To find enlightenment."

"That's what you want?"

"Sure."

"But what do you think it is?"

"I don't know . . . To be free from mental and external demands. Something like that, I guess."

Her answer is so vapid and half-hearted I think she's just fucking with me.

"What do you think it means?" she says.

She's provided me with a golden moment to shine and I search myself for some kind of pithy wisdom that can be condensed into a digestible, aphoristic phrase, but I have nothing. Maybe it's the beer. Maybe it's some lingering, brain-eating effect of the pretreat. It feels hard to think. I have to say something.

"To me, I think it means the freedom to not want anything. But I don't know if that's enlightenment or depression."

"Maybe . . ." Now she's staring into the depths of her mostly full beer. "Maybe it means only wanting what you *need* . . . and maybe things like this exist to help you figure out what you need."

"I can tell you what I don't need," I say, trying to lighten the mood, trying to get us off this uncomfortable subject. "Another wet lettuce sandwich."

This doesn't elicit the laugh I was going for but she at least smiles and says, "I don't think anyone needs any more of those."

Then we lapse into a surprisingly comfortable silence. I appreciate the carbonated bitterness of the beer on my tongue, enjoy the slow release of serotonin it's coaxing from my brain.

I polish off the second beer and go for a third. I look at Fee's glass, intending to offer to fill her up, but her beer is still virtually untouched. It must be warm by now and I think about asking if she wants a fresh one but I'm enjoying the silence. I take my beer back to the stool and sit down. Normally, a few beers in, I'm thinking about what I'm going to do the next day. Or I think about what happened that day. I think of the climb, the struggle, the hustle, how I can get *more* of what I already have. But, right now, my mind just feels blank and part of me thinks this could go on forever and I wouldn't mind. Could this be the beginning of enlightenment? Would being enlightened mean feeling like this all the time, even without the beer, even if I wasn't on a spiritual retreat? Would it be possible to just stay here forever?

After a while, I say, "The silence is . . . kind of nice." It's barely a whisper but it seems booming.

"Huh," Fee says. "I was just thinking this feels like the saddest bar in the world."

I immediately remember I don't like her.

"Who's making it sad?" I say.

"I think I'm ready to get out of here."

I still kind of want to stay here forever but, I don't know, maybe I think I still have a shot with her so I polish off my beer and get up from the stool on wobbly legs.

"Give me a second," she says. "I have to pee."

"I'll wait," I say.

Her eyes flutter and she says, "Okay, I'm ready."

I hear the trickle of her urine run from the stool and onto the floor. The crotch of her pants is dark.

"That's one way, I guess."

"A little more piss isn't going to hurt."

And, like that, I feel attracted to her again.

"Back to the retreat?" I say.

"Let's walk around for a bit."

"Okay." She's not ready for the night to end.

I follow her out of the taproom and into the steamy night. There's a far-off rumble of thunder and a deep purple flash of lightning in the distance. The air smells like rain.

"We might get wet," I say.

"I'm okay with that," she says.

Maybe the rain will tamp down her odor a bit. I still haven't gotten used to it. I follow her off the deck and onto what appears to be a bike path. Tall trees eclipse the dark, milky looking sky. As we walk along, I realize I have no idea how to have a conversation with anyone and am not sure I ever did. In college, hanging out with my friends, we just regurgitated what we learned from our professors, bits from our favorite shows and comedians, or interviews with musicians who were probably about the same age as us. Beyond that, it was mostly just gossip, although we would have probably thought it sounded too feminine to call it that.

"Who do you think's the most enlightened person at the retreat?" I say.

"Are you . . . serious?" she says.

"I guess, yeah. Why wouldn't I be?"

"I don't know. I guess I've just never really seen it as a competition before."

"Everything's a competition."

"That's . . ."

"Darwinian. Science."

"I'm not sure."

"Obviously I mean besides Blastneesh. He's supposed to be the most enlightened. That's why we're paying him, right?"

"To teach something doesn't make you the best at it."

"It's not Tall Rex. I'm sure of that. That guy has problems."

"I think he's a sadist. Definitely not a seeker."

"So who do you think it is? Gus? He really seems like a free spirit. Likeable. Probably doesn't have a care in the world. Thomas is kind of a mystery and he seems really serious and focused. I could see him becoming the most enlightened. Although, after tonight, I'd have to throw Nikola into the running too . . ." It feels weird not to think of her as the dark-haired woman anymore. With the lubrication of the beer and thinking about Nikola dancing around the fire, I find myself aroused.

"Are you mad that I didn't even put you in the top three?" I ask.

"Are you trying to make me mad?"

"I don't know. It wouldn't be very enlightened of you to

get mad at me for being honest."

"I'm not mad," she says. "I'm still not going to fuck you."

"I never said I wanted that to happen."

"But you would, right? If I asked you to?"

"Sure," I say. "I need to do something to get over my disastrous marriage. And, quite honestly, you need something to get over your boyfriend too."

"Still not happening."

"Why not? Is it because I'm not enlightened enough?"

"No. It's just that . . . if you were a book or a movie, you'd be completely irrelevant."

"What's that mean?"

"Your . . . act . . . or personality or whatever it is . . . it feels tired. Like I could find ten carbon copies of you in any large crowd. I think that's why you're ultimately here. To pay a price and make yourself sound more interesting to your rich professional friends. In the long run, you'll go back to being exactly who you were before, you'll just be spending money on different things."

"Maybe I liked who I was before. Maybe I'm doing all this to get back to who I was before."

"Do you want to change your brain or do you want to change your life?"

I have to think about this. There's a louder, closer rumble of thunder and the first whisper of rain in the trees.

"Hm. Well, I guess I'd have to say I want to change myself since I don't really remember much about what my life was like."

"And how does that feel?"

"I haven't really thought about it but . . . pretty good, I guess. Like getting rid of a bunch of stuff I don't need."

"Brainwashing doesn't have to be a bad thing."

I think about the term "brainwashing" in its most literal

sense.

"To be brainwashed by advertising and the media," Fee says, "is to have your head filled with voices you don't need in there. Voices and images and promises that encourage you to go out and spend spend spend. Like the perfect life can be purchased. And maybe it can be, if you believe those voices. Blastneesh is truly washing your brain. Making it cleaner."

"I guess you have a point."

"There's too much coming at us for a lot of people to handle. That's Carol's problem. I don't think she's really schizophrenic. I think she's taking in everything she hears and reads and sees and that bizarre life story she's constructed is how she makes sense of things."

"She told me women don't grow nipples until they have a kid."

"And I'm sure she heard that somewhere. She probably didn't just make it up."

"Why hasn't she forgotten her past?"

"Because it's not real. Starting to make sense now?"

"Hm."

"You can't remember your wife or kid's names, but you could probably tell me what kind of car you drive. You could probably even tell me your phone number and those are, really, like some of the least important things in life."

Now the rain is dripping from the trees and we're starting to get wet.

"Wait a minute," I say, "are you trying to get in the top three?"

She lets out an exasperated sigh and says, "Talking to you is really difficult."

"Yeah, I'm pretty sure I've heard that before."

For what feels like the next several minutes, she doesn't say anything at all. We reach a bit of a clearing in the trees and get soaked fairly rapidly. The thunderstorm seems to have dissipated but there is still plenty of rain. I glance over at Fee to see the way the rain has glued her shirt to her small breasts and nipples. I think about touching them, sucking them into my mouth. Then I think about the warm release of milk and I'm oddly thinking about being back in the cabin again and I feel very confused with everything. I don't know what I'm doing here. I don't know why I'm wasting my time with Fee. I don't know why I can't think of anything to say to her that sounds wiser than what she has said to me. I don't think Blastneesh has all the answers and I feel like a dupe for paying so much money to be here. I want to lash out in some way but feel like I've run out of options.

"So you must be looking pretty forward to your one-on-one consultation, huh?" I say and it sounds a bit more aggressive than I intend it to.

"Sure, I guess," she says.

"I mean," I say, "I'm guessing that's what you're saving yourself for."

"What are you talking about?"

"For Blastneesh to fuck you. I know how these things work. The leaders tell their followers they can't have sex amongst themselves so they get all the men or women they want."

"So . . . wait . . . that's what you think happens at special counsel?"

"Pretty sure."

"Well . . . that's not how I plan on spending mine."

"But if he wanted to fuck you, you'd let him, right?"

She doesn't even have to think about it. "Well, sure. It would probably feel like going to the moon."

I don't know why her saying that makes me so mad but I can't spend another second around her. I just want to get back to the cabin, get bloated on Carol's breast milk, and fall asleep to Jorry's antics.

"I can't take this anymore," I say. "For your information, fucking me would be like going to *Saturn*, at least."

Then I storm off. I feel like maybe there's still a glimmer of hope with Fee but it just feels too emasculating to keep talking to her.

I'm pretty sure I hear her laughing at me. She does not follow me back to the cabin.

twenty-eight

I ogle Nikola as she digs. I'm not sure why I wasted so much time with Fee when Nikola was really the one deserving of my attention from the beginning. More age appropriate. Probably bathes with regularity.

The sky is gray. The air is heavy and damp. The Power Hole is a giant mud pit from last night's rains. Nikola's shirt is already plastered to her skin. The lithe muscles in her arms flex as she heaves shovel after shovel of mud. She clearly has so much more elegance and poise and maturity than Fee could ever be capable of. Plus, despite her consultation with Blastneesh yesterday and her ecstatic dancing around the bonfire, I don't see any possibility of her ever becoming more enlightened than me. She has an artsy vibe to her and it makes me think she would be far too self-involved with her mental state and individual pursuits to be a fully enlightened being. Like being "happy" or "blissed out" would run so counter to her dark, introverted vibe she could never accept it.

I pause from my shoveling to take a deep breath and appreciate those words: fully enlightened being. I'm on my way.

I woke up feeling great this morning, eager to dig and not as angry as I'd felt the previous mornings. I'd only had a couple beers last night, so I knew it wasn't the cause of resignation that can seem like calm acceptance from drinking too much the night before.

I was one of the first ones at the Power Hole. Of course Tall Rex was already there. Nikola was the third or fourth person to show up. I made it a point to position myself as close to her as possible so Fee would hopefully get jealous when she showed up. This had nothing to do with trying to make me more attractive to Fee. It had more to do with trying to rattle her, toss her from the road of enlightenment that seems to come too easily for people like her. Nikola tried moving farther away from me a couple of times. I had to wait until nearly everyone was there to surreptitiously assume this position behind her. Fee was usually not the last person to show up so when everyone besides her and Thomas were there, I found myself furious. Today must be her special counsel day. Why wouldn't she have told me that? And if it *was* her consultation day, where was Thomas? Had something happened to him?

The Example Circle was plainly visible from the Power Hole and, for the first time since arriving, it was empty. That was somewhat surprising. Someone had to have known that Fee and I had sneaked out last night. If that wasn't deserving of being thrown in the Example Circle, I wasn't sure what was. At least we wouldn't have to share the space for the entire day. That would have been unbearable. I wasn't sure if the rain and the dampness would tamp down her stench or just add some other, weirder layer on top of it.

We're probably about an hour into the dig when a woman's scream rips through the otherwise tranquil morning. We all stop digging to look in the direction the scream came from. Cassie appears at the perimeter of the Power Hole looking frantic. I hadn't even noticed she was missing. She and Thomas were definitely front runners in the "most boring" category, although I think Hildy has to be the leader there.

"I need help!" she yells. "Dear god, somebody please come quick."

We all just kind of stand there leaning on our shovels until Tall Rex approaches her and says something. I can't hear the exchange. Cassie begins walking away from the Power Hole and Tall Rex follows her. The seriousness of Tall Rex abandoning his post at the Power Hole resonates through the gathering of seekers and we all shamble out of the hole in pursuit.

The first thing I notice when I get to the cabin and elbow a couple seekers out of the way is the blood. A lot of it.

"I just woke up and she was . . . like this."

I lean my head into the cabin to see what Cassie and Tall Rex are looking at.

It's Fee.

Or what used to be Fee.

Or parts of Fee . . . dismantled and lying on the bed.

I immediately feel like I'm going to be sick but, having never really seen anything quite like this, I can't look away.

Tall Rex calmly nods his head and says, "Get back to the Power Hole. We'll take care of it."

I want to interject and ask Tall Rex what he means about *getting back* to the Power Hole, since Cassie hadn't been there, but think now might not be the best time to bring it up. Maybe if I can get a personal consultation, I'll mention it. Cassie oversleeps. Therefore, she cannot possibly be considered a serious candidate for enlightenment.

"Take care of it?" Cassie looks appalled.

"That's what I said," Tall Rex says.

"You *need* to call the *police*," Cassie says.

"You know we can't do that."

"Then I'll find a phone and do it myself."

Tall Rex looks up from the gore-soaked bed and notices they have an audience. He brandishes his discipline stick at us and says, "Get back to the Power Hole. All of you." Calmly. Not yelling.

As aggressively as I elbowed my way to the front of the group of spectators, I now make sure I lead the charge back to the Power Hole and hope Tall Rex makes note of my ultra-enlightened discipline and relays it back to Blastneesh.

Later, Cassie takes her place in the Example Circle and Tall Rex brings Fee's remains over to it in a wheelbarrow and dumps them in the circle.

"Extreme grieving," I think, and continue digging with the slightest of smiles on my face.

Today, for whatever reason, it's a lot easier to dig effortlessly while losing myself in my meditative thoughts. Some wise person, at some time, said to "know thyself." This has to be one of the main tenets of enlightenment and I find it very easy to think about myself, especially as my memories continue to drop away at an even faster pace. I can barely remember my first day here. I know I had a wife. I think she came here with me. But not only can I no longer remember her name, I can barely remember her face. I'm sure she's beautiful.

Speaking of beauty, I feel like a beautiful man. A bit worn and dirty, sure, but in the days or weeks I've been here digging, my beer paunch has melted away. I can no longer feel the flab under my arms swinging as I heave the shovel. My jawline has undoubtedly tightened. I'd been contemplating regrowing my beard—a look tailor-made for the discerning craft beer and whiskey enthusiast—but now I don't think that will be necessary. I probably won't even need to think about bringing back the razor beard. I can feel my pecs bulging like two tight little balls with each plunge of the shovel into the mud. This healthy self-assessment, I'm sure, means I'm making good progress on my path to enlightenment.

Another thing I've always heard is that it's important to remain in the present. I don't think I'm quite at the level of feeling re-born with each new breath but, again possibly due to the lack of memories and lack of research of any kind that would prepare me for what is going to happen during my remaining time at the retreat, I find this relatively easy to do.

Presently, I am thinking about my pursuit of Nikola. I know nothing about her and, if she's going through the same things as me, this is okay because she probably knows virtually nothing about herself. In order to woo Nikola I'll need to either catch the attention of one of the other women at the retreat or establish myself as the dominant male. There's always the possibility she could be a lesbian so let's just go ahead and say I'll need to establish myself as the dominant person. It occurs to me I could really play up the Carol and Jorry angle, let it be known I partake of Carol's breast milk every evening and have become something of a big brother figure to Jorry, but part of me thinks that might just come off as sad and weird.

Depressingly, were I to try and make her jealous, the only two remaining women I could bestow my attention on would be either Gemini or Cassie. Then it begins to once again hit home how absolutely pathetic this retreat is, that Cassie and Gemini are two of the three most fuckable women here. Gemini—cute and bubbly and fun-loving, for sure—but also a good thirty to forty pounds overweight and that's only by the absolute loosest of American standards. Cassie—blocky and stoic, the very definition of a wallflower. Inexplicably, Big Labia pops into my head as a potential candidate and I have to wonder why. I don't think women think of their labial size as anything equivalent to the way men think of their penis size. Women want big breasts, plump asses, and tight pussies. Most of them do, I'm pretty sure. Maybe it's the flair of having an oversized labium. Like the guy who's shaped weird but has the uncanny ability to use this to make people laugh. But that wears off. No one is envious of a carnival act.

I'm so lost in my own thoughts I don't realize how much time has passed until Tall Rex raises his discipline stick above his head and barks, "To the Example Circle!"

My first thought—so cynical—is "More of this shit" but that's immediately replaced with something purer and more rational. What is it going to be today? The occupants of the Example Circle—Fee's remains and Cassie—offer limitless possibilities. Are we going to shit on Cassie? Is she going to have to strip and masturbate with Fee's still flesh-covered bones? As I scrabble up the narrow ledge to the perimeter of the Power Hole—rushing to get to the top so I can turn and offer Nikola a hand (which she refuses)—my head is swimming with the possibilities.

I fall behind Nikola on the way to the Power Hole, though not too far behind. If I were pantsless and erect, the tip of my penis would be grazing her lower back. As we approach the Example Circle, I realize I'm muttering "I'm a nice guy" with absolutely nothing to qualify it. Just "I'm a nice guy. I'm a nice guy," over and over again like a fucking psychopath.

When I reach the Example Circle and draw close to Nikola's side, she breathes an exasperated sigh, rolls her eyes, and moves as far away from me as possible. I have no idea what's wrong with her. She seemed so open and free last night and that's when I realize, with a skipped heartbeat of horror, I might have missed my shot.

In the Example Circle, Cassie is the exact opposite example

than Fee was yesterday. Whereas Fee was blissed out and be-atific, Cassie looks panicked. Granted, things have not turned out well for the examples. With Fee now being a collection of dismembered bones and hunks of gory flesh, I'm technically the only example who is still alive. Maybe the only example I provided was that of a false sense of security. Cassie shuffles from foot to foot, her eyes bouncing from seeker to seeker. Tall Rex raises his discipline stick and I find myself almost giddy with his expected pronouncement. I don't think of myself as a habitually cruel person but, when being part of everyone else's sadistic excitement, I can kind of get into it.

Cassie makes a sound, almost like a bark, and bolts out of the Example Circle and into the woods.

"Want me to go after her?" Gus says.

"Yeah, let's get that bitch," Big Labia snarls.

Tall Rex, still brandishing the discipline stick, turns from the Example Circle to face the seekers and says, "No no. She is free to go. Let that be an example to you all." He lowers the discipline stick and drops his head in thought. I feel like he's in this position because he is psychically linked to Blastneesh. I feel as though I have Blastneesh's voice in my head at times and wonder if I have the ability to rise to such a position of power. The voice in my head has become so ubiquitous I've stopped noticing it. Again, I feel like this is yet another step to becoming fully enlightened. Tall Rex is looking at the pile of Fee and most of the seekers' eyes track his gaze to stare at the same thing.

"No one has to stay here. While we will not offer a refund if you choose to go, you are not here involuntarily." He points the discipline stick at the pile of Fee. "However, it should be noted that to leave the grounds without Blastneesh's blessing can have very dire consequences. Probably so riddled with guilt she fell apart."

I suddenly find myself more nervous than I probably should be. After all, I was with Fee last night. Was I not in the Example Circle because I came back first, showing initiative? Did Fee come back on her own, or was she caught, brutally dismantled, and returned to her bed? Did someone butcher her or did she . . . self-dismantle?

I'm snapped out of my thoughts by the discipline stick lashing across my chest. I belt out a bark of pain and experience just the slightest flash of anger.

"I know what you're thinking," Tall Rex says. "Don't think you've gotten away with anything. You are not in the Example Circle because you have Blastneesh's permission to leave whenever you want to. He has made it clear to me he doesn't want you here. If Seeker Fee had left with anyone else, she would not have met the same fate, I'm sure. However, because she chose to spend her time with you, she was set too far back on her path to enlightenment that . . . well, it's easy enough to see what happened to her. You, Seeker Scott, will never achieve enlightenment and are therefore no longer worthy of being made an example of. Actually, I shouldn't even refer to you as a seeker. So let us now turn our attention to Seeker Fee. One of the most faithful servants until her most recent life-ending decisions. She let the doubt and the weakness in and it destroyed her. It quite literally ripped her apart . . . And now there's no coming back. So I would like each of you to get on your knees and tell Seeker Fee what she meant to you. Do not let her self-destruction be in vain. Yesterday, she sat coated in your urine. Today, she resides in the Example Circle in pieces, a shattered relic of her former self. Let her also rise from the urine to live in each of your hearts. Come forth, enter the Example Circle to grab a bone or organ. Let the life still contained in the tissue sustain you."

Thomas, that old freak, is the first to step into the Example

Circle. Of course he grabs her pelvis and pulls it close to his chest, the rest of us still standing outside the Example Circle, watching him.

"Come on now," Tall Rex says. "Everyone at the same time. We've got a lot of digging to do."

Now everyone else descends on the pile of Fee and I have my hand on one of her breasts until it's snatched out of my hand by Gus, who immediately drops to his knees and says, "Fee, I'm pretty sure you were a good friend but I have absolutely no recollection of that. Because of this, I do not even have the ability to feel sad. I'm sure you were really great though." He pulls the breast close to his bearded face and kisses it. Then, I'm pretty sure he says, "Being brainwashed is awesome."

I end up with her head because it's been kind of kicked to the side and no one seems to have any interest in it. Granted, it is pretty disturbing. Holding it in both hands, I pull it up to my own face and stop just short of kissing it. There's something about the eyes, fully open and clouded over, that creeps me out too much. I immediately think about taking it back to the cabin and fucking it in the mouth before realizing how hard up I must be. Also, regrettably, this isn't the kind of retreat where I could do that in front of everybody. What a bunch of repressed prudes. I really should have done my research.

Everyone else is talking to their respective body parts and I'm only half-listening to them so I can find some cue as to what to say because I can't think of anything.

Maybe it's the eyes. I turn the head away from me so I'm staring at the back of it. It makes it a little better but now she doesn't even feel like a person. Looking at only so much hair, it feels artificial, like a Halloween prop or something.

Big Labia is standing to my right. She says, "It's okay to

grieve in silence."

Her saying that relieves me of the burden of saying any-thing. I still need my grief to be performative in some way so my fellow seekers don't think I'm an emotionless ghoul. I pull Fee's head closer to mine and gently lean my forehead against it until I'm sure at least a few other seekers have seen me. Then I let it drop into the mud and cross the Example Circle to where Nikola stands holding one of Fee's feet. I put my arm around her shoulders and say, "It's okay to grieve in silence," hoping she didn't hear Big Labia say the same thing to me only a couple of minutes ago. Surprisingly, she doesn't shake me off or attempt to move away.

"You're a horrible man," she says and I wonder if Tall Rex's denunciation of me has done something to heighten my appeal. Am I the retreat bad boy? Is this the type of person someone like Nikola desires?

"I know," I say. "I know . . . but I'm trying to change. That's why I'm here."

"That's not what your wife said."

"I know," I say. "But she was a cunt . . . and she's not my wife anymore. To be honest, I stopped finding her attractive. I suppose this was a last-ditch effort to save our marriage." I take a dramatic pause. "Now I know the real reason I came was so that I could meet you. I think you drove a wedge be-tween us."

"This is a really inappropriate time to be hitting on me," she says.

"The best things happen at the most inappropriate times." I think this sounds pretty wise.

"Why don't you just leave? Nobody wants you here."

"That's not true." And I realize this is my golden oppor-tunity to make her slightly jealous. To prove to her I'm not some loser who doesn't know how to have friends or maintain a relationship. "Carol and Jorry need me. That's why I'm sticking around."

Now she finally shakes my arm off and moves away and I'm left wondering if what I said had the desired effect or if it just really disgusted her. To make myself seem less like a liar, I go back to retrieve Fee's head and take it over to Jorry, who's holding what looks like a femur with some ropes of skin and bloody sinew hanging from it. His face is scrunched up in a horribly woeful expression and he's sobbing in chest-racking bursts, snot hanging out of his nose and coating his mouth and chin. I fight the urge to gag.

"How you holding up, big guy?" I say.

He looks at me in a confused way before throwing his head toward the leaden sky and howling and moaning his sadness.

"Here," I say, handing him the head. "Try this one. It'll make you feel better."

I'm doubting this is what he wants. I'm just trying to distract him so he stops with the caterwauling. To my surprise, his howls cease, he drops the femur and eagerly reaches for the head. Once he's holding the head in both hands, he's genuinely smiling and using his huge tongue to lap up the snot surrounding his mouth and I have to move away from him before I'm sick.

The clouds break up some time after noon, the heat rises, and the humidity is completely enervating. I'm digging within a few feet of Nikola. When we came back after our time in the Example Circle, she spent about an hour trying to move away from me but I think she got too exhausted and gave up. I'm trying to harness the powers of my mind dread alternately cast sensual thoughts toward Nikola while glancing over at Jorry, who is still holding onto Fee's decapitated head. Carol's mouth moves constantly as she digs and she has a small group of people around her—Gus, Hildy, and Big Labia. I can't hear what she's saying.

Thomas is still missing, presumably at special counsel, and Gemini is off by herself on the far end of the Power Hole, digging and smiling like an idiot.

"Why don't you like Gemini?" I ask Nikola.

"Why are you talking to me?"

"Because I like you. I think you're really special." I decide to use the word "special" so my interest is not immediately taken as sexual, even though I'm pretty sure she's well aware it is. If she knows I want to fuck her, she'll just keep stringing me along. We probably wouldn't be here long enough for her to relent out of sheer carnal need.

"I don't even know who you're talking about," she says.

"Gemini. The girl over there."

Nikola doesn't even stop her digging long enough to turn around and look.

"It's not that I don't like her. I guess we just haven't had the chance to hang out."

That seems like a pretty weak answer.

"I get it," I say. "You're not here to make friends. Me either. I'm here to become the most enlightened."

She rolls her eyes and continues digging without saying anything. I wonder why Gemini has been happy and blissed out since her special counsel session and, less than twenty-four hours after hers, Nikola already seems like the raging cunt she was before. Okay, maybe not a raging cunt. She seems to lack the energy necessary to rage. Just a cunt.

Women tell men they should not make continual advances if the woman isn't interested but, chances are, if a guy is doing this, it's because it's worked in the past. We know that, eventually, they'll become vulnerable. Nikola will reach a point where she craves focused attention. Sure, she may dance for us again tonight, and having those eyes on her will feel good, but she'll need more than that. Being the most conventionally attractive man here, I know it's only a matter of time until she relents.

"Would you like me to stop trying to talk to you? You seem really put out." This is my way of trying to get her to admit that she's a cunt. If she says yes, then not only does that leave no room for interpretation, it'll also make her think she's being too harsh and possibly even feel a glimmer of guilt.

"I'm just really in a groove," she says. "Really focused."

"I get it," I say. "You just want to be alone." I know she won't agree with me because no one actually wants to be alone. "I hope you enjoy the rest of your day."

I swing my shovel up to rest on my shoulder and walk across the Power Hole to where Gemini is digging. She moves fluidly, like a smooth machine. Of the remaining seekers, she seems to be the only one who is actually enjoying the digging. Maybe I can absorb some of her positive energy. Also, as I draw closer to her, I realize she's shed a few pounds over the last couple of days. I would probably now describe her as "thick" rather than chubby.

"Hey there," she says, welcoming. The dreads and tattoos aren't really my thing and I think this must be the reason I didn't notice how pretty she was before.

"Hey," I say.

"I'm Gemini," she says.

"Oh . . . I know. I'm Scott. We introduced ourselves a couple of days ago . . . I think."

"Yeah." She smiles more broadly and it lights up her face even further. "You're probably right. I can't remember anything."

"It's okay. I think that's pretty common around here. To be honest, I'm surprised I remember your name."

"We gotta strip the brain before we can re-wire it, right?"

"Sure," I say, but I'm eager to change the subject. She's going to want to engage me in some hippie-dippy philosophical discussion and I'm not ready to go there just yet. I briefly imagine her and Fee and Gus sitting around and having the most stoner discussions possible and it makes me a little queasy.

"Really, besides Tall Rex and Blastneesh, the only people's names I can remember are Jorry and Carol—besides yours, of course." And now I have to wonder if I did know her name or had forgotten it until she told me and then just reverse engineered it into my memories. Then it occurs to me we meet a few types of people our entire life. Those whose names we know before meeting them in the flesh and those people we talk to before ever knowing their names. There are some people whose names are the only thing we ever know about them and there are some people whose names we *never* know, regardless of how many times we come in contact with them.

I realize Gemini has said something to me but I was completely zoned out.

"Huh?"

"Carol and Jorry—are they the old lady and her son?"

"Oh . . . yeah. I'm kind of like a big brother to the kid and another son to Carol. They're really lonely."

"That's sweet. He kind of gives me the creeps."

"Ah, he's harmless."

"I'm kind of surprised you don't know Nikola's name."

"Who?"

"You know . . . over there. The woman you were just talking to. The one you haven't been able to take your eyes off of?"

I throw a shovelful of dirt over my shoulder and try to laugh it off. I didn't realize I'd been so obvious.

"Oh, her . . . No, I didn't know her name was . . . what did you say? Nicole?"

"Nikola."

"Ah. No. I thought I knew her from someplace closer to home but I think I was mistaken."

"And where do you call home?"

"I really don't know."

"Sorry about your divorce, man. That was pretty harsh, if you ask me."

"Oh, it's okay. We'd grown apart. This was a last-ditch kind of thing. I'm pretty sure she was wanting to sleep around, if I'm being honest."

"That sucks. Everything about it. Marriage sucks."

"I'm not planning on doing it again."

"Not gonna give it the old college try?"

"No. I'm a romantic. All or nothing. She was my college sweetheart. We had a kid together. There's no love like young love. I don't think I can rewind the clock to experience that again."

"Maybe you'll just have to take on a younger lover."

I pretend to mull it over even though the first thing I want to say is "Is that an invitation?" Instead, I say, "I don't know. It'll be a while before I try that again."

"Yeah," she says. "Get out there and have fun. You're not too old. You're a good-looking guy. You'll do fine."

"It just . . . feels like a lot of work."

"Tell me about it. Americans have a way of making sex feel like a marathon. A very expensive marathon. I mean, we should all just meet and fuck whoever we want. Over and over. It's a physical need. A basic human right. But we're taught that it's something we should be ashamed of. We're not taught to be ashamed to work ourselves to death just to buy the same shit everyone else has. That's embarrassing to me."

I spend the rest of the dig time near Gemini. She's the type of girl I've never really had a conversation with and find myself regretting not ever trying to get into that scene in college. I'd only ever been to one Phish concert and found myself aesthetically opposed to most of the other attendees and never went to another one. I don't remember what the music sounded like. Gemini has a refreshingly liberating way of looking at the world while also trying to navigate her staggering gaps in recent memories. Occasionally, I glance over at Nikola to see if she's looking in this direction. Gemini talks a lot and I find myself tuning out quite a bit but have to pretend to be more interested than I really am so Nikola recognizes the impending threat.

Then Gemini says, "So, what do you do?" and I'm immediately lost.

"I . . . have a job," I say. "Doing stuff." I'm pretty sure I work in an office but I can't remember what state it's in, let alone what it looks like or what I actually do.

"No . . . I mean, most people work. That's all boring stuff. What do you do for fun?"

Since I can barely remember anything, I reframe her question as: "What would I like to do for fun?" Still, I have to think hard.

"Last night I had some beers with Fee. That was pretty fun, I guess. Other than that . . ." I'm blanking. Even if I can't remember what I did for fun on a daily basis I have a pretty good idea of the person I was and what that type of person does. But I can't tell someone like Gemini about that. If I were being honest, I'd say I liked to win for fun, or that I just kind of like . . . feeling like a winner since birth and doing the things I think winners do. "Travel . . ." I stammer. "I like to travel quite a bit." I do not elaborate because this is yet another form of competition, wanting to be the most well-traveled amongst my family and friends. But it sounds better than saying that when I go out drinking with friends, I want to drink the most, I want to be holding the best cocaine/weed/whatever, I want to be the last one awake. Or that I had to have the biggest house in the best location. Or that I had to be the most ripped, most disciplined person at the gym. Or that, when playing competitive sports, I'd play until I was ahead. I'd take a loss sometimes but made sure to win the majority. Even in college, if I were taking an art or literary class, I'd scour the internet the night before to figure out the important talking points about whatever subject a person my age was supposed to be interested in and make sure to bring them up in class and pass it off as though I'd actually read, watched, or understood those things.

I come to a personal realization that's so wise I have to share it with Gemini even though I'm pretty sure she's talking when I say it, "I think I like to exhaust people for fun."

"That's . . . weird," she says. "Maybe the people you're around just don't have enough energy to handle you."

I naturally take this, and everything else she's been talking about, to mean she wants to sleep with me and decide I will wait until the most opportune time to make a move on her.

By the time Tall Rex bellows that it's time for dinner, I'm pretty convinced Gemini is a sure thing, yet Nikola still commands my attention. Also, I can't stop thinking about Carol, but that might just be because I'm hungry or that I'm pretty sure, over the course of the afternoon, Nikola had gradually moved closer and closer to Carol's burgeoning group of listeners.

I clamber out of the Power Hole and extend a hand to Gemini to help her up. I follow her to the dining hall and sit down next to her at the back of the table. The chatter is subdued until Blastneesh glides out to the stage and lifts his hands in that triangle gesture until everyone claps. Thomas wanders out from beside the stage, looking happier than I've seen him since we got here. The mood at the table shifts from quietly exhausted to energetically anticipatory.

I want what Blastneesh has. I want the ability to command a room, to have people hanging on my every word. I don't know why this hasn't happened for me yet. On the rare occasion I've had to speak in front of a group of people, it's met with chilly silence or complete indifference. Sometimes it's days before the people listening to me even make eye contact with me, if ever.

"Death . . ." Blastneesh says and, surprisingly, everyone around the table laughs like he's just made an awesome joke. "It's unavoidable. We must . . . forget. We must move on. But . . . it can set a tone . . . a mood . . . and so we must lighten the mood."

My eyes go to the cart of food Tall Rex wheels out and, for a second, my hopes are through the roof because it looks like the cart is heaped with a mountain of cocaine. Then Blastneesh keeps talking and my hopes are shattered.

"For dinner . . . the perfect thing . . . Sugar!" Blastneesh smiles and opens his arms and I guess we're supposed to get it ourselves because everyone is standing up and moving toward the head of the table where the cart of sugar sits.

The line is significantly smaller than it was only a few days ago and I'm at the back, behind Gemini. She's smiling, radiant, and I can tell she's excited about tonight's dinner. Realizing this might be the opportunity I've been waiting for, I put my hands on her hips, lean into her ear, and whisper, "We should try and go off alone later."

Her easy demeanor is immediately gone as she angrily pushes my hands off her hips and says, "Fuck off, creep."

I find myself dropping back a few feet and wondering what I did wrong. I tell myself I didn't do anything wrong, she's just crazy.

I become hyperaware of the other seekers, hoping they're not laughing at me.

"Good lord," Thomas says, "I hope this doesn't kill me. I'm diabetic."

"Me too," Big Labia says.

"Pre-diabetic here," Gus says. "Maybe this'll send me over the edge."

"At least it's vegan and fat free," Hildy says.

One by one, we load up our exceptionally large bowls with sugar and head back to the table. I imagine Gemini will find someplace else to sit after my unwanted advance but she returns to the same spot and I'm left shoveling spoonful after spoonful of sugar into my mouth under a heavy cloak of awkward silence.

Surprisingly, after scooping several spoonfuls into her mouth, it's Gemini who breaks the silence.

"Sugar makes me so horny," she says.

"It's . . . really sweet," I say.

I've avoided sugar as much as possible most of my adult life. I take a little spoonful and let it dissolve on my tongue. It's more of a sensation than a flavor.

"You'd think they could have at least done cotton candy or something fun," I say.

"You complain too much," Gemini says. "Sugar is sugar. I'm so wet right now."

I take another little spoonful. It already feels like it's making my teeth fuzzy. I'm probably going to wake up with cavities.

"You're . . . very confusing," I say.

"Hm. What are you confused about?"

I lower my voice so none of the other seekers can hear. I'm pretty sure they already think I'm a sexual predator anyway.

"Do you want to fuck or not?"

She takes another heaping spoonful of sugar and is acting like one of those girls who gets drunk after the first few sips of a drink. She's bouncing the spoon, shiny with her saliva, in her hand, loosely pointing it at me.

"I *always* want to fuck," she says. "Just not you, not here."

"We could get out of here."

She rolls her eyes. "You're not getting it. That's *why* I'm here."

After only a few small spoons of sugar, I'm already feeling the effects. With no fat or actual substance to balance it, it has an almost speed-like element to it. I can feel my thoughts fracturing and jumping around.

"Wait . . . why are you here?" I say to Gemini but it could have just as easily been something I asked myself.

"To deal with my problem."

"You have a . . . fucking problem?"

She laughs. Her eyes look insane and her cheeks are rosy red. In this moment, she looks beautiful.

"That's right, mister. I have a *fucking* problem."

"Fucking okay then."

"I'll fuck anything that *moves*," she says in a man's voice and I feel like she's referencing something I don't get.

A few of the other seekers turn their heads toward us. Nikola is one of them and I hope she heard Gemini, takes it completely out of context, and thinks I'm making progress.

"You came here because you fuck too much. I get it."

"So I made a deal with myself that I would not be doing any fucking while here."

"You must be going crazy," I say.

"Oh, I am," she says. "No masturbation either."

The sugar is not making me hyper. It's making me disoriented and confused.

"Yeah," I say. "I haven't jerked off either."

"But you've had sex? I'd like to hear about it."

I have the vague recollection of a sloppy blowjob administered by Carol but it's not something I want to think about and would never admit to. Instead, I glance at Nikola, who thankfully is not looking at us, and say, "Well . . . I have needs."

Gemini shovels in another spoonful and leans excitedly forward. "Oh shit, you fucked Nikola?"

I quickly motion for her to keep her voice down. She covers her mouth with both hands in mock embarrassment and then raises one and says, "High five!"

I give her the high five. It feels good. Now at least one person will think I've slept with Nikola even though it isn't true. I'm pretty sure Gemini is jealous of Nikola, so hopefully it never comes up in conversation.

"But wait . . . I thought you fucked Blastneesh. I'd like to hear what that was like."

She shakes her head and says, "No no no. He taught me a very special trick to make it easier for me."

"What was it?"

She smiles a broad, genuine smile and it's too easy for me to imagine being in her, having her under me, trying to make that expression grow into something even more ecstatic.

She reaches out with her spoon and taps the end of my nose with it. "It's a *secret* trick. Something he only taught to me."

Now it's my turn to roll my eyes and say, "You totally fucked him."

It's hard to tell if people are finishing up with their "dinner" or if everyone is doing what Gemini and I are doing— casually and absently absorbing spoonfuls of the stuff. I guess that's what sugar is there for. It's always there, waiting for you to get bored, quenching that quick craving to stick something into your mouth but never satisfying any actual hunger. In fact, I think I'm hungrier now than before I began.

Our attention goes to the stage when Blastneesh clears his throat.

"There are . . . eight of you left . . . Who will become the most enlightened?" Then he flashes that goofy smile and I count the remaining seekers seated around the table. He's definitely counting Carol and Jorry as one . . . unless he's not counting me. I take another hit of sugar and feel my fury rise. I thought I'd been doing so well at keeping it tamped down.

"I kid," Blastneesh says. "Enlightenment . . . is not a competition. I do not . . . pretend to be . . . any more *enlightened* . . . than the rest of you . . . Except . . . maybe . . . Seeker Scott."

The rest of the seekers laugh quietly and turn their reddened faces toward me. I try to self-deprecatingly lower my head and raise my hand as if to say "Guilty as charged" but my fury is now off the charts and I'm sure it's apparent to the rest of the seekers, especially Gemini, who is closest to me. And while my head is lowered, I just keep thinking, "This is not the retreat I wanted."

"You've heard it said before but . . . enlightenment . . . is a journey. Once you realize this . . . you are already on the way. When . . . every moment could be the . . . moment . . . that changes everything . . . you begin to appreciate every . . . second . . . of every day. You do . . . only what you want . . . only when you want. But know this . . . as you become . . . more enlightened . . . you will begin . . . to find the same . . . sense of purpose . . . in everything you do."

Does anyone else think he's speaking impossibly slowly tonight? I feel like I'm high on crack, which I've only done a couple of times. I want to get up and run around. I either want to fuck someone or punch someone. White trash pretty much lives off this stuff. Is that why they have so many kids and seem angry all the time?

"That is the . . . goal of life, if you will. To enjoy . . . to be aware . . . to be *awake* . . . every second of every day . . . . . ."

Now he takes an exceptionally long pause and I think to myself, "Whoa! Double ellipsis!"

"If you've ever . . . stared into the eyes of a dying person . . . you will recognize . . . that look . . . What is it? Fear . . .? Regret . . .? Resignation . . .? A sense of duty . . .? It's . . . the same look you get when you ask people . . . what they do for a living."

More gentle laughter. Gus says, "Ugh," and places his head on the table. He's shaky and I can tell even from where I am that he's drenched in sweat. Hildy, sitting next to him, places her hand on his back and leans down to whisper something into his ear, probably just checking to see if he's okay. Blastneesh makes no acknowledgment of the commotion.

"Very few people . . . do what they want to do. They do . . . the easiest . . . or the highest paid . . . *job*. It's always a job. To be . . . paid for doing anything . . . makes it a job."

I'm trying hard to pay attention but I'm too distracted by my racing heart and my fellow seekers. I'm starting to wonder if something had been added to the sugar. I feel really weird. Then again, I've never attempted to eat an entire bowl of sugar before—not even when I was a kid. It seems like no one is paying attention. Gemini continues to slowly eat spoon after spoon of sugar. Each time she pulls the spoon slowly from her mouth elicits the warmest, most blissed-out expression. I'm pretty sure she's thinking about sex and I'm thinking about how happy the first person she fucks after leaving here is going to be.

"I guess . . . for most . . . a job is a necessary thing."

I wonder if Blastneesh knows no one is paying attention and is being intentionally boring. Nikola has pushed her bowl away from her and is picking at her hands. Big Labia is staring at the ceiling with her thick hands folded over her chest.

"There are . . . all kinds of jobs . . . Important jobs . . . not important jobs. What I do . . . is not a job."

Jorry is practically vibrating, rubbing his hands together and muttering something that sounds like "Can we go?" while Carol spoons more sugar into his mouth. I find myself looking forward to getting back to the cabin, of partaking in Carol's breast, and I wonder if that's because I was never breastfed as a child.

"While I am . . . compensated for speaking with you . . . I would never do this . . . if it were a job . . ."

And now he's talking about his daily routine: what time he gets out of bed, what he has for breakfast, how he plans out his day. The seekers are fading hard. Big Labia stands up from the table and again stares at the high ceiling. Thomas, who has finally stopped grinning, also stands up from the table and drifts to the stage where he drops to his knees and bows to Blastneesh like he's at a Pentecostal altar or something.

Why should I be the one to sit quietly and listen to Blastneesh talk about how he picks his footwear for the day? I stand too.

Gemini sucks the last bit of sugar from her spoon and says, "Go get em," and growls softly and now I know I can't sit back down.

I walk toward the stage.

Blastneesh continues talking, not even looking at me. I wonder how hard it is for him to remember everyone's names and I tell myself to stop being so negative. I've paid good money to be here and Blastneesh is helping me on my path to enlightenment. I have a brief glimpse of the life I led before coming here and imagine returning to the exact same life without all the anger and hostility and anxiety. Being here has, at least momentarily, made me realize how good I probably had it before. Maybe that's the true intent of the retreat.

Now Blastneesh is saying, "Words are like magic incantations. The meaning is meaningless."

I'm standing at the base of the stage realizing this is the closest I've been to Blastneesh . . . I think. Except I have the vague memory of him being in my house, the architecture and location of which I cannot recall. Thomas is bent over on the floor beside me and I wonder if he hasn't slid off into a diabetic coma.

"What matters is . . . what manifests when you put all the words together . . . when you slowly absorb—"

"When do I get my special counsel?" I shout.

Now Tall Rex is paying attention to me, coming at me with the discipline stick.

"Oh, Jesus Christ, sit down," Nikola says.

Blastneesh is still talking even though no one is paying attention. Tall Rex raises the discipline stick but I'm not backing down.

Now I have a more immediate concern. I turn to Nikola and say, "Why do you hate me so much?"

Then the discipline stick crashes across my back and I tell myself I'm going to hit Tall Rex with my shovel the next time I get the chance.

I don't know if the discipline stick knocks something loose in my brain or if our sugar dinner really was spiked with something but I'm feeling completely out of my head and loving it. The jarring pauses are gone from Blastneesh's voice and it's as though he's speaking directly into my head. I lie on my back and turn my head to see Thomas, who I'm sure is dead.

Someone, I think it's Nikola, screams.

"Ultimately, not to dwell on it, but I know when I make all these decisions throughout the day that I am going to die. And this leads me to wonder if it is not all these decisions that will lead me into death. The only thing you can really do to combat this is to make no decisions. That is how I started on my spiritual path. Of course, even the decision to make no decisions is a decision. But it is a bigger decision. I was told to go to a cave for thirty days. The amount of time did not matter because after the seventh day—no food, no water, very little sleep—everything I'd known about my previous life died. I no longer kept track of time. It became as meaningless as everything else. By the time my master came to retrieve me from the cave, I was a different person. By doing nothing for a month, I became aware of what I was able to do."

Listening to Blastneesh, I once again feel like a seeker. I'm not sure if he is unenlightened or if he just lacks imagination. Then he says something that completely changes my mind.

"All this death is not without purpose. It is not even death. It is ascension. Being here has made a few people realize they are ready to ascend to the new plane. Unlike seekers Corinne and Brent, they have decided to move upward rather than sideways. They take their electricity with them but leave behind a certain life force that will help aid you in your enlightenment. But this . . ."

And as his voice returns to normal, I'm starting to gain more of a sense of being in my right mind.

". . . is not like other retreats . . ."

I groggily stand up. Thomas has now fallen forward, his face on the floor, his butt up in the air. His bowels have let go and stained his pants. I return to the table where the remaining seekers are once again gathered as though nothing out of the ordinary has occurred.

"For there can only be one who leaves here enlightened . . . Why so competitive, you ask? And to that . . . I say . . . why not? Enjoy the rest of your evening. Tomorrow . . . things will be different."

I feel bleary and exhausted as I make my way back to the cabin.

"I'm going to win the whole thing," I mutter to myself. I wish I had memories of all my past resentments to compel me forward.

When I get back to the cabin, Carol and Jorry are already there. I didn't even see them leave. Jorry has removed the flesh from Fee's skull and is wearing it like a mask. He's dancing around at the foot of Carol's bed and laughing excitedly. I don't think I've ever seen him this happy, although the skin mask gives him a kind of deranged quality. I remember what Fee had said about her pussy last night at the bar and I think about going out to the Example Circle to look for it. I think my brief conversation with Gemini earlier has thrown me into an even bigger sexual frenzy than usual.

Carol is already talking.

"I did not choose to move to Florence, Kentucky. I met a man in a church in Lawrenceville, Indiana, who drove a very old bus for the church. I told him I am here to do the Lord's work and he could take me where I could best serve."

She rolls up the bottom of her t-shirt and I eagerly place my head on her lap and suckle. Jorry, still excited, comes over to do the same. He's able to take the teat while wearing the mask and I find myself grateful for this. As disturbing as it is, it's more pleasing to look at than his actual face. The warm breast milk immediately calms me. The sexual frenzy dissipates.

"He drove me straight to the house in Florence, Kentucky,

and that's when I realized it was where I'd always lived. He said there was no one living in it and it was mine for as long as I wanted. I immediately knew I belonged there. Even when people were breaking in at night to perform experiments on me, I wasn't going to forsake my calling. Then they implanted Jorry inside me and I knew I'd be there for good. The number of satanic people in the neighborhood increased. I ate my oatmeal every morning and watched them. I ate all that oatmeal every morning and I never once remembered buying any of it. I never remember buying any food. I ate what was in the cupboards and the cupboards were always full. At first I thought this had something to do with Clark, the holy church bus driver. Then I realized it wasn't Clark at all. It was the satanic night people. It was part of their experiments. The food. The evil is in the food. That's how they put it in us. They've found out how to liquefy computer chips. They're in all the health food, all the food, even the organic stuff. This is the food eaten by the animals we eat, so it's just more liquefied computer chips in their muscle tissue. Then it gets inside us and hardens. They're trying to turn us into robots from the inside out. That's why everyone carries phones now. It's connecting them to the towers. But the towers are just the tip of the iceberg. They go all the way to the center of the earth. All the way to the pits of hell. And when they're finished running the scripts on our phones, that's when they'll activate the signal and all of our free will will dissolve along with the brains we were born with. Our doctors will all be online because they'll be avatars just like us. A million scripts all running at different times to give the illusion that humanity is continuing as it was before. Not even brainwashing. Total brain replacement. And we'll be paying for every bit of it. That's why I don't eat anything anymore. That's why my breast milk is so fresh and delicious. I live off air that's filtered through the device in my throat. My breast milk is the purest thing in the world."

She's gently stroking my hair as she talks to me and this tiny bit of kindness offsets all the crazy gibberish spewing from her mouth and when I've drained her of milk completely, I make my way to my own bed and collapse, feeling calm and relaxed, like tomorrow is going to be a new day. Jorry is bouncing from foot to foot beside my bed like a goddamn nightmare and Carol says, "He wants to know if he can sleep in your bed tonight."

I'm too tired to care. I shove myself against the wall and say, "Come on, buddy," and he leaps into the bed with me and stares up at the ceiling.

From across the room, Carol says, "Like one big, happy family."

part three
THE PREPARATION

twenty-nine

I follow Tall Rex past the Power Hole en route to the dining hall and main building. I'm not entirely surprised to see Thomas still slumped in front of the stage. I haven't been in this building when it was empty. It feels like it's poised for something. Last night was kind of wild. It seems like each night is getting a little wilder and maybe that's why I haven't left yet.

Tall Rex knocks on the door I've seen all the other blissed-out people exit through before dinner. Today is the day. Tall Rex woke me up by slapping my knees with the discipline stick and telling me it was my special counsel day. I couldn't get out of bed fast enough. Jorry, still sleeping soundly, made this somewhat of a challenge.

"Yes?" I hear from the other side of the door.

"Master, I've brought the 'seeker.'" He doesn't even need to use air quotes. I can hear them.

"Send him in."

Tall Rex turns the knob and lets the door swing inward before motioning me to go on ahead. Blastneesh is leaning against his desk wearing Adidas track pants, no shoes, and a t-shirt that says "Saratoga Springs '98." He looks like any other reasonably fit, late middle-age man.

Tall Rex appears in the doorway and says, "Do you need me to stick around?"

"We'll be okay," Blastneesh says in a voice not as affected as the one he uses to address all of us before dinner.

"Are you sure?" Tall Rex says.

"Close the door," Blastneesh says with maybe just a hint of force.

The door clicks shut and I immediately panic. I am not afraid of Blastneesh, but he makes me nervous because he has what I want. I just don't know if that's spiritual knowledge, prowess, and wisdom or just the ability to ruthlessly manipulate people into giving you all of their money, respect, and time. I guess if I could have both, that would be great, even if I don't really need the money. The money, I figure, is kind of like a contract of faith. Proof that someone wants what you have the ability to give them.

Not knowing what else to do, but having a pretty good idea of what goes on in here, I shuck my pants down and get on all fours.

I close my eyes and say, "I've never done anything like this with a guy, so please be gentle."

He walks around behind me and I turn my head to look at him over my shoulder. Do I even want to know how big it is? Would it be better if I didn't know?

He doesn't tug down his pants to reveal his magical penis. Instead, he kicks me in the ass with his bare foot.

"Stand and pull up your pants. Have some dignity."

I do what he says, now completely thrown for a loop.

"I'm sorry," I say. "I think I misunderstood what happens here."

I say this to cover for my embarrassment. I fight the urge to kick or punch something.

Blastneesh doesn't say anything, he just keeps staring at me intently.

"What . . . what does happen here?" I say.

"What would you like to happen here?" When he asks me this, it has a weird effect. Like in stereo. I'm hearing him as that voice inside my head while watching his lips move and hearing him with my ears. It's disorienting.

"You mean . . . like, in this room—today—or at the retreat?"

He shrugs. "You tell me."

Now I'm suddenly nervous. I feel like I've been put on the spot. I start playing with a long string dangling from my shirt. "Well, I don't really know . . . The retreat is really expensive. I was expecting more . . . *something*. I don't know."

"What do you think it's a retreat from?"

Unable to help it, I roll my eyes and say, "*Life*. I wanted a retreat from life and . . . and . . ." I let myself trail off before I say anything too insulting.

"But isn't this a retreat from your life? Do you not appreciate the life you had before more? What I am doing is giving you the spiritual tools to get the most out of that life when you return to it."

I want to tell him it feels like he's constructed some sort of work camp with virtually no overhead so he can talk for a few minutes a night and walk away with bags full of money. Instead, I say, "That's the thing—I don't remember what life was like before."

"Even better. You can return to a blank slate. Only this time you'll approach it with newfound spiritual tools."

I fall silent. He has a point. If I were happy with whatever life I had before, I wouldn't have made the decision to come here. The voice inside and outside my head confuses me. It makes me think I'm talking to myself. It makes me immediately want to agree with it.

After a few more seconds of heavy silence, he finally says, "I brought you here to show you something."

"I'm ready," I say because it almost sounds like I'm telling myself that.

He leads me into another, smaller room with a desk, a monitor, and an ergonomic office chair. I feel like he's going to ask me to be his secretary or something. Then I have a moment of profound fear. What if this is some science fiction shit? What if he's about to show me images of all the worst moments from my life? Like, all the times I've thought I was glad there wasn't anyone around to witness my actions. What if Blastneesh is a god-like figure and what he's about to show me is why I'll never be enlightened?

The monitor comes on and I'm watching some very high-resolution video of a family. There's a very attractive blond woman who seems incredibly familiar, a good-looking dark-haired man, and a boy who's maybe four or five all sitting on a living room floor and playing a game. I hope I don't have to watch this very long.

"What am I seeing?"

He points to the woman. "That's Corinne, your ex-wife." He points to the man and says, "That's Brent, her new husband."

I look at the boy, try to tear up, fail, and say, "Is . . . is that my son?"

"No," he says. "You had a daughter. You set her free. She'll be starting college in the fall. Very precocious. Corinne's parents are helping her out. That's Brent's child from a previous marriage. Your daughter, Wendy, will be summering with them until she graduates."

"Hm." I don't know what else to say.

And, like that, he's gone. Everything else is gone too. Again, I find myself disoriented. There's a single window in the room. Wood floor. Walls that were once white but haven't been painted in a very long time. I think about trying the door but I'm afraid it'll be open. What happens then? Do I open the door and find him standing on the other side, telling me I blew it? Do I go back out and join the other seekers? What would be the point of begging for my special counsel session if that was the end result?

I sit down in the middle of the floor. I look around the room trying to find . . . what? Cameras? I don't know. I don't see anything.

I don't know what the point of this is. I'm bored after the first two minutes. I lie back and stare up at the ceiling. I close my eyes. I'm still seeing images of the last thing I saw. My ex-wife's new life. I feel like I should be able to think of something more interesting. I try to think of Nikola. I try to think of myself when I leave here—not just this room, but the retreat—fit and blissed out. People will know something is different. But I keep returning to those images of my ex-wife's new family. I see it as though it's on a monitor, not even like I'm there, not even like a ghost or an invisible man.

I'm imagining watching them in real time. It's like a montage of the most boring parts of *her* new life but then I have to stop and think that maybe that just *is* her new life. Whenever one of them breaks off from the group—which is rare—they show up in another window or another camera. Why can't I think of anything else? This is like torture. Even though Blastneesh just said it, I still can't remember my ex-wife's name. I decide not to fight it. Who knows how long I'll be in here. I vaguely remember the guided meditation from the Wellnevermindfulness app. It instructed me not to seize

on a single thought. To not consciously try to think of anything. Let the thoughts come and go. I don't know if that's
what I'm supposed to do or if I'm just too lazy to try thinking
of anything else.

I watch Brent and wait for him to sneak off and snort a
bump of coke in the bathroom or reach into the liquor cabinet
for a nip. I don't even think I see a liquor cabinet. Every time
he checks his phone, which is hardly ever, I imagine he's sending a sext to a mistress or watching a few seconds of porn. But
he's not and I know this because whatever I'm watching in
my head does that thing they do in movies where the text
pops up on the screen the way subtitles do. It'll be the son
from the next room texting him something like, "I love you,
Daddy." I watch him sit on the couch and stare at the floor
for like ten minutes before saying to his wife and son, "This is
a really beautiful floor." I listen to him appreciate the flush of
the toilet, the heft of the silverware, the plushness of his reading chair, the book he's reading, which looks boring as fuck.
It is clear that Brent appreciates things and I wonder if that's
the point of Blastneesh showing me this. Because I'm convinced that's what's happening. If Blastneesh can put his
voice inside my head, it only stands to reason he can put images in my head as well. Another reason not to fight it. I just
don't know why it has to be so boring.

I'm thirsty and my stomach is rumbling. Lying on the floor
is making me restless and I realize, with just the faintest of
shudders, that I miss being out in the Power Hole with my
fellow seekers. I was thirsty and hungry then too, but I could
find ways to distract myself. I miss ogling Nikola and, I guess,
Gemini. No, definitely Gemini. Ever since she had announced
her retreat celibacy to me, I've been unable to stop thinking
about fucking her.

I watch the boy go into his bedroom and do normal things:

play with some stuffed animals, flip through some baseball cards, draw a shitty drawing with some crayons. Kid's probably never going to be an artist. He removes an iPad from its charging cord and crawls into bed. The screen of the iPad becomes a new window on the screen I'm watching. Maybe this is where I'll get the good stuff. I wonder what he's into? Bondage? Rape porn? Milfs? Torture? Maybe he likes to watch school shooting footage or bum fights. I get nothing. It's a stupid game featuring cute, fat frogs.

Now I'm watching Karen (or whatever her name is) and feel like I'll get something good. Though I've forgotten her name, I can remember much of what happened over the course of our marriage. I wait with bated breath when she goes into the restroom and opens the medicine cabinet. Here it is, I think, every shelf should be stuffed with prescription medicine. But, no, just the usual medicine-cabinet stuff. I maybe spy some Tylenol or allergy medication. Maybe she has another medicine cabinet that's more fun. Maybe she's had to graduate to a whole medicine trunk or chest or something requiring a lock. Maybe she carries everything around in a giant freezer bag. But, no, again, I don't see her get into anything like this.

Brent reads the kid bedtime stories. Karen's in the shower but that "camera" has gone dark and the unfairness of this makes me feel cheated. Brent and Karen retire to the bedroom in their pajamas and I wait for some action to begin and I think I'm probably going to masturbate if this gets sexual. I haven't done it since I've arrived and feel like I deserve it. But they just get under the covers and lie on their respective sides of the bed, Brent reading his boring ass book and Karen flipping through a gardening magazine.

Thankfully, I don't have to watch them sleep. The footage begins at a random interval on some other random, boring day. It's almost exactly the same as the previous day. Maybe they just haven't had enough time together to realize how boring their lives are? Maybe things just haven't been given enough time to derail. I mean, I know how awful Karen is. Blastneesh mentioned Brent's kid was from a previous marriage, so things couldn't have been too perfect there. Besides, it's only a matter of time before Karen gets tired of raising a child that did not come directly from her vagina and starts acting out again. *Nice try, Blastneesh,* I think. Show me what happens five years down the road.

Despite being bored out of my skull, I'm not the slightest bit tired, so I can't even go to sleep, one of my default weapons against boredom. This is usually easier because I'm maybe a little hungover and sleep deprived most of the time. I don't know. That life feels like so long ago and it's been mostly eaten along with my other memories.

I find myself focusing on Karen. The image is crystal clear and some of the angles are fairly close-up so it has that almost textural quality to it, yet I can't control it. I can't bring her any closer to me. I can't change my perspective. I'm slowly massaging my cock through my pants while I ogle her going routinely throughout the day, waiting for her to reach over her head so her shirt lifts and a strip of skin is revealed or waiting for her to crouch down so the waistband of her jeans slides down just enough for me to be able to tell what color underwear she's wearing. This is something I try to be covert about in real life but when the subject of my ogling isn't even in the room with me, there's no reason to look away, no reason to deprive myself of that pleasure.

Not at all to my surprise, this makes the time pass more quickly. It's why I'm just rubbing myself, never getting completely hard, not even thinking about fully masturbating to completion. That would ruin it. All my interest would be gone and the rest of the day—or at least the next couple hours—would be excruciating.

I again wonder what Blastneesh's intent with making me do this is. I guess he's not really making me do anything. Supposedly, I'm free to leave but I'm not so sure about that. Of course, I'm all paid up so I guess it doesn't really matter. I find myself fixating on Karen(?) . . . Kelsey(?) . . . Corinne(?) . . . I'm really struggling to remember. It *can't* be Karen. I would have fucked someone named Karen, although it sounds like the name of a much older woman, but I would probably not have dated and would definitely never have married someone named Karen. These things matter. I'm not sure why I'm given the entire domestic situation. Does this at all resemble my life when I lived with her? I can't imagine doing anything this boring but I do have to realize I've been digging a hole for the past several days. But's it's not just any hole, it's a Power Hole. What's the purpose of that? Is it supposed to symbolize the central mystery at the heart of most world religions? Is it going to be used for something? Maybe Twin Springs, Ohio, is going to be home to the Wellnevermindfulness Institute (Spirituality for Gen Xers!). Sometimes, I guess, a hole can just be a hole.

I continue to rub myself as I watch them. I form an acrimonious relationship with the husband and son. I feel like they are hamstringing my ex-wife with, like, really boring superpowers. I can't stand them. I can't believe Corinne(?) fell for it and there's a huge part of me that feels great schadenfreude given her current situation. Just wait until her unchecked mental illness surfaces. It's going to be like a powder keg going off in that house, wherever it might be.

During one segment, Corinne (I am now pretty certain that is her correct name and, if not, it's wildly preferable to "Karen," which I will no longer use to address her even if that is her name, which I'm almost absolutely certain it is not) is dressed down in a pair of very tight-fitting khaki shorts and a black tank top and I'm harder than I've been since closing my eyes. How long has it been since I've come? I have vague memories of receiving a blowjob from Carol but that doesn't seem like something I would let happen. And even if it did, it was for nutrition rather than pleasure. I know there's a group of choades who highly value semen retention—the no fappers—and they tie this into health and wellness somehow but I've always thought there was some sort of underlying religious reason for this. I will not do anything for religious reasons because it seems silly and antiquated. But then I also wonder if they try and reduce sexual stimuli and, if that's the case, then it seems to be exceptionally religious, or at least Victorian or puritanical in nature, and not necessarily fair to those of us who can turn mundane domestic scenes or a trip to the mall into something of truly pornographic proportions. Obviously, as with any drugs or alcohol, one should never expect sex to solve all one's problems, but if approached with means, maturity, and a healthy attitude, it can be managed just as well as anything else.

The harder and more aroused I become, the more I begin to think maybe the semen retention people are onto something. Much like investors or penny pinchers—two other things I've been fortunate to never have to be—they want to hold onto everything waiting for the big payoff. Like, I truly feel like the next time I come is going to be epic. It might just split the world open.

No amount of voyeurism can replace the physical act of touch or the actual act of sex. There's always a level of frustration when one is removed from the scents and physical sensations of another person. This is why so many people date and marry people who are gross when they could easily masturbate to the most beautiful people in the world. This is how incels are created. Men using all the tools of the internet to make themselves rich or as physically perfect as they can be, and are then surprised when women do not swoon over them. It's that physical component—it can be brain chemicals, anything. Something about them doesn't sit well with people. It's their sense of entitlement. They've put all this work into something and they're shocked and angered when they don't get the results they want. Maybe entitled isn't the right word for it, since they *have* actually worked for it. Maybe thinking of it as a failed speculation is better. I'm probably more entitled than any of those guys. I've never had to work for anything in my life. I usually get at least some version of what I want but usually end up wanting more. I know this about myself and feel like this makes me more enlightened than most individuals. Enlightenment through entitlement— that would be my modern spiritual approach. You don't just *want* to be enlightened, friend, you deserve it.

And I find myself phasing out what's going on even though Corinne is still wearing that skin-revealing outfit. I could pull my cock out and run through mental scenarios of undressing her and fucking her but what if that opened something darker, something painful? What if it sent me on a spiral down whatever memory hole we existed in together? What if, dear god, I remembered all the times we lived, loved, and laughed together? And the fact that it's over would throw a layer of sadness on all of it. Like those old movies—something from the seventies—that have that certain light or film quality or something about them that renders them not just inherently sad, but emotionally devastating.

Sadness is the real enemy. Enlightenment teaches us to never be sad. It teaches us to lie to ourselves. But isn't that preferable to being lied to by . . . nearly everyone?

It's working. It really is. I do not feel sad at the moment. Even thinking about sadness only lasted for a few seconds and now I'm back in the moment, absently rubbing myself as Corinne sips a cup of tea, and thinking about what's coming next. And I feel like I have a lot of things coming up because I'm not a depressed person. Depressed people lack imagination. They can't see anything positive happening in their future. They are unenlightened. If they were truly enlightened, they would never be depressed because they'd know they were always in control of their own future. More importantly, they are in control of how they think about that future. These are people who do things because they think they have to or they're supposed to. The truly depressed person sees no end to the oppressive misery. The more normal person is like the semen-retention enthusiast. They think if they buckle down and commit to misery for an inordinately long period of time, things will be better on the other side. The enlightened individual says fuck all that, I don't have to do anything except make myself happy. If not happy, at least content. If not content, at least engaged.

I have never not been engaged. Maybe I am a hedonist, but I've always wanted to eat and drink everything in the world and I've been fortunate enough to march down that path in an extremely unbalanced way. This is my gift to people. This is why I feel like the most enlightened person here.

I take my hand off my cock. I can still feel it jerk and slide around in my pants until it gradually softens and returns to just being another appendage. I now see Corinne and her new family as though from above. Do they know I'm watching them? Does it matter? I feel such pity for them. Brent and Corinne were both here. They could have experienced the great breakthrough if they'd just stuck it out. I guess there's also the distinct possibility they could have died but wouldn't that be preferable to whatever existence they've chosen to live?

I watch them as though from the ether.

I let myself . . . feel happy for them. And this makes me feel really good about myself. I mutter, "Win win."

I have no idea how long I've been in this room watching Corinne and her family. Maybe that's part of the idea. When I first lay down and closed my eyes, admittedly, I thought something was going to happen. Those are our expectations, especially when something is framed like this—as entertainment or education or something. I no longer have those expectations. No sex is happening. No violence is happening. There's no intrigue. Someone is not going to abduct the child. I'm not going to see so much as a hint of ass cleavage from Corinne. What's Blastneesh trying to teach me? That people are not here for my amusement? For my entertainment? Fuck him. I already knew that. Rather, I knew people were not *put here* to be my entertainment. But I can choose to view them as entertainment if I want, even if it is really boring entertainment. Because to be enlightened means you can see the world how you want and no one can question you. Or, rather, you want that reality to be questioned every day. You want it to be a constantly shifting and unstable thing. At least I do.

I imagine Blastneesh entering the room, asking me how things are going.

"Good," I'd say. "I'm feeling pretty enlightened right now," and he would probably think of a million reasons as to why I am *not* enlightened.

I spend the next however long putting myself in Blastneesh's position. I could totally be a guru. My mind is blank, pure. This quiet moment in a tiny room in Twin Springs, Ohio, is where I discover my true purpose in life. I've been a pawn. Doing mostly whatever I wanted to do, sure, but within someone else's framework. I knew where I'd end up working when I got out of college, never mind that I can't remember where I went to college or what I was doing when I got out. Perhaps if I'd had to work for it, had to struggle for it, I'd remember now. I've never had any problems getting to the top, but I've never really *won* anything. Sure, I could win the party. Sure, I could have, like, a co-CEO position created for me so I'd have a great title and a great office and a great salary to do something that I, quite honestly, was never really able to figure out. Then of course I realize my life was made so easy because people are *afraid* of me. They know what I'm capable of. If they give me anything I want, they think I'll just occupy myself with my own interests and not interfere too much in the fabric of their reality. Well, none of them ever imagined me becoming this enlightened. None of them could ever see me wanting to step up and—*gasp*—take a leadership role. But what I've accomplished while in this little room is truly life changing. Not just for me but for every person I'll come into contact with from this moment forward. I feel higher and more powerful now than I can ever recall feeling and I'm in a room by myself and can't remember the last time I came or did drugs or smoked a cigarette or drank. Not that I ever thought these things were me. Sure, sometimes I'd fall into my phone and feel like I was living someone else's life, but sometimes we have to learn by emulation. I'm not a copycat. I'm a scholar, learning by doing.

Now it's time to remove the excess, to clean out the toolbox until I'm left with only the essentials.

And I'm back to thinking about the Power Hole. If anything, it is a metaphor for the human spirit we've all spent a lifetime hollowing out. This is why talk of the soul is mentioned so much around a person's death. It's not because the dying person is worried about where their soul will end up, it's because they're wondering what happened to their soul as they look back on their poorly lived lives.

An almost euphoric wash of sensation runs through me like the first warm breeze of spring. My skin prickles into gooseflesh, my scalp tingles, my scrotum tightens. I take a deep breath and it feels as good as the first breath I took outside of the womb.

That's people's real problem. They spend their lives trying to re-create the womb—build comfort, insulate themselves, retreat from the knowledge of the world. My biological mother died during my birth. The importance of that is not lost on me.

thirty

I'm expecting Blastneesh to come and have another chat with me before releasing me so I'm somewhat surprised when Tall Rex opens the door, brandishes the discipline stick, and says, "Let's go."

I'm dazed, lost in revery, blissed out, and feeling amazing. Who knew that hunger, boredom, and thwarted humiliation could have such a curative effect? In my mind, this retreat is already over because I've already won.

I exit Blastneesh's private quarters into the dining hall as I've seen so many seekers do before me. I hope the ones who have not had special counsel feel the same desperate rush of jealousy or envy or whatever it was I felt. The first person I seek out is Nikola, so she can see how I've changed, how I've transformed. All she does is roll her eyes and scoff audibly. I glance up at the stage, expecting to see Blastneesh in his chair. He's not there. The chair isn't there either.

Most people who've left special counsel have chosen to sit toward the front of the table. Since Blastneesh isn't there, I decide not to do this. I find Gemini in her usual spot at the back of the table and go there. There's a different feeling to-night, like everything has changed.

Gemini is beaming. "Was it *amazing?*"

The first thing I want to say is that I lay on the floor for who knows how many hours and astral projected into my ex-wife's boring current living situation but know that sounds negative. And it really wasn't a negative experience. So when I take a second to think about it, I say, "Yeah." Just saying that word feels so positive and good that a completely spontaneous and unforced laugh comes from somewhere deep within me. "Yeah, it really was."

"I can tell," she says. "You seem . . . lighter."

"I feel that way."

I'm looking around the table. Carol and Jorry are about mid-way up. Jorry's still wearing Fee's face and Carol is staring fixedly at Nikola. Gus sits on the other side of Jorry and I hope he's not trying to move into my territory. That milk is mine. Big Labia sits beside Carol, looking as content and vapid as usual. Someone's missing but I can't figure out who.

I lean closer to Gemini and ask, "Who's missing?"

"Hildy," she says.

There must be no recognition in my eyes and, honestly, I have no idea who she's talking about so she decides to clarify. "The older woman. Very quiet."

"Ah," I say. "That's probably why I didn't notice her."

Thankfully, Gemini doesn't elaborate because I realize what I said could be taken two ways and I meant the most insensitive one. I didn't notice she was missing because she's an old woman. Not because she was quiet.

"Did she . . .?"

"She ascended," Gemini says.

"So she died," I say.

"She *ascended,*" Gemini insists.

"Was she in the Example Circle?"

Gemini nods. I wait for her to say why and when she doesn't, I have to ask.

"For being too quiet and boring. Not contributing."

"How did she die?"

"I don't know." Gemini's expression goes blank like it's not even something she's thought about. Then she breaks into a laugh and says, "Probably old age," and we're both laughing and I'm thinking Gemini doesn't even know how lucky she is to be talking to me post-transformation. She could very well be talking to the next great spiritual leader of her generation.

"Looks like she's not the only one missing," I say.

"Yeah. Where's Blastneesh? You didn't kill him, did you?"

And we're both laughing but I have to seriously try hard to remember the last several hours. While I remember the feeling I walked away with, the specifics of what went on already seem vague.

"I killed him and ate his chair," I say.

This sends her laughing even harder.

She places a hand on mine and says, "I just want you to know that I've come three times since talking to you. What Blastneesh said would happen is happening. Once I stopped letting people take advantage of me and stopped abusing myself, I can have an orgasm almost on demand. Today has been . . . something else."

Obviously, I want to probe her about this but we're interrupted by the loud screech of the microphone. Tall Rex doesn't bother bringing it up to his level. He bends way down, seems more nervous than I've seen him since our arrival, and says, "The Wisdom Master will not be joining us for the remainder of the retreat."

An even deeper silence falls over the already silent table and I can only imagine what the other seekers think. Do they think they've disappointed Blastneesh and, therefore, he's forsaken them? Do they think I had something to do with this? I hope they do. I feel like that gives me power. Did Blastneesh know this? Is he trying to sabotage me? Is this something he had planned since the first night of the retreat? Or is it something he planned out well in advance? Was I more or less scapegoated into the retreat?

Nikola is now looking at me like I'm the devil. Then she turns her attention to Tall Rex and says more loudly than I've heard her say anything, "This is not acceptable."

Tall Rex, now standing up straight again, stares blankly at her.

"I'm *here* because of *Blastneesh*," Nikola says.

"Where's the food?" Big Labia muses, seemingly to the table in general.

Tall Rex turns to her, raising a finger and again leaning down to the microphone as if to say something but is interrupted by a piercing scream from Nikola.

"He was supposed to change my life!"

She stands up from the table, shaking and crying with emotion.

Gemini, choking back a laugh, leans into me and says, "Oh shit, I think she's gonna rush the stage."

Then, gathering all of her strength, Nikola rushes the stage. Tall Rex immediately falls into a defensive stance, wielding the discipline stick. As though she has nearly superhuman strength, Nikola whips the discipline stick out of his hand and, for a second, stands there holding it, a stricken expression of surprise on her face. She wraps another hand around the discipline stick and holds it pointed against her chest. Before any of us can even comprehend what's going on, she falls forward, driving the discipline stick through her chest until it appears through her back, blood bubbling up all around it.

There's a collective groan from the seekers as blood runs off the stage and onto Thomas's corpse, still resting at the bottom.

"Wild day," Gemini says before moaning with what I believe is another orgasm.

I wonder if I can find a position for her in the organization I'm putting together in my head.

No one really moves. We stare at the stage silently. Nikola's body is twitching. Tall Rex approaches her and seizes the discipline stick with a somewhat disgusted look on his face. He pulls it out of her body and a geyser of blood shoots into the air and then showers down on him. He throws up his hands in resignation and storms off the stage.

We all continue to sit in a collective daze for an uncomfortably long period of time.

Gus stands up and says, "I'm going to the gas station in town for some food. Anybody want anything?"

No one answers right away. I'm staring at Carol's chest and she's looking at me like she has all of my nutrition right there and I have a brief moment where I imagine all the remaining seekers partaking from her breast but I'm much too greedy to encourage this behavior. I may be the most enlightened person here but I'm not an idiot.

"I'll take some Sno-balls and a big Mtn Dew," Big Labia says. "And whatever the cheapest cigarettes they got is. Do you need any money?"

"Nah," Gus says. "I just steal everything. Anybody else?"

No one else shouts their orders at him so he heads off, alone, to the entrance of the retreat, hopefully feeling neutered and worthless.

"These woods are filled with all kinds of animals," Gemini says, her eyes wide. "I'm going to see if I can find a rabbit."

What she says seems so random it doesn't really warrant a response so I just stare blankly at her.

She elaborates. "I'm going to kill it with my bare hands and eat it raw. I'm already soaked. I'm going to come so hard."

"That sounds . . . fun?" I say. But it really doesn't. It sounds like work.

She stands up from the table and says, "I feel so alive right now," before throwing her arms up in the air, releasing a barbaric yawp, and running out of the dining hall.

That leaves Carol, Jorry, Big Labia, and myself.

I look at Carol to see her looking at me. She cups one of her breasts with her hand as though beckoning me. I look at Big Labia as if to say, "What about her?" and Carol makes a face that says, "Don't worry about her," so I stand up and move over to the trio.

I stand between Big Labia and Carol. Big Labia is staring absently forward into the middle distance, looking content but dazed so I tap her on the shoulder and she snaps out of it.

"I don't think we've met," I say. "I'm Scott Champion."

"Bonnie Carpenter," she says.

"It's nice to meet you, Bonnie." I'm trying to use my people skills. I'll need them if I'm going to recruit people to the cause.

"I know who you are," she says. "The retreat asshole."

"Is that . . . a bad thing?" I've heard that asking questions is better than being defensive or combative and, obviously, if I were to make my caustic quips about the size of her genitalia, she would probably make a withering comment about mine, even though she doesn't seem particularly quick or bright.

She just shrugs her shoulders and says, "Least you're still here."

"Do you mind if I sit here?"

She makes a chuffing sound and looks really put out before heaving herself a couple feet down the bench.

"Thanks." I sit down next to Carol, who already has her shirt up.

Jorry and I both fall on those nutritional powerhouses like we haven't eaten in days, the greedy slurping filling the nearly empty dining hall.

"Oh my," Bonnie says. "This isn't right at all."

I don't care what Big Labia Bonnie thinks about this but I also know her negative reaction to our behavior is because it's foreign to her, something she's never experienced before. Or hasn't experienced in a very long time. While I don't want to give up an ounce of Carol's precious liquid, I also don't want anyone to feel excluded so, with a mouthful of milk, I turn to Bonnie and cup her chin in my hand. I don't want her to feel like I'm sexually assaulting her but also think she is not going to pass up the chance to press her lips to mine.

I'm not wrong.

She opens her mouth and moves into me like she's going to kiss me and I press my lips against hers and feel the milk, now warmed by both Carol's and my bodies, pass into her and think, "This is what sharing feels like," and a tingling sensation passes through my body and I feel almost holy.

She swallows the milk and sits back and says, "Oh my."

I place a hand on her shoulder and say, "Your life will never be the same."

Some hardened expression breaks, her eyes get glassy, as though she's on the verge of tears, and she says, "I think you're right. I misjudged you."

"Everyone has," I say. "I'm easily the most enlightened person here."

Then I go back to Carol's breast. During the feeding, Jorry

grabs my hand and clasps onto it. My first instinct is to yank my hand away from his hot, sweaty claw but I'm overcome with a weird sensation before I can do that. I let him hang onto it, squeezing and releasing it like a cat's paw as it nurses from its mother. It's like my brain has been entirely rearranged throughout the course of the day and some deeper part of me, something beyond the brain, tells me I'm on the right path. It's the most leisurely, satisfying feeling I've had thus far.

When we're finished, Carol and Jorry head to the cabin and Bonnie says she's going to go look for Gus.

This has been a life-altering day and I don't want to let it end. I think about going off into the woods and calling for Gemini, joining her in the hunt. Then I'm drawn to the sound of flies hovering around Thomas and, beyond that, Nikola's beautiful corpse.

I think, "My bride."

I approach the stage and lift her frail body. Just touching her is enough to make me swoon.

"In the new world, there will be no marriage, only constant commitments. If I say you are my constant companion, then it is such."

She doesn't protest.

I drag her still leaking body to a nearby cabin—empty— and we consummate our new relationship. But not completely. I'm not sure if I can handle it, so I make sure not to come. I tell her I don't want the spell to be broken but that's not completely true. Now that I've had her, now that I know I can have her whenever I want, my interest is already waning somewhat. The truth is, I'm saving my semen for something else, something truly monumental.

thirty-one

The Power Hole seems to be completely desolate. I didn't par-
ticipate in the dig yesterday but it looks like the people who
did were working in reverse. It looks like an even shallower
hole than it did on my last day of digging. There are so few of
us left. Gus and Bonnie are on the end of the hole closest to
the dining hall. Carol and Jorry are somewhere toward the
middle of the hole. Carol mutters to herself but there's no one
besides Jorry to hear her. I feel like she knows what happened
last night and is giving me the cold shoulder because of it but
I'm so in my own head that may not be the case at all. Gemini,
apparently, never came back. Tall Rex circles the Power Hole
but seems diminished compared to his previous self.

I checked out the Example Circle before coming to the
Hole, just to make sure Gemini wasn't in there. The only thing
occupying the Example Circle was Hildy's corpse, which
looked like it had been picked at by wild animals, and what
was left of Fee's remains. I had a vision of Gemini falling on
Hildy's corpse and removing hunks of flesh with her teeth.

The total lack of leadership is palpable.

Even though I don't feel like it, I immediately get to digging, plunging my shovel into the soil and tossing it up onto the rim of the hole. Tall Rex reaches my end of the hole and stops.

"What the fuck are you doing?" he says.

"I'm digging."

"I can see that. You're digging the wrong way. We're filling in the Power Hole now."

"What? Then it won't be a Power Hole. It'll just be the ground." I remember thinking yesterday that by digging the Power Hole, we were hollowing out our soul, which I guess would mean that we are now making ourselves whole again. I look at the other seekers and see that they are indeed dragging the soil back into the hole.

"It's in the contract Blastneesh made with the owners of the land," Tall Rex says.

I think that's the most mundane, banal thing I've heard since being here and something about it makes me unreasonably angry.

"When I get the chance," I say, "I'm going to hit you with this shovel. Like, really hard."

"Oh, fuck off," he says before hitting me with the discipline stick. "By the way, hope you had a lot of fun last night. You know you're going to pay for it."

"Really? Then why am I not in the Example Circle? Is it because you don't have the power to put me there?"

"The Example Circle is being reserved for Seeker Gemini upon her arrival."

Then, almost on cue, a loud shriek tears out of the woods and a blur charges across the lawn and drives itself into Tall Rex. It's Gemini. She's been gone less than twenty-four hours and already looks like she's gone completely feral. I can only imagine the number of orgasms she's had since the last time I saw her. Before any of us can stop her—not that we would—she's tearing at Tall Rex's throat with her teeth, great gouts of blood spewing into the air before cascading down. Tall Rex, still holding onto the discipline stick, is convulsing in the throes of death.

I think, "I did not see that happening."

Gemini straddles Tall Rex's dying body, grinding her crotch into him, and punches her hand into his torso until she pulls out his still-beating heart and takes a bite out of it. Then she charges back off into the woods.

I turn to face the other seekers. They've stopped digging or . . . undigging or whatever they were doing. They slowly come toward me and at first I think it's because of my powerful appeal and then realize it's just so they can get a closer look at Tall Rex's body.

"Huh," Gus says. "Do we keep filling in the hole or not? Feels pretty useless. I'm really disillusioned right now."

I have yet to try out my leadership skills so I say, "Keep filling it in," thinking there will be some protest.

Surprisingly, there isn't.

"Yeah. Might as well," Gus says.

"We don't want Blastneesh to have to pay any unwanted fees," Bonnie says.

Jorry, still wearing Fee's face, says, "Backwards dirt," and goes back to the spot with Carol.

In an energetic burst, I clamber up the side of the hole, wrest the discipline stick from Tall Rex's hand, and spend the next minute or so beating him with it until kicking him into the hole and covering him with dirt. I don't know if Blastneesh is coming back or not but, if he does, this will be one fewer thing to explain.

For some reason, spending the morning covering Tall Rex's corpse feels much more purposeful than digging a pointless hole. Even if you wanted to call it a Power Hole, it was still pretty pointless. Although when I think about all the power I received from everyone digging the hole, how I probably realized that power around the same time they started filling the hole back in, I might doubt how powerful it is a little less than the remaining seekers.

Before Tall Rex is completely covered, I toss the discipline stick in next to him and cover that up, as well. Not only is this less incriminating, it's not like the discipline stick is some sort of baton, passed on to the next person in charge of discipline. And it certainly isn't something someone with my power needs to yield. Tall Rex was a toady, a failure. Why would someone like me want to use anything someone like him had? I guess I could give it to Jorry but, even though he hasn't really displayed any violent tendencies, it still doesn't seem like a great idea.

Thinking about Jorry gives me another idea. I straighten up, let the shovel rest on my shoulder, and mop the sweat from my brow with the back of my hand. It truly is a beautiful day. We've made virtually no progress in filling in the Power Hole and that's just fine. If it's not filled in, it will just be a reminder that we were here, like one of those ancient religious sites.

I walk over to Carol and Jorry.

"Is it okay if I borrow Jorry for a minute?"

He's standing beside Carol as she works to fill in the hole, bouncing from foot to foot.

"I don't care," Carol says and it strikes me that it might be the most conversational thing I've heard her say.

I look at Jorry and say, "You want to come with me?"

He starts fiddling with his loincloth and even though I don't really care if he wants to expose and then play with himself until he ejaculates, I'm not sure how well Gus or Bonnie would take that.

"No, no, not that," I say. "Grab a shovel and follow me."

I begin walking to the far side of the Power Hole even though it would be much easier to get out at the part Carol has already filled in. I throw my shovel up to the grass and heave myself out of the hole. I turn to help Jorry up. He still seems so excited. He's going to love what I have planned.

He follows me to the Example Circle.

"Okay," I say. "We're going to destroy the Example Circle."

Jorry's shoulders slump and his head dips down. I think he might be sad but it's hard to read his facial expressions under Fee's face.

"Wait," I say, overcome with an uncharacteristic stroke of empathy. "Do you want to be the example?"

He claps his hands the best he can and jumps up and down a little. This wasn't at all what I was expecting but I guess it seems harmless enough.

"Okay. Hop in there."

He nearly squeals with delight before hopping into the Example Circle. Then he just kind of stands there looking around and muttering, "Where they?"

Great, I think. *He wants an audience.*

"Stay right here," I say before walking back to the others in the Power Hole. Once there, I shout, "Everyone to the Example Circle!"

There are no protests. They all dutifully begin walking to my side of the hole.

I stand at the Example Circle and wait for the others. Bonnie pulls up beside me and says, "I thought we was done with this shit."

"We're going to destroy it when we're finished."

Gus, noticing Jorry in the circle, says, "Dude, this just

seems cruel."

"He wanted it," I say.

I glance at Carol. I've never seen her look so proud.

I feel like I need to say something soon before they start pissing on Jorry or pelting him with rocks or something even worse. I figure it's as good a time as any to practice my oratory skills.

"Today," I say, "in the Example Circle, we have an *example* of everything good and pure in the world. I cannot refer to him as *Seeker* Jorry because he is no longer in search of anything. He has found exactly what he was looking for, he just doesn't quite know it yet. Pure of mind and pure of heart, Jorry will venture forth to do amazing things." I feel like I could keep going. I don't actually know Jorry well and have never tried to have a conversation with him, but I feel like I could just spew those hollow platitudes all day long. It's so much easier than coming up with something real or honest and, ultimately, it's what people want to hear. It's the art of talking without saying anything of any substance or importance. But I can tell everyone is already getting bored so I just start clapping my hands and chanting, "Jorry! Jorry! Jorry!" and, as the other seekers take up the chant, it looks like Jorry is in pure heaven. He raises his arms to the sky like a prize fighter and turns in circles, openly welcoming the attention.

I get pretty bored with it and, to put an end to it, say, "Now let's bust up the Example Circle!"

Jorry is the first person to leap into action. Taking up his shovel, he wastes no time in laying into his showcase. The other seekers join in with gusto and it occurs to me I am the only one here who's actually been made an example of. That is why I will come out on top. It's like, with no one to impress, the others no longer even see this as a competition. What they don't know is that they should be trying to impress *me*. I am their leader now. Jorry and Carol are part of my staff. Jorry is in charge of inducing empathy and Carol is in charge of nutrition. I've already won. There's no question about that. I'm not a contestant anymore. It's between Gus and Bonnie and I'm going to need one of them to step up and dazzle me.

The problem with destroying a small circle of dirt filled with body parts is that you have no real idea of when you've actually accomplished the task. Much like anything else, I guess, it's finished when you get tired of doing it. I briefly wonder if we're living in a world of half-finished inventions. Like, if Alexander Graham Bell hadn't been so lazy, couldn't he have just invented the smartphone right out of the gate?

While I have everyone gathered around, I say, "We should drag Thomas into the hole before we finish up today. It just seems like the right thing to do."

Everyone seems so tired and beaten down I expect there to be protests, but Gus says, "I'll do it," and heads off toward the dining hall.

"What about Nikola?" Bonnie says.

I'd hoped they would have forgotten about her because I'm not entirely finished with her and now I feel exposed, rushed. I had planned on burying Nikola eventually. After all, she can't really come with us. I suppose we could eat her or burn her and incorporate her ashes into something but her energy seemed pretty toxic so I'm much more comfortable with her just being a dead sex doll.

"I'll take care of it," I say, heading off in the direction of the cabin where I left her.

Sometimes fate really does work in my favor. I'd been feeling slightly put out and on edge all morning, didn't really know why, and it was like Bonnie identified the problem for me. There had been a complete lack of sexual energy. I was not physically attracted to Bonnie, Carol, Jorry, or Gus and that left me with nothing to ogle, nothing to obsess upon. I'd almost completely forgotten that Nikola's near perfect body was still around. I should have taken advantage of it first thing.

I open the door to the cabin and join her on the bed. Thankfully, she hasn't started to smell yet. I wish I had my phone on me so I could take some commemorative footage of our act but, alas, I don't. I'll have to try and remember it but memory has been elusive as of late. I reassure myself I will remember because I've consciously started a new chapter of my life. All that old stuff, it doesn't matter if I remember any of that anyway. It's all in the past. It's the old me, stumbling blindly through life completely unaware of my self and its desires. What happens with me going forward will all be part of my *legacy*. If I become too old to remember it, there will have been someone documenting everything and, not that I'll ever die, but I'll be able to reflect on my past self in whatever evolving media it's captured in. The thought is dizzying.

Again, I do not allow myself to come.

When I'm finished with Nikola, I drag her out to the Power Hole because I wore myself out and am too tired to carry her. There are four mounds of dirt in the Power Hole. I'm assuming two of them are Tall Rex and Thomas so I'm not sure what the others could be.

Bonnie, noticing my confusion, says, "We went back for Hildy and Fee . . . Well, what remained of them anyway."

I glance at Jorry, still wearing Fee's face.

"Yeah," Bonnie says. "Didn't have the heart to ask him for it."

"I guess this one's next." I let go of Nikola's hands and nudge her to the edge of the Power Hole. No one comes to lift her down so I keep nudging until she tumbles down the side. I then scramble down to join them. At least at this phase, I want to be a leader who isn't afraid to help out.

Once we get Nikola at least semi-covered, no one seems to want to do any more digging or filling in or whatever.

"You know," Gus says, "I know a guy with a backhoe. He'd fill this in for us if I asked."

Gus's practical and utilitarian approach infuriates me but I'm also tired of trying to fill in the hole. I'm ready to start the next leg of my spiritual journey.

"Maybe we should call it a day. See how we're feeling tomorrow."

Gus glances around at the remaining seekers before looking at the ground, kicking a small rock, and taking a tentative, shaky breath.

"Yeah," he says. "About that . . . I think I'm gonna take off tonight. It's just not the same without any of my friends."

My first instinct is rage. I do not try to understand what he is saying. He should know this isn't acceptable.

"You're betraying us," I say and don't expect the other seekers to come to my aid with such ease.

Bonnie is by my side, saying flatly, "Traitor."

Jorry and Carol are also moving closer to where Gus and I stand face to face.

Gus throws up his hands and says, "There's just nothing more for me to get out of this."

Before thinking any more, even trying to think of anything to say to him, I lift my shovel and bring the heavy metal part down on his head. I'm not sure my intent is to kill him but I don't have time to even think about that before the other seekers are surrounding the bleeding Gus and beating him with their shovels. Even Jorry is getting into it. I watch with the most serious and somber expression I can muster but, inside, my ego is bursting. I've never felt more loved. These are not merely seekers now. They are my *followers*.

We stand around looking down at Gus's battered corpse. I suppose I've seen some pretty horrific things since arriving here but don't feel as though I've caused any of it. I can sense how keyed up my followers are. Jorry, apparently not finished yet, takes another swing at Gus, the sound of the shovel hitting his already compromised head ringing out amidst the afternoon quiet. I can't hold it in anymore. I move a few feet away from the group, double over, and vomit. It only happens once and then I dry heave a few times.

Bonnie comes over and rubs my back, says, "You did the right thing."

I don't have to ask her how she knows because I know it's true. I took the first swing and my devoted followers were right there behind me, pledging their allegiance. It feels so good. I imagine how Blastneesh must feel with all his millions of followers, even if most of them are just connected to him through an app.

Something else hits me. I stand up straight and wipe the bile from my chin.

"We're . . . we're all here because of an app, aren't we?"

"Sure are, hon," Bonnie says.

"What's an app?" Carol says.

"It's like a website on your phone," I say. "So you can just click an icon and go right to something without using a browser. I guess they're pretty revolutionary. Think of all the seconds we've saved."

"I've never had a smartphone," Carol says. "The tower behind my house probably put the signal right into my head."

Carol's completely deranged and I love that about her.

"So what's your point about the app?" Bonnie says to me.

"It's just . . . it feels kind of dumb."

"Nah. It's technology. The future."

I try to stand up straighter and address my three followers.

"You are no longer Blastneesh's seekers," I say. "You're my followers now."

"Of course," Carol says. And I thought she was going to be the tough one.

"I just go where my passion leads me," Bonnie says. "I only came here cause my husband wanted me to."

"Your husband?" I say.

"Yeah," she says. "The good-looking guy."

"Brent?"

She chuckles. "The one who ran off with your wife."

I'm not sure how to take this and am stuck processing it for a few uncomfortable seconds.

Brent was really good-looking and Bonnie is . . . not. Plus there's the age difference. She has to be twenty years older than Brent. Then I think about that giant labial fold and think maybe Brent's a sexual freak.

"I know what you're thinkin," she says. "I ain't too much to look at and I'm kinda old. I'm pretty sure he was just after my money but . . . well, he kept me satisfied."

I move toward Bonnie and bring her into my arms. "You're self-aware," I say. I can't bestow any false platitudes on her. "That's perfect."

Suddenly, I'm very thankful I did not come during my time with Nikola because I can feel my penis stiffening against Bonnie and I think, "It might not be the ideal scenario, but group sex is imminent."

Now I know I'm in tune with nature and the whole fucking universe because right after thinking that I can hear a rumble of thunder in the distance and a cool breeze picks up and I know that if I'm able to consummate my relationship with my followers then I will truly be as powerful as I feel.

Blastneesh's absence has created a void and I'm here to fill it. I have a flash of Bonnie touching my penis and don't know if it's a memory or a prophetic vision.

I pull back from Bonnie and look into her sad, unfocused eyes.

"We must seal our bond." I look at Jorry and Carol. "We are the beginning!"

I move toward Bonnie again, bend my head down to kiss her, and lower my hand to stroke her oversized labial fold. I'm harder than I've ever been and I feel like this is really going to happen. I don't even care if it's not with the ideal participants. Fee, Gemini, Nikola—they would have just ended up betraying me and moving on. The three people currently surrounding me know what I've been through.

Bonnie's mouth tastes like cigarettes and tartar build-up but I don't let that bother me at all. I break the kiss with Bonnie, look at Carol and Jorry, and say, "We'll be together forever," and I hope Carol and Jorry find this comforting.

Carol doesn't have to say anything. She lifts her shirt and Jorry is already giddy, hopping up and down and clapping his claw-like hands.

"I'm so glad I'm finally gonna get fucked," Bonnie's voice is husky, her breath rancid against my face.

In the distance, a dark cloud is headed for the retreat and I think a storm is coming to charge the Power Hole, and that, combined with our sexual energy, will be what breaks the universe open and makes it suitable for people like us. Perhaps my one mistake in life has been surrounding myself with beautiful people. Perhaps Bonnie realizes this as well. She glances down at my cock and I'm pretty sure I see a look of appreciation there. She strips off her clothes before dropping to her knees, part of her labia resting in the dirt of the Power Hole. Jorry whips off his loincloth and tosses it over his head. Carol slides her pants and adult diaper down and off. I didn't even know she wore an adult diaper. I can't get my clothes off fast enough.

Bonnie takes the oversized part of her labia in her hand and wraps it around the base of my rock-hard cock before taking me in her mouth. I probably taste like Nikola but she doesn't seem to mind. It feels amazing but I don't even worry about coming prematurely. Carol moves over and lifts one of her breasts to my mouth. I take the nipple between my lips and begin sucking.

She looks as feverish and intense as always, says, "My front door's busted so you'll have to come in through the back. Jorry was nearly full grown when he came out. Ruined me down there."

"I like knowing these things about you," I say before reaching out to stroke a papery cheek. "You're a very special person."

I think she almost smiles.

I go back to her nipple. Just the first two swallows of her milk seem to light my insides. Rapidly approaching dark clouds consume the blue sky. Magenta and blue flashes of lightning streak across the clouds. I take a mouthful of Carol's milk and spit it into my hand. I pull my cock out of Bonnie's mouth, let the milk dribble out of my hand, and use it to lube up Carol's asshole, which might be a little prolapsed.

The wind picks up even more, blowing the dirt and making it sting against my skin.

I throw my head to the heavens and shout, "I feel so alive!"

"Amen!" my beautiful followers shout back.

This is not just the beginning of something magnificent, I think as I work my cock into Carol's baggy asshole. *This is a celebration of victory.*

Carol makes a sound like "Oof," and then says, "That's

exactly how I like it."

Thus far, Jorry has mostly just been watching, excitedly hopping from foot to foot and rubbing his hands together. Now Carol takes his tube-like penis and inserts it into her mouth. Bonnie, back on her feet, moves behind me and smacks my tight ass. I'm fully inside Carol at this point and reach back to spread my ass cheeks. Bonnie presses her big labial fold against my asshole and slowly works it in, the grit from the dirt adding an odd—not entirely unpleasant—sensation. Carol takes in more and more of Jorry's tube-like appendage. It seems like it's getting longer and longer. Bonnie's big, rough hands grip my hips while she thrusts against me, pounding my prostate. I feel an odd sensation at the tip of my penis, now deep in Carol's bowels, and I imagine the tip of Jorry's appendage touching the tip of my cock. I've never had sex like this before. Didn't even know it was possible. Maybe this will be the central mystery of our new religion.

The rain comes down all at once. Combined with the wind and the deliciously cool breeze, it's like being surrounded by beautiful chaos. Thunder crashes and blinding light flashes around us as we all move together; we all move as one. Carol flops one of her breasts over her shoulder and I suck her sweet milk as Bonnie grunts behind me and Carol gags on Jorry's tube. I can feel my orgasm building. I'm not going to stop it this time.

My balls tighten and I shout, "Holy shit! I'm coming!"

Everyone else grunts with, I guess, pleasure, and I unload into Carol's ass, Jorry's tube milking every drop of semen from my cock. It's like having anal sex and the best blowjob in the world, not to mention the fact that Bonnie has fully stimulated my prostate to further take my pleasure off the charts.

We continue slowly writhing against each other until we

slowly pull apart. I feel like the universe has been shattered and we are the early pioneers in a new dimension.

Exhausted, we collapse into the mud, a feeling of euphoria wrapped around all of us. The thunder and rain have stopped and I look up at the light clouds racing across the dark sky. We must have been at it much longer than I thought. I do not allow even a second of regret to seep into my thoughts. Those doubts could be sown by the old me and I imagine I just dumped whatever was left of that person into Jorry, where his complete love of life and lack of rationality will find some way to get rid of it.

"Where's Gus?" Bonnie says out of nowhere, sounding kind of stoned.

I sit up and look toward the spot where Gus fell after I hit him with the shovel.

"He was definitely dead, right?" I say.

"Pretty sure," Bonnie says.

"Hm," I say.

Then Carol says, "He's bathed in the source. He can't die. There are people like him spread all over the world. I knew he was like that when I first saw him."

This makes no sense. This makes perfect sense.

"Well," I say, "of the many things we'll be capable of, doing harm will not be one of them."

I feel even more certain of my future vision.

I say, "We'll get out of here tomorrow."

thirty-two

Of course now you all know me as Super Supreme Leader
Scott Champion, host of the popular reality competition
show, *Dreaditation*, where we take thirteen seekers and lead
them through a series of contests to see who is the most spiritually superior, the most enlightened. "Who will become enlightened and what will be left of them?" I came up with that.
I think it's a pretty good tagline. Part of me wants to say I
never thought I'd see myself on TV while another part of me
knows I was always supposed to be famous. It's the final piece
in my glorious bubble. Once I realized that, my life was truly
exactly good. I can't wait until we get to do a celebrity version. Maybe I'll swap out the robe for a uniform and throw
myself into the retreat. Probably not. One man can only win
so much in his life.

The preceding is the story of my own spiritual journey. My
people suggested it. They said viewers would want to hear it.
They said it would be an important component of the show.
Bonus content. They may have said something about an extra
"revenue stream." They suggested hiring a ghost writer to

assist me even though they understood I'm more than capable of writing a brilliant memoir. They said it was a time thing. I met with a few of them. They all seemed like untalented losers so I opted to do it myself.

They were right though. It was really time consuming . . . and boring. It was interesting, as I started, how the memories came flooding back. A couple hours later, I knew I wouldn't have the capacity of sitting my ass in a chair and staring at a monitor for hours at a time. I had more important things to do. Spiritual things. So I more or less ended up dictating the entire thing to Carol and Jorry.

Speaking of Jorry, he gave birth to my second child. It was sort of a subplot running throughout the first season of *Dreaditation*. I can't really tell you any more than that about it. Since becoming famous, I've had to reaffirm some boundaries. I have to guard my private life. What you see on the television and read on the gossip sites will have to be enough. I'm the loveable guru with the broken tooth. My people told me not to fix it. Said it made me more relatable.

The Wellnevermindfulness app is still up and running although no one has seen or heard from Blastneesh since the retreat. That's another component of the show comprised in roughly five-minute segments we film shortly before the season begins and splice in later. A spiritual leader searches for his master. I argued against this but the studio execs told me it had to stay. They said it would add humility to my "character." I think they're just trying to piggyback on the success of the Wellnevermindfulness app. So the first season took place on the outskirts of Mumbai and those segments featured Bonnie and I traveling through India and looking for the reclusive spiritual leader. Eventually the *Dreaditation* app will overtake the Wellnevermindfulness app in downloads and, hopefully, this part of the show will just kind of fade away.

I'm pretty sure Blastneesh resides inside me anyway.

We're just a few days away from starting our second season. All the seekers have been chosen. We don't call them contestants. This is such a small representation of the hundreds of thousands of people who flock to my retreat summits throughout the world. The adoration never gets old. I always knew I was powerful and I always did well in competition, but I'd never truly won anything until Blastneesh's retreat. Not anything meaningful anyway. And now I am able to share my power with people, give *them* the opportunity to become the most enlightened person of the year.

I am here to tell the world each one of us is entitled to enlightenment . . . But I am not without my obstacles. What I have realized is that winning feels good and is best if it's done again and again. One of the only reasons we tune in to anything is to see who's going to win. To get through life, we *need* an opponent. My opponent, the *Dreaditation* nemesis, is Gus the Immortal. People think I made him up. I have to explain to them how immortality is not enlightenment. It is the anti-enlightenment. How, when you remove the fear of death, you remove any desire whatsoever to become enlightened. So Gus the Immortal is the one person walking the earth who is not entitled to enlightenment.

Once each of you achieves your enlightenment, you will see how much easier your life becomes. You will not need money or a house or healthcare or anything that people waste their time searching for. You'll realize we've had everything we need all along, it's just a matter of tuning out the chatter and focusing on it.

Let's begin now . . .

Close your eyes . . .

Take a deep breath . . .

Now, slowly exhale . . .

Other Grindhouse Press Titles

#047__*Halloween Fiend* by C.V. Hunt

#046__*Limbs: A Love Story* by Tim Meyer

#045__*As Seen On T.V.* by John Wayne Comunale

#044__*Where Stars Won't Shine* by Patrick Lacey

#043__*Kinfolk* by Matt Kurtz

#042__*Kill For Satan!* by Bryan Smith

#041__*Dead Stripper Storage* by Bryan Smith

#040__*Triple Axe* by Scott Cole

#039__*Scummer* by John Wayne Comunale

#038__*Cockblock* by C.V. Hunt

#037__*Irrationalia* by Andersen Prunty

#036__*Full Brutal* by Kristopher Triana

#035__*Office Mutant* by Pete Risley

#034__*Death Pacts and Left-Hand Paths* by John Wayne Comunale

#033__*Home Is Where the Horror Is* by C.V. Hunt

#032__*This Town Needs A Monster* by Andersen Prunty

#031__*The Fetishists* by A.S. Coomer

#030__*Ritualistic Human Sacrifice* by C.V. Hunt

#029__*The Atrocity Vendor* by Nick Cato

#028__*Burn Down the House and Everyone In It* by Zachary T. Owen

#027__*Misery and Death and Everything Depressing* by C.V. Hunt

#026__*Naked Friends* by Justin Grimbol

#025__*Ghost Chant* by Gina Ranalli

#024__*Hearers of the Constant Hum* by William Pauley III

#023__*Hell's Waiting Room* by C.V. Hunt

#022__*Creep House: Horror Stories* by Andersen Prunty

#021__*Other People's Shit* by C.V. Hunt

#020__*The Party Lords* by Justin Grimbol

#019__*Sociopaths In Love* by Andersen Prunty

#018__*The Last Porno Theater* by Nick Cato

#017__*Zombieville* by C.V. Hunt

#016__*Samurai Vs. Robo-Dick* by Steve Lowe

#015__*The Warm Glow of Happy Homes* by Andersen Prunty

#014__*How To Kill Yourself* by C.V. Hunt

#013__*Bury the Children in the Yard: Horror Stories* by Andersen Prunty

#012__*Return to Devil Town (Vampires in Devil Town Book Three)* by Wayne Hixon

#011__*Pray You Die Alone: Horror Stories* by Andersen Prunty

#010__*King of the Perverts* by Steve Lowe

#009__*Sunruined: Horror Stories* by Andersen Prunty

#008__*Bright Black Moon (Vampires in Devil Town Book Two)* by Wayne Hixon

#007__*Hi I'm a Social Disease: Horror Stories* by Andersen Prunty

#006__*A Life On Fire* by Chris Bowsman

#005__*The Sorrow King* by Andersen Prunty
#004__*The Brothers Crunk* by William Pauley III
#003__*The Horribles* by Nathaniel Lambert
#002__*Vampires in Devil Town* by Wayne Hixon
#001__*House of Fallen Trees* by Gina Ranalli
#000__*Morning is Dead* by Andersen Prunty